A PUBLISHER'S NOTE

To my dearest readers:

Triple Crown Publications provides you with the best reads in hip-hop fiction. Each novel is hand-selected in its purest form with you, the reader, in mind. *Let That Be the Reason*, an insta-classic, pioneered the hip-hop genre. Always innovative, you can count on Triple Crown's growth: manuscript notes — published books — audio — film.

Triple Crown has also gone international, with novels distributed around the globe. In Tokyo, the books have been translated into Japanese. Triple Crown's revolutionary brand has garnered attention from prominent news media, with features in ABC News, The New York Times, Newsweek, MTV, Publisher's Weekly, The Boston Globe, Vibe, Essence, Entrepreneur Magazine, Inc Magazine, Black Enterprise Magazine, The Washington Post, Millionaire Blueprints Magazine and Writer's Digest, just to name a few. I recently earned Ball State University's Ascent Award for Entrepreneurial Business Excellence and was named by Book Magazine as one of publishing's 50 most influential women. Those prestigious honors have taken me from street corner to boardroom accreditation.

Undisputedly, Triple Crown is the leader of the urban fiction renaissance, boasting more than one million sizzling books sold and counting...

Without you, our readers, there is no us,

Vickie Stringer
Publisher

Karma II

A Novel

By

Sabrina A. Eubanks

Compilation and Introduction copyright © 2010 by
Triple Crown Publications
PO Box 247378
Columbus, Ohio 43224
www.TripleCrownPublications.com

Library of Congress Control Number: 2010920094
ISBN 13: 978-0-9825888-2-6

Author: Sabrina Eubanks
Graphics Design: Valerie Thompson, Leap Graphics
Photography: Treagen Kier
Editor-in-Chief: Vickie Stringer
Editor: Maxine Thompson
Editorial Assistants: Christina Carter and Matthew Allan Roberson

First Trade Paperback Edition Printing 2010

10 9 8 7 6 5 4 3 2 1

Printed in the United States of America

Acknowledgements

As I do every day of my life, all through the day, I would like to thank God for all that I am, all that I have, and all that I hope to achieve. Without Him, nothing is possible. With Him, everything is. Thank you, Lord. You move mountains.

Thanks always and eternally to my wonderful, much missed parents, Mary and Julius Sr. You guys were gone way too soon. Having a wonderful time, wish you were here.

To my sweet boy, D.J. You are my reason for everything. You'll never know how much your mama loves you. To my brother, Jay – I love you much. Are you ready? Derrick Sr., thanks for the absolute best gift I ever got. My son, D.J.

To my family, my uncles and aunts, all my cousins, I love you guys. Each and every one of you. Thanks for my crown, Kim. Niecy, stay strong. I'm here if you need me. Pamela! There, I shouted you. Get it? Hey, Uncle June! Aunt Kadie, you are a godsend. My nephew Jayson (Pookie), and my niece Joli – I love you. Always know that your dream is attainable. Hey, we got a black president! Thanks, Jan!

Karyn, it's like we said, life happens. I'm sure we'll find a way to get back. Peace and love to you and Marly. Vera, just buy the damned shoes and take off some of them freakin' hats! I'm waitin' on you. Love you much. Brenda, your crazy ass holds me down more than you know. Mad love. Desiree, you know how we do, when you're a Jet... Jesus loves you, and so do I. Douglas and Winston, I always love you guys.

George, James, Sherryl (2 r's), Chuck, Craig and dem, Priscilla,

Eileen, Kim S., Mo (Mo, Mo, Mo! I said it 3 times, okay?) Dee Dee, and Darlene. All of you are special to me for different reasons. Y'all are still some badass kids… I love y'all.

Vickie, Barbara, Larry and the rest of y'all. I guess we'll be friends forever. Crazy Love.

Mrs. Davis, you are a unique and wonderful person. Everyone should know someone like you. Thanks so much for your unwavering faith in me. Dr. B.D. Lewin, what more can I say? Thanks for always being there. You're one of my all-time favorites.

T.A. family, thanks for holding me down! You guys always know who you are. Much love and crazy respect!

Lastly, I'd like to thank my family at Triple Crown Publications. To Ms. Vickie Stringer, I'll always be grateful to you for believing in me and giving me this wonderful chance. Thanks so much. You're the best! Ms. Christina Carter, as always, it's truly a joy to work with you. I couldn't ask for anyone better. A special thanks for seeing me and Needmore through our "moments." Much love, mad respect. Thank you Maxine Thompson for teaching me some tricks of the trade that I didn't know. I think I got it now. I appreciate the insight. Thanks to all who worked hard to get this book on the shelves.

If I didn't mention you, you live in my heart.

GOD BLESS THE READERS!!! That was a loud shout out. Did you hear me?

Dedication

To my love and my life.
Mama's beautiful baby boy-child, Derrick Jr.

Chapter One

Rock Stars

Nicole Hardaway hung up her cell phone in frustration. This day had gone into a long downhill slide since her feet hit the floor. When she woke up that morning, Keith hadn't been in bed beside her. Keith Childs. She couldn't believe she'd wasted almost three good years on his ass. She should have never started shacking up with him. Why buy the cow when you could get the milk for free? That saying was so true. Keith had been spending less and less time at home. He wasn't even getting the milk for free. Not from her, anyway.

Her beautiful hair fit neatly into a ponytail and settled into a tight knot at the nape of her neck. A face like hers, striking and serious, required no makeup, though she applied a little anyway. She'd been perfectly aware, all her life, of how she looked. It was advantageous when it came to dealing with men in a romantic sense, and a hindrance when it came to dealing with women in every way possible. When she was at work, she always downplayed her looks. The majority of people she worked with were men, and she demanded to be taken seriously for her good work rather than her damn fine face.

Even if she didn't want to admit it, she had a few nerves in her stomach about the important meeting later that morning. In order to be taken seriously, Nicole selected a black turtleneck and slipped into a pair of charcoal gray tailored slacks. Her shoes were sensible and black. She got up and was about to finish when she heard Keith enter the apartment. Nick stopped what she was doing and waited.

He breezed into the room like nothing was wrong. "Hey, Nicky. On your way to work?"

She didn't look at him, and didn't answer. The last time he'd shown up after being out all night, he'd carried the unmistakable scent of another woman on his breath. Nick wasn't a fool. She knew he was stepping out on her.

"I asked you a question."

Not only was he wrong, he also wanted to fight. She went to the dresser and strapped on her shoulder holster. She hung her ID around her neck and clipped her badge next to her cell phone.

"You're not talking to me?" He asked.

Nick left the room and went into the foyer. She opened the closet and put on her coat. Keith put his hand on her arm. She snatched it away and finally acknowledged his presence. This time she didn't melt when she looked at him, standing there with his fine ass. Tall and muscular with beautiful bronze skin, big brown eyes and that dark moustache. When he smiled, his dimples were sinful. He touched her again and she shook him off.

"Don't touch me. I'm going to be late."

He looked at her like he knew her iciness was just bravado.

"It's not what you think, babe. I was just playing a little poker and it got late,"

"Yeah, Keith. It's a little late. You come in here at eight in the morning with some bullshit line, expecting me to fall for your weak shit all over again. Not today, playa."

He looked a little shocked at her reaction. "Nicky, be nice. I'm telling you the truth."

"Tell it to the next one. Who put the hickey on your neck? One of your poker buddies?"

She tried to stay cool, but that hickey had pissed her off. She pulled her gloves on, and felt the hot sting of angry tears welling up.

"Damn, Keith, you're a grown man. You could at least have told that bitch not to mark you up. I'm tired of crying over you, trying to figure out why you don't love me, and wondering what I did wrong. I think it's time to wrap this shit up."

His mouth dropped open in disbelief. "What?"

"I didn't stutter. You're kicked to the curb, Keith. You are a waste of my life."

He blinked. "What?" He repeated.

"Next time I see you, we'll be discussing whose shit has to go."

She went out the door quickly toward the elevator. Nick wasn't disappointed when he didn't follow her. She was done. She got into her car and drove to Midtown South. Nick tried to push Keith to the back of her mind, but he refused to go. Although she mourned the death of the relationship, she could have kicked herself for having blindly put her faith in Keith for so long. She didn't wish anything bad on him. She just wanted him to leave her alone.

Nick was sitting there stewing when someone knocked on the window.

"You're late." Leah said in a flat voice.

"No, I'm not." She got out the car and walked into the precinct with Leah. Leah looked at her, frowning.

"What happened? Keith didn't come home?"

"Oh, he came home. At eight the morning."

Leah's look of displeasure darkened her face. "You know I hate his ass, right?"

"At this point, so do I."

Leah looked skeptical. "Sure."

"I'm serious." Leah made no comment and Nick got defensive. "I told him we have to part company."

"Yeah, but did you tell him it was over?"

"I told him it was a wrap."

"I hope you mean it this time."

Leah didn't believe her. When it came to Keith, Nick's track record wasn't that great. She'd let him walk all over her for almost three years. They'd broken up and she'd let him crawl back more times than she cared to count. Leah had watched all this play out, and she was constantly pissed at Nick for letting Keith treat her like that. She always took him back, so Nick could understand why Leah wasn't taking her seriously.

Leah ran a hand through her short, pixie-cut hair, her brown eyes sparkling mischievously, and changed the subject.

"You ready to meet the rock stars?"

"Please, Leah. Rock stars? We're all good detectives, with good busts."

"Yeah, but they took Nine down. That was huge, Nick." She paused and took her lipstick out of her pocket and applied it perfectly without a mirror.

"What are you primping for?"

"They're really fuckin' cute. I've had a crush on Noah for years. I may finally get a chance to hem his ass up."

Nick laughed and shook her head.

"You need more lipstick." Leah said, looking at her critically.

"I'm not putting on lipstick for those two. Forget it. I'm not gonna be one of their groupies."

"Suit yourself, but you need to be looking for a new man, and Lucas Cain is a damn fine specimen. He's also available."

Nick sucked her teeth. She followed Leah down the hall to Captain Myers' office. She'd heard the celebrated tale of the takedown many times. It was a memorable bust. A notorious drug empire fell, and its CEO, the rapper Nine – no small potato in the rap game – was in jail for the duration. With his numerous convictions, he was looking hard at 25-to-life. The bust elevated Cain and Ramsey to rock star status, at least in Midtown South. Nick also remembered fallout afterward. Nine's girlfriend had murdered Cain's fiancé, Justine Greer, the news reporter. Ramsey had blown Nine's girlfriend away, but not before she'd managed to pump two bullets into Cain. Cain and Ramsey had flown low for a time, then they resurfaced with a gigantic bust last year. If truth be told, Nick was a little impressed, but she wasn't overly so, because she'd been involved with some pretty good busts herself. Leah knocked on Myers' door.

"Come in." Captain Myers was a tall, beefy man, with salt and pepper hair and merry blue eyes. He was cheery and unpretentious, though his reputation preceded him. He was legendary.

"Good morning, ladies," He shook their hands. "Have a seat. We have coffee and danish. Help yourselves. You're the first ones here. That gives us a chance to get acquainted."

Myers eyed them both. His appraisal had no sexual overtones - just an overall evaluation. Myers took a bite of his cheese danish.

"I heard about the work you guys did to help put Damon Brooks out of business. That kid owned Alphabet City for years. Very impressive. A lot of cops are good with buy–and-bust surveillance and operations, that type of thing, but it takes a certain type to go deep and mingle with the criminals and get involved with their lives, earn their trust."

They'd gone fairly deep bringing down Brooks, insinuating themselves into the everyday lives of drug dealers, posing as gold-diggers and girlfriends. Pretty humiliating stuff, but necessary infiltration.

"We can deliver." Leah said.

Myers smiled shrewdly. "I know you can. That's why you were requested."

There was a brief knock at the door. It opened before Myers could answer. In walked a tall, clean-shaven, brown-skinned man. He was generically good-looking, with quick, sharp eyes.

"Captain Myers? I'm special investigator Dexter Griffin from the New York office of the Drug Enforcement Agency. I'm here to discuss the Draco sting with you," he said briskly, and then offered Myers his hand. Myers took a moment to look at it, and then back up at him. He stood up and took it. You could tell he was pissed about Griffin barging into his office like that.

"Nice to meet you. Detectives Nicole Hardaway and Leah Wheeler."

"Ladies. Where are the other two? Ramsey and Cain?"

Myers looked at Griffin coolly. "They've got 10 minutes. Have a seat. Eat a danish. Please."

Myers waved in the general direction of a chair as they regarded each other. It was more than obvious that Griffin had just earned a top spot on Myers' shit list. There was another knock and Myers glanced distastefully at Griffin as he moved to answer it himself.

"Cain, Ramsey. We've been waiting for you."

He swung the door open, and in walked the rock stars. "You fellas get a cup of coffee and help yourselves to the pastries." Ramsey's gray eyes passed over Nick and Leah. He gave them a beguiling little smile.

"Don't mind if I do." He had the exact voice of a grown up smartaleck. Nick hid a smile.

"Just go get your coffee, Ramsey." Myers chided, not without amusement.

Cain skipped the coffee and sat next to Nick. He

leaned forward, resting his elbows on his knees and began to enter something on his cell phone. All that crap she'd heard around the water cooler and out in the field was true. They were like fucking rock stars! They'd barely said anything, but they were like magnets. Cain hadn't spoken at all and he had his back to her, but he had a masculine virility that emanated from him in waves. She looked over at Ramsey, standing there, whistling low and pouring his coffee. He must have felt her watching him, because he turned suddenly and threw those clear gray eyes on her. He smiled a little, like he was used to women watching him, and sat down next to Cain.

Nick's attention returned to Cain. Nice shoulders. He stopped what he was doing and clipped his phone on his belt. Nice flat stomach. She knew there had to be a six-pack hiding under that sweater. He leaned back in his chair and turned toward Ramsey. They had a short conversation in low tones. He smiled and a small dimple appeared in his right cheek. He still had his head turned away from her, so she couldn't see his face full on. But it was one hell of a profile. He wore his hair in a short, neat natural, freshly cut and curled up at the back of his neck. He smelled good, too. She glanced at Leah, and saw that she was watching with subdued enjoyment.

Karma II

Myers sat down at his desk and his hands. "First things first. Let's get the introductions out of the way."

After they'd all been introduced, he paused and gave Griffin a nod. "The floor is yours."

Griffin stood up and unbuttoned his suit jacket. He put his hands in his pockets and scrutinized the four of them. He stopped in front of the rock stars and folded his arms across his chest. "The Nine case?"

Noah looked at him like he thought he was a bit peculiar. "Yeah, that was us."

"Spectacular bust. A little trouble afterward?" He looked pointedly at Lucas.

Lucas stared back and shrugged. "Not really." His

voice was smooth, rich, and quiet.

"Not really? What do you mean by that?"

"I mean not really."

"Shortly after the trial began, didn't Eric Dillard's girlfriend murder your fiancé? She also shot you twice, didn't she?"

Lucas' gaze didn't falter. "Yes."

Griffin looked at Noah. "You took her down?"

"Sure did. One in the head. Two in the chest."

"You seem happy about it."

Noah actually laughed. "I am."

"What makes you so happy about that?"

"I didn't miss."

Griffin's eyebrows went up. He stared at Noah a moment. When he turned his attention back to Lucas, he was wearing a small smile of his own.

"Are you comfortable going deep again?"

"If you think I'm not capable of doing my job because of a situation that had nothing to do with the Dillard case, then you're wrong."

"I meant no offense. I know you lost someone very dear to you. Going deep involves a lot of risk. If you're not up to the task…"

Lucas stood up. "I'm always up to task. One case had nothing to do with the other."

"Both cases had a common thread. Simone Bainbridge."

"One case had nothing to do with the other." Lucas repeated.

"Then what was the Bainbridge case about?"

Lucas advanced on him. Noah and Captain Myers both jumped out of their seats. Lucas stopped just shy of Griffin.

"It's a matter of public record. What's your problem?" Lucas said.

Myers held out his hand. "Have a seat, Cain. Please. You too, Ramsey." He turned toward Griffin as they seated themselves. "Why are you badgering my detective?"

"I apologize, Captain Myers, to you and your officer. Badgering was not my intention."

"Then what was your intention? Oh, and Cain's a detective first-grade, by the way. A damn good one."

"I was merely trying to ascertain Detective Cain's fitness for this case. We can't afford any emotional slip-ups."

"Cain is more than mentally fit. The Dillard case was not the last major case he's worked on. We've had five excellent busts since then. This Bainbridge thing has nothing to do with anything. It was a separate tragic incident. I guarantee you the incident was handled fairly and ethically. I dealt with it personally. Is there anything else we need to clear up before we get to the matter at hand?"

"I can respect your protectiveness of your detectives, Captain but, you have to understand, we cannot afford any loose cannon behavior. The Draco crew is dangerous and this case is tremendously important. Do you understand?"

Karma II

The red flush of anger started to leave Myers' face as he nodded.

"Yeah, I got you. It's political."

"So we understand each other?"

"Sure, but like I said, I won't stand for abuse of my detectives. They were hand-picked by me. Respect my judgment."

"I certainly do. May we start?"

"By all means."

Griffin handed out a set of photographs. "I regret starting off on the wrong foot. I hope we'll be able to work together as a cohesive unit."

Noah snickered rudely. Both Myers and Griffin gave him a sharp look. Griffin continued.

"First of all, Draco is the well-earned name of this drug empire. It's named for the code of Draco. It means harsh, severe, brutal. This is how they deal with people, from the upper echelon to the addict on the street. Every offense is punishable by death. That includes informants, theft, insubordination and so on. There are no deals, no pleading, only swift execution. They have a penchant for scalping."

He paused and looked at them. Something in his demeanor softened, and his eyes didn't seem quite so hard. "This is serious shit, guys. That's why I have to make sure there are problems, no slip ups. You cannot make errors in judgment. Your cover cannot be blown. If it is, they will kill you, and it won't pretty."

Leah fidgeted with her empty coffee cup. "You're pretty sure about that, huh?"

Griffin looked at her directly. "Damn sure. We tried to infiltrate before. They sent one agent's head back to us in a box. He had a happy-face sticker stuck to his forehead and his genitals stuffed in his mouth. It came with a cheery little note – 'Go fuck yourself.'"

Noah let out a whistle and Lucas shook his head.

"Damn," Noah mumbled.

Griffin nodded. "Yeah. Damn."

They all exchanged glances. It was the first opportunity Nick had to look Lucas in the face. His eyes were captivating - they pulled her in. She looked away quickly.

Noah addressed Captain Myers. "Any special reason why you picked us? Any of us give a hint we want to stop breathin'?"

"Ramsey, you, Cain and I go back a ways. We've made some fantastic busts. You guys are four of the best detectives here. I know you can get the job done. Period."

The room until was quiet until Griffin spoke again.

"Draco started in the projects in East New York. Back then, they were known as the Bullet Crew. They built the empire in the 80's off the crack epidemic. The head of the empire was a man named Jasper Trinidad. They called him the Overlord. We tried to bust him several different times. In 2000 he was found dead in his bed from a heroin overdose."

Lucas raised an eyebrow. "He was using?"

Griffin smiled grimly. "Technically, no. That day they found 10 needles stuck in his body. Plungers down."

They exchanged glances again. Lucas hit her once more with those gorgeous eyes. Nick glanced away. When she looked back, he was still looking at her. Nick felt heat creep into her face.

"Hopefully, this whole operation won't be too long. We're not interested in losing any of you. We want to take Draco down with the least amount of time and minimum effort," Myers said.

Griffin nodded and indicated another photograph.

"These two guys inherited the empire after Jasper's demise. Tate and Troy Trinidad. Jasper's two younger brothers."

"His brothers took him out?" Noah asked.

Griffin nodded. "Without question."

Nick looked down at the photo. They seemed to be on a cruise somewhere. They both were leaned back on the rail with raised champagne glasses, grinning into the camera, while the ocean sparkled a crisp cerulean blue in the background. They were twins.

"Which one is which?" Noah asked.

"Troy is on the left. Tate on the right. Troy is in charge of enforcement. Tate is the brains."

Nick couldn't see much of a difference between the two. Lucas must have read her mind and got the question out first. "How do we tell them apart?"

"Troy has Draco tattooed on his neck."

Noah smiled. "Okay. What if he's wearing a turtleneck? Like Nick here."

Nick self-consciously touched the neck of her sweater. Griffin surprised her by
smiling at Noah's remark.

"Good one, Ramsey. Troy is a little shorter and a little heavier than Tate. As you get to interact with them, you'll notice different nuances about them, like Tate's voice being heavier."

"How do you plan on going in?" Lucas asked.

"We're still working out the kinks on that. We haven't decided what level we want to infiltrate on. We're also still selecting the proper backup."

Leah frowned. "So when are you talking about all of this going down?"

"It'll take as long as it takes. We want the least chance for failure before we make an attempt. But we also want you all back safe."

Myers leaned back in his chair and tented his fingers. "In the meantime, all of you are off any current cases you're on. This interim period will be spent wrapping up any paperwork pertaining to those cases, and preparing for the Draco sting. I want you to get to know each other. Well. Your lives could depend on it."

Griffin nodded. "We'll send you out on a few buy-and-busts to see how well you work together. Today, we're sending you to the range."

He paused and looked at his watch. "We'll break for now and meet again in a couple of days. Once again, I regret the rocky start. You can talk to me and I will listen. If there's anything I can do for you, give me a call."

He took the time to shake everyone's hands and then made his exit. Myers leaned against his desk and folded his arms across his chest.

"I want you guys to operate with extreme caution at all times. I would take it personally if anything happened to any one of you. Please be careful."

He turned and looked at Noah pointedly. "Be sure you watch that big mouth of yours, Ramsey."

Noah dropped his eyes and put his hands in the pockets of his hoodie. Nick noticed that even when he wasn't smiling, he tended to look slightly amused most of the time.

"With any luck, this will be quick. Go pick up an unmarked and take it to the range. I'll see you all in a couple of days."

They left his office and Nick and Leah picked up the keys for the unmarked and waited outside for Lucas and Noah.

"So what do you think?" Leah asked.

She was smiling impishly. Nick knew that smile well. She knew Leah wasn't talking about the case.

"About what?"

"Don't try to act like you don't know what I'm talking about, Nick. I saw your cool ass staring at them and damn near drooling. That shit was priceless!" Leah erupted into a burst of giggles, and Nick was annoyed.

"I don't know what you're talking about."

They stared at each other.

Leah cracked a smile first. "They are fine, though."

Nick smiled back.

"You ain't lying. Let's not talk about them here. We don't want to swell their heads up any bigger than they already are."

Leah smiled. "Why do you say that?"

"I'm pretty sure they're so full of themselves you can barely stay in the room with them. Don't fawn over them either, Leah. I know they probably get enough of that."

"Why are you being so cynical?"

"I'm in the middle of breaking up with somebody. I'm not real fond of devastatingly handsome men right now."

"You looked pretty fond of Cain's devastatingly handsome ass in there."

"Leave me alone, Leah."

Leah looked over Nick's shoulder. "Here they come. Lord, have mercy." She said longingly.

They were deep in conversation about something. Noah was smoking a cigarette. Leah took the car keys out of her pocket. "Ready?" She asked.

Noah flicked his cigarette away.

"Yep. Let's go." Leah opened the door on the driver's side and sat down. Before she could close the door, Noah grabbed it by the frame.

"Whoa, wait a minute."

Leah blinked at him. "What?"

He waved for her to get up. "You two gotta sit in the back. Come on, get up."

Leah popped out of the car like a jack-in-the-box. "What did you just say?"

"I said," he started, like he was talking to a slow child, "You two gotta sit in the back. We don't do back seats."

Leah put her hands on her hips. "You're kidding me, right?"

He smiled. "Nope."

Nick looked at Lucas. He was already looking at her, a small smile on his lips. Feeling a bit exposed, she crossed her arms over her chest. He noted the gesture and laughed a little. She turned to Noah.

"You want us to ride in the back because we're women. What are you? A caveman?"

Before Noah could answer her, Leah got in his face. "Yeah, what kind of shit is that? I guess you want us to walk three feet behind you, too."

Noah's head went back in surprise. His gray eyes fell over Leah a bit sinfully. "Kinda feisty, huh?" He looked at her ass rather boldly. "I like that."

Leah gave him a knowing look. "I bet you do."

Noah smiled at her. "You still gotta ride in the back."

Leah stuck her chin out defiantly. "I don't think so." Noah rolled up on her so close, Nick thought he was going to kiss her.

"Ride in the back."

Leah lost her cool and got distinctively girly, pushing him away from her with a shaky hand. "Stop! Don't roll up on me like that."

Nick held back a smile. She knew that came out a lot

whinier and highpitched than Leah had intended.

Lucas started laughing. "Alright, Noah. That's enough."

"I was just havin' a little fun." He looked at Leah with that same sinful look. "Sorry," he said unapologetically. Nick moved next to Leah.

"I guess you'd have to be a man to appreciate that type of childish humor, Ramsey." She said.

Noah turned his smile on her. "You can call me Noah."

Lucas spoke up. "He really was just joking. If you want to drive, go ahead. We'll take the back seat."

Leah stuck her tongue out at Noah. He frowned at her. "Now that's childish... but kinda sexy too."

Lucas hit his friend lightly on the shoulder. "Get in the car, man."

Chapter Two

Burying the dead

A few days after the initial Draco meeting, Lucas and Noah sat in Captain Myers' office, wating for the final go-ahead for Lucas to be on the Draco team. They sat in companionable silence, neither one particularly worried about the outcome. They had been in this hot seat together many times. They'd always come out clean because they were good detectives. Hell, two of the best narcs Midtown South had to offer, and that always kept them in good favor with their commanding officer, Captain Myers. He knew them well enough to know, maybe they wouldn't go strictly by the book, but he never had to worry about them being dirty or on the take.

"This is takin' forever," Noah mumbled, looking annoyed.

"You know it's a waiting game."

Myers walked into his office, and sat across from them

at his desk, looking at them sternly. "Good to go. Justified and righteous."

"Thanks, boss. See you tomorrow."

They headed toward the elevator. Noah checked his boy. "You alright, Luke?"

Lucas was looking out the window. "Just fine."

Noah stared at him, a touch of concern in his eyes. Lucas ran his hand over his beard, and returned his gaze to the window. Noah spoke in a low voice. "Snap out of it. Don't keep goin' back there, bro. It'll eat you up."

Lucas stared at him. Noah stared back. "Keep it movin'."

"Keep it moving, Noah?"

Noah looked Lucas straight in the eye. "I didn't stutter. You can't live in the past. I know it hurts, but this shit you're doin' to yourself is no good. She's dead, Luke. She ain't comin' back."

Lucas was instantly irritated with him. He'd known Noah for the better part of 10 years. They were like brothers. It was times like these, though, that Lucas really

didn't appreciate Noah's brutal candor.

"Shut up, Noah." He said under his breath.

Noah frowned. "Forget that. This shit is ridiculous! I told you the day of Justine's memorial, you need to start livin' again. It's six months later."

"I've been out." Lucas mumbled.

"You got laid."

Lucas smiled. "Mission accomplished."

Noah smirked. "I bet it was. Ain't you lonely, bro?"

Lucas shook his head. "I don't know... I still miss her."

Noah's eyes softened a bit. "You can't grieve for the rest of life. Listen to me. It's time you pick your game back up, Luke."

"You don't understand."

Surprise and anger flooded Noah's face. "Don't tell me I don't understand. I was there. Right up to the end when I blasted Simone's sick ass straight to hell."

"Yeah, I know. I'm sorry for that, man."

"Ain't no need to be sorry, bro. I was happy to bust a few caps in her ass after what she did to you and Justine. Crazy bitch."

Lucas laughed softly, though he was not amused. "That's sick."

Noah shrugged. "It is what it is."

Lucas fell silent and turned back to the window again. He closed his eyes and let his mind take him back.

It had been Halloween when Justine breezed into Gideon's and stole his heart. He'd loved her at first sight, and he believed in his heart she'd felt the same. Then along came Simone Bainbridge.

Simone had set her sights on him as hard as he'd set his on Justine. She'd thrown herself at him constantly, but he'd been good at resisting her. Problem was, Simone had been wet-dream fine, and she had a habit of hemming him up. Things had happened. He took Justine to Jamaica and proposed. They were happy. Then came that goddamn Nine case.

Karma II

He felt a sting on his cheek. He reflexively put his hand to it and sat straight up. Lucas looked at Noah, who was grinning and about to pop another one.

"What's the matter with you?" Noah laughed and let the rubber band fly.

"I was awake."

Noah looked at him solemnly. "So you say. Seems to me, you haven't been awake in a long time. Snap out of it. I'm serious, man. Keep the good things close, but it's time to let go. You goin' home?"

"Nah... figured I'd hang out with you."

"Well, shit, it's about time. Come on, Lazarus."

Noah was grinning at him. Lucas smiled back.

"Shut up, fool. Let's go."

They ended up at a popular club in Chelsea. Lucas wasn't blind to the fact that Noah always steered clear of every place he'd ever gone with Justine. Good man. Better friend. They hit the bar. Heads turned. They walked in side by side with their usual swagger. They were men, not boys. They didn't bop and dip with their heads down. They walked in, heads high, checking out the joint, aware of their surroundings, with a masculine, vaguely gangster stride.

I'm here, I'm fine, and I'm a bad bad man. Ladies, get wet. Men, don't fuck with me.

They were also well aware of men watching them, wondering who they were. Some a little jealous, holding their women a little tighter. Some wary, a little intimidated. The others, bold and frowning, thinking, 'Who this nigga think he is?' Straightening themselves up a bit taller and puffing their chests out.

Women paused whatever they were doing, or stopped completely. Some staring inconspicuously, some brazenly. They gave their lips tentative licks, trying to decide which flavor was better. Vanilla or chocolate. They had their choice, because they were just as different as they were alike. The only thing they had in common in the looks department were their general physiques. Both were tall with muscular, athletic bodies, though Noah was just a bit smaller than Lucas, who had him by about an inch. Noah was light with dark black, curly hair. He had large and lively eyes that were light and twinkly when he was happy and dark and steely when he was not. His features were mostly chiseled, but softened by a heavy dose of Mother Africa. His mouth was rudely sexy, his lips usually tilted up in a semipermanent smirk, and complimented by a nicely trimmed moustache and goatee. Noah was so classically good-looking, he was almost pretty, but there was nothing feminine about him. Noah's masculinity exuded out of him like a strong cologne.

Lucas, on the other hand, was a deep, rich brown. He

had large chocolate eyes fringed with thick, lush lashes. He wore a light beard, and the darkness of his hair was a gorgeous contrast against his dark skin. He possessed a sexy mouth, too, and though his smile was not as quick as Noah's, when he did, he had the major wattage of a movie star. Light or dark, you couldn't lose. Noah was the pretty boy. Lucas was just downright handsome.

They ordered single malts and settled in. Noah turned to survey the inventory, and Lucas did the same. Old habits rushed back when that single malt slid smoothly down Lucas' throat. He took another sip and found himself reverting back to his player days. A brown sister in a tacky fuchsia dress. She'd crossed herself out with that damning dress. Dark sister in a black mini skirt. Nice legs. Pretty face. Not bad. She threw back her head and laughed. Sounded like she was baying at the moon.

"How's it lookin'?" Noah asked, sipping his drink.

Lucas shrugged. "Fair to middling. I think I see a few howler monkeys." They shared a laugh.

"Damn. That's cold, bro."

"They're okay. Nothing spectacular."

A pretty honey-colored cutie in a red dress walked by. She gave Noah the once over and smiled invitingly. He smiled back.

"Nothing wrong with her." Lucas said, picking his glass up.

"I see. You alright?"

Lucas nodded. "I'm straight."

Noah tossed back the rest of his drink. "I'm out."

Lucas watched him as he followed that girl and started getting his mack on. Noah leaned over and spoke to her. She blushed as Noah's mouth went very close to her ear. He'd be taking her home tonight. That is, if Liz wasn't there. Noah was still very much involved with Lissette Maldonado. Had been since Lucas and Justine had been together. If Liz knew what Noah was up to, she'd skin his ass alive. Then again, maybe not. She had to know

21

Karma II

somewhere deep inside of herself that Noah would never be faithful to her. It just wasn't in him.

Noah lived to see how much ass he could get. He'd tried to commit. Even got married and had a couple of kids with Nadine. It ended badly. Nadine caught him in his car with some chick with her legs in the air, a block from his house. Nadine had been in such a rage, that she'd walked back to the house and gotten a baseball bat. She'd knocked out the windshield and a side window trying to get to his ass. Noah had to damn near break her arm to get the bat from her.

Lucas wasn't mad at Noah. He completely understood him. Matter of fact, he'd been exactly the same way, maybe a little worse. Half the time, Lucas couldn't even remember women's names, hardly ever called them back. Last name? Not if he could help it. Yes, yes. He'd been a cold, calculated ass bandit. Then came Justine...

Justine had shown him he wasn't as much of a player as he thought he was. She'd shown him how to let his guard down and let someone in. Taught him that everyone needs love. Craves it, no matter how much they think they're just fine without it. In the split second in which he'd met her, he was open. He hadn't been that way since his mother left he and his father when he was eight years old. He'd come home from school one day and she was gone. Lucas watched his father drink himself to death in record time. His grandfather finished raising him, and although he doted on him, he was a very busy man. The head of cardiology at a prestigious New York hospital. Lucas was virtually left to his own devices. When he got out of high school, he headed straight to the Marines. He'd wanted to stay out of trouble and felt it would give him structure. His senior year had been wild. Hanging out until all hours, drinking and chasing girls. His grandfather had been so busy, if he noticed what was going on, he never mentioned it.

The Marines made a man out of him and gave him the

discipline he needed. While he was there, his grandfather died and left his estate to him. Two brownstones in Brooklyn's Carroll Gardens, the money he had in the bank, his investment portfolio and all his insurance. At only 22 years old, Lucas Cain suddenly found himself rich.

Instead of letting his newfound wealth turn his head, he enrolled at NYU. He started out wanting to be a lawyer, but he got bored very quickly. He took the test for the NYPD and dropped out. He needed some excitement in his life. If something happened to him, he had no one waiting at home to miss him. He was financially secure, young and good-looking, but he was also very much alone. Sure, he had friends, the same people he'd known all his life, but they knew his circumstances and tended to take advantage. Women were the same way, at least he'd always thought so. Lucas attracted women like honey does bees, and he was fine with that, but he also felt women were put on this earth to hurt you. He kept them at arm's length and intentionally refused to give them any piece of himself emotionally. They could thank his mother for that. He wasn't putting his heart out there just to get crushed. Just for that person to leave him.

Or die, he thought.

Lucas finished his drink as Justine's face flashed in his mind. He looked down and gripped the end of the bar. He still couldn't put her in a place where he could still love her, but move on.

"Oh, God. Not again." Noah said, leaning with his back against the bar.

"What's wrong? You couldn't make it happen?" He asked with a smile.

Noah smirked. "You know I'm gonna hit it. I just can't do it tonight."

Lucas raised an eyebrow. "Liz got you on a short leash tonight?"

Noah laughed. "You know ain't no woman got me on a short leash. I'd chew right through that shit every time." They shared a laugh. "Nah, she's married. Gotta get home."

Lucas shook his head. "Damn, Noah."

Noah feigned shock. "What? ' Cause she's married? Nobody ever turned me away when I was married. Married people need love, too."

Lucas laughed. "That's not love, Noah."

Noah shrugged. "Not that I need to ask, but why were you looking so glum when I got back here?"

"Just thinking."

"Stop all that thinkin' and loosen up."

"I'm loose."

Noah smirked again. "Man, I walked over here and you were tighter than a virgin. A sad virgin."

Lucas laughed. "Fuck you, Noah."

Noah grinned. "Fuck you back."

They finished their drinks and Lucas looked at his watch.

"No offense, bro, but I'm out."

Noah gave him the screw face. "You just got here."

"I been here long enough. I'm out."

"Go 'head, then. Go home and be sad. Lookin' at sad pictures, and sad movies, listenin' to sad music. Smellin' her clothes. Cryin' in the corner. Go 'head and take your sad ass on home."

Noah turned back to the bartender and asked for two more. Lucas felt his jaw tighten. His hand curled into a fist. Noah's eyes dropped to Lucas' hand and bounced back up to his eyes. A small smile crept across his face and his eyes grew steely.

"Oh, what? You gonna hit me? Go 'head."

Lucas didn't think he'd ever been this angry at Noah. He knew he really shouldn't be mad at Noah. He was just being Noah. Brutally honest and subject to a lack of tact. Lucas wanted to swing on him because those words hurt, mostly because they had been so true. Noah had called him out. Lucas stepped to him and glared into his eyes.

Noah didn't fall back.

"Go 'head. I know you been needin' to hit somebody for a long time. Might as well be me for tellin' you the truth."

The bartender paused in front of them. "Everything cool over here, fellas?"

Noah didn't look at him as he answered. "It's all good," he said.

The bartender looked at them warily, then moved on. Lucas opened his hand and stepped away from Noah.

Lucas sighed deeply and leaned on the bar with his elbows. He put his face in his hands. Noah put his hand in the middle of Lucas' back and spoke close to his ear.

"You alright?" He asked.

Lucas nodded, then shook his head.

"Okay. You ready to get shitfaced?" Noah asked. "Alright. Tonight, we grieve this shit out. Tomorrow you're gonna get up, dust yourself off, and put Justine where she belongs, okay?"

Lucas nodded.

"Good. You're not gonna cry, are you?"

Lucas stood up straight and looked at him in resignation: "Probably."

Noah smiled. "I probably will, too. Let's get outta here before we get a DWI. That definitely wouldn't be a good look for us."

Noah ended up crashing in one of the spare bedrooms. It was one of the longest nights of Lucas' life, but it was worth it. When he woke up, he was hungover, but his heart was much lighter. He'd always love Justine, but maybe now he could try to move on.

Karma II

Chapter Three

Karma II

Caught off guard

Lucas pulled up at Noah's house and blew the horn for him to come out. They were supposed to meet Leah and Nicole. It was raining so hard he could barely see. It didn't help his mood. He'd been feeling strange all day. Not a bad strange, yet not a particularly good strange either.

It was starting again and Lucas didn't want it. He wasn't ready. He thought back to when he'd first met Justine. She'd caught his player ass off guard and given him butterflies, like he was in high school. This was different It wasn't love at first sight, like it had been with Justine. Instead of that tingly, fluttery feeling of butterflies, Nicole was pulling him into her orbit like a planet. He didn't think she even realized it. She was too busy trying to act tough and unaffected.

Her bravado made him chuckle quietly.

He smiled as he remembered the day they went to the

range. Nicole had been impressed with him, but did her damn hardest to do better. She'd fallen a little short. When she asked himwhere he'd learned to shoot, he told her he'd been a sharpshooter since he'd been on the force and a Marine sniper. Nicole had rolled her eyes and sucked her teeth. Lucas had watched her perfect mouth form an unconscious pout, and he literally had to find something else to do with his hands to keep from reaching out and touching her.

"Fuck you, Noah! Go then! Don't come back!"

Lucas looked up, out of his daydream by the sound of Lissette screaming.

"Stop, okay? Jesus Christ! I have to go, Liz." He heard Noah yell back.

When Noah got to the car, he was soaked. He got in, slammed the door, and ran his hands through his wet hair.

"Everything alright, No?"

Noah used his hands to wipe the excess water off his face. "Fuckin' peachy."

"Yeah? What's up with Liz throwing you out of your own house?"

Noah wiped his hands on his jeans and lit a Dunhill. He inhaled deeply and cracked the window. "She lives there."

Okay. Lucas didn't see that one coming. "Yeah? Since when?"

"Since she told me she was pregnant."

Both of Lucas' eyebrows went up. He really didn't see that one coming. "You feel like talkin' about it?"

Noah shook his head. "Nah." He mumbled.

Lucas glanced again at his brooding friend. "So, what's up, Noah? You happy about this or not?"

"No. It's not really the baby I'm not happy about. It's Liz."

"Liz?"

"Yeah, Liz. I mean I'm not pissed that she's pregnant.

It was bound to happen eventually. We were goin' at it like rabbits, but I told her in the beginning what I was willin' to do. I was straight with her. Now she's tryin' to flex on me."

"Flex how? She wants to get married?"

"Yeah."

"You love her, right?"

"She's alright."

"Come on, No. You been with Liz for two years."

"Okay. Alright. Maybe I do. Shit, I love your ass, too. That don't mean I want to marry you."

They laughed. "Seriously, Luke, that's the shit we were arguing about. I tried that shit with Nadine. It wasn't her. It was me. I don't like being married. It just ain't for me."

Lucas smiled. "Why not? Too restrictive?"

"Yes. Yes, it is. I gotta do me. I ain't never been a one-woman man. I tried, Luke. I swear to God I did. I tried as hard as I could with Nadine, but I just couldn't do it."

"Maybe you just didn't want to."

"You know what? You're right."

"Why?"

"'Cause I don't like makin' promises I know I can't keep, that's why. I really wanted things to work with Nadine. I mean, I loved her like that, Luke. I still do."

Lucas nodded. He knew Noah still loved Nadine. That was why he took so much shit off her now. Noah knew he was responsible for the demise of their relationship, so he took what she dished out, even though he'd bitch about it.

"Liz has been remindin' me a lot of Nadine, lately. She's pregnant, so naturally she wants to get at least some type of commitment from me. I told her to come live with me, which I think was a colossal mistake, but I can't give her more than that. I won't. I fucked up then, I'll fuck up now."

"You don't know that. Maybe not."

29

Karma II

"Come on, man. This is me we're talkin' about. I don't think I'm capable of restraint when it comes to women."

Lucas shrugged. "Maybe you never tried hard enough."

"I tried. Shit, so did you. Sometimes, no matter how hard you try, you fail anyway. Some chick comes along with a tasty piece of ass you've just gotta have... and you fail, Luke. You fail."

Lucas didn't appreciate the slight reference to Simone, and him failing Justine by sleeping with Simone, but he let it go. He let it go because it was true.

"It comes with the curse, Luke."

"What curse?"

Noah laughed. "You know, the curse. I know you know what I'm talkin' about."

Lucas smiled. He was sure he did, but he decided to play dumb. "Not a clue. Explain."

Noah gave him a look that let him know he wasn't buying his dumb act at all. "Okay, I'll break it down to you, even though I know you're bein' ignorant on purpose."

Lucas laughed. "I am?"

"Yeah, Luke, you are, 'cause you've got the gift of the curse, too."

"How can a gift be a curse?"

Noah smiled decadently. "Oh, it's a gift, bro. Damn straight."

Lucas smiled and nodded. "Go 'head, son. Break it down, then."

"Alright. I'll tell you about the gift first. I ain't gotta tell you that women ain't never been a problem for me, 'cause you understand. It ain't never been a problem for you, either. Think back as far as you can, Luke. Stories your folks told you about bein' the prettiest baby in the nursery, when you were five or six, little girls wantin' to play house or doctor with you. Getting' a little older, maybe nine or 10, and those girls lettin' you kiss 'em in the coat closet. Then 12 or 13, and they were lettin' you feel 'em up and do some dry-humpin' at their house. Any older, and you were probably hittin' every honey that would let you. I'm talkin' about fine girls, not the homely ones with big asses that let anybody touch 'em. After that, it was on. Every time you looked up, women were throwin' ass at you, and you were catchin' every piece that came your way."

Lucas laughed. Noah's ass was crazy, but so far he was right. "Keep going. I'm listening."

"Then you get a little more mature and start sleepin' with women instead of girls. You start gettin' some finesse and pick up some skills. All of a sudden, you ain't just some really cute boy anymore. Now you're a bonafide lover, too. Playa, playa! You do a little more maturin', step your game up and get a job decent enough to keep you fly. Now you're a man and you ain't cute

at all no more. Everything else you got goin' for you makes you even more attractive. Congratulations! You just graduated to a Mack!"

They laughed and gave each other dap.

"Now comes the curse," Lucas said, once he stopped laughing at No's definition of the gift.

"Yep. While you're quietly enjoying your pleasant, Mack Daddy lifestyle, those girls and women you screw around with are doin' two things."

He paused and took out a roll of peppermint Lifesavers. He popped one in his mouth and offered one to Lucas. Lucas took it and parked the car.

"What two things?"

"Gettin' older and makin' wish lists. See, while we're out there enjoying gettin' a little honey from every flower we decide to sink our stingers in, they're wishin' they'll hurry up and get married, get a nice house and a couple of kids before the shine wears off their asses. Next thing we know, one of 'em decides she wants us to be her knight in shinin' armor. Just like we do, a woman knows how to get the man she wants. Especially if the sex is good. They hit us over the head with that shit. We might not make 'em exclusive at first, maybe just the main one. Sooner or later, she starts edging everybody else out and beggin' for commitment. It ain't even like we don't think about the same thing, but our time frames are different than what women have in mind. It's much further down the road, 'cause we're still screwin'. Anyway, to make a long story short, if we give in, we get hit with the curse."

"Which is?"

They got out of the car and Noah walked over to his side.

"Once a mack, always a mack. You get so used to women always bein' available to you, throwin' themselves at you, so used to the game, that when you finally want to make that move, you got a big surprise in store for your ass."

"What's that?"

"You find out it's almost impossible for you to be completely faithful. You find out you've been mackin' so long, it's ingrained in you."

"I don't agree."

Karma II

Noah shrugged, but looked at him with empathy. "Then don't, but it's true. You know it's true. Even when you have the best intentions. The circumstances may not always be the same, but the basic principle stands, Luke."

They walked into Leah's building and rang for the elevator.

"Damn, No. You tryin' that hard not to get married? You made up a curse?"

They stepped into the elevator and Noah punched the button for Leah's floor.

"I ain't makin' up shit."

Lucas knew he was right to a certain extent. As much as he'd loved Justine, he'd still slept with Simone. "Yeah, maybe you're right."

"I know I'm right."

They stepped off the elevator and glanced around the hallway for her apartment number. "You seen the ass on Leah?"

Lucas smiled and nodded. "Yeah, No, I saw it. Hard to miss it."

"I gotta tap it."

Lucas shook his head and laughed. "Come on, Noah,"

Noah cut him off. "I have to, Luke. She fuckin' looks like Janet Jackson."

"More like Nia Long."

"Still a winner. I gotta get it."

"What about Liz?"

"Liz ain't here."

"Besides, you don't even know if she's feeling you like that."

"She is. I ain't new to this game, Luke. Neither are you. You're just tryin' to stick up for Liz. Shit, Leah's feelin' me as hard as Nick's feelin' you. Don't try and act like you don't know that, either. She's feelin' you so hard, she can't even look at you. Really nice ass on her, too, by the way."

Lucas smiled and shook his head.

"You got issues, Noah," he said as he rang the bell.

"Yeah, okay. The first one bein', how do I get Leah's legs in the air?"

"Shut up, man. We're right here at the door."

Noah smiled devilishly. "Good. If she hears me, it'll already be out there. Less work for me."

"Like I said, you got issues, bro. You need to calm your ass down."

Noah shrugged. "I keep tryin' to tell you, Luke. Noah don't change."

The door popped open and Leah greeted them with a smile. She was wearing a tight pair of low-riding jeans and sage-colored sweater, just short enough to give you a glimpse of the golden-brown skin of her flat belly.

"Hey, fellas. Come on in. I hope it wasn't too hard to find me."

"Not at all. How you doin'?" Lucas said, stepping

33

Karma II

over the threshold.

"I'm good. We were just waiting for you guys."

Lucas and Noah removed their jackets and Leah turned and hung Lucas' in the foyer closet. Both of their eyes fell to those jeans. Lucas glanced at Noah and gave him a look that said *I ain't mad at you*. Noah smiled shrewdly as Leah reached for his jacket.

"Sorry. It's a little wet." Noah locked her in his gray gaze and changed his shrewd smile to charming.

Leah smiled back and batted her eyelashes. "I'll just bet it is."

"You have no idea." He mumbled, suggestively.

They followed her down the hall into the bright and airy kitchen. Nicole was at the counter, chopping vegetables. She looked up when they came in and smiled.

"Hope you like lasagna," she said by the way of greeting.

Her eyes hopped on Lucas and hopped off just as quickly. She was wearing jeans, too, and a fitted white shirt - a far cry from the mostly androgynous stuff she wore at work. The shirt accentuated her curvy figure, her full breasts and tiny waist. It seemed starkly white against her cinnamon skin. Her hair was lush, dark and glossy, pulled back in a ponytail. It fell down her back in loose bouncy curls. She looked over at him with huge, slightly uptilted eyes that were so dark they were almost black.

"Well, do you?" Nick asked him.

Lucas blinked. "Do I what?"

Something that was not quite a smile touched her perfect lips. "Do you like lasagna?"

Lucas realized he must have been looking at her a little too hard. "It's fine," he said.

Leah stepped between him and Noah. "Did you bring wine?"

Lucas and Noah exchanged a puzzled look. "Wine?" Noah asked.

Leah placed her hands on her hips. "Yes, wine.

Remember, you asked if I wanted you to bring anything? I said wine, Noah."

"I got sidetracked. I forgot."

"Then I suggest you skip yourself down to the liquor store and get some."

Noah's smile shrunk down to a smirk.

"I don't skip, baby." He said in a low voice and took a step toward her.

"Okay, okay. Forget it."

Noah reached out like he was going to grab her, and Leah jumped out of his way so fast she collided with Lucas.

"You're crazy." She said, moving behind Lucas.

Noah laughed at her wickedly. "And you're a coward," he replied.

Nick sighed loudly. "Alright, already. Enough you two. I'll make the liquor run. Leah, if you and Noah could tear yourselves away from each other and find the time to finish chopping this stuff while I'm gone, I'd appreciate it."

Karma II

She paused to wash her hands, "Come on, Lucas, let's go."

Before he could say anything she had her hand on his shoulder, leading him out of the room. Leah reached into her pocket and pulled out a fifty and handed it to Nick.

"Here. Get a merlot, while you leave me alone here with the wolf."

Nick plucked the money out of Leah's hand and flipped her ponytail out of her coat. "You can take care of yourself," she said.

She walked out of the apartment. Lucas followed her elevator and pushed the button.

"They're probably all over each other by now," Nick stated, putting her hands in her pockets.

"Probably."

The door opened and Nick walked in first. "That's a little soon, don't you think?"

"Soon for what?"

He positioned himself a bit behind her. Lucas was never as blatant as Noah, but he checked her out just the same. Noah was right again. Pretty nice ass.

"For them to be at each other like that."

"I'm not a judge. They're both grown."

"What's up with Noah? What's his story?"

She turned around and looked up at him. "You know what I mean. What's his story?"

The elevator opened into the lobby. He caught the scent of her. Some soft smell… like strawberries. "If you want Noah's story, you're gonna have to ask Noah for it."

She sighed. "You're difficult, aren't you?"

Lucas laughed. "Not really."

Nick was walking slowly. Lucas fell into pace beside her. He studied her profile. Her cheekbones were elegant, her nose, small and dainty. Her lips a full and sublime pout. She was exotically beautiful, and once again, Lucas felt himself wanting to reach out and touch her to see if she was real or a figment of his imagination.

"You know, they call you guys rock stars."

He smiled. "Oh, yeah?"

"Yeah, they do."

"I wonder why?"

"I know why. Well, now I do. Apart from your stellar careers in police work, I mean. You guys remind me of music."

Lucas laughed. "Now, that's a first. You want to explain that to me?"

Nick looked thoughtful, then started giving him her take on things.

"Well… Noah's that in your face, blatant sex music. You know, that R. Kelly, Bump n' Grind, throw your panties on the stage type of deal. Fine as hell, sexy and most likely, can deliver the goods."

Lucas stopped walking. "Damn, girl, you feelin' Noah like that?"

She stopped walking too "Noah's pretty cool. He only gets on my nerves when his machismo gets in the way. But no, I'm not feeling Noah like that. Why do you ask?"

Lucas looked down at her. She was feeling him out, obviously. As much as he wanted to kiss those pouty lips of hers, he decided not to let her inside of his head just now.

"I just asked. That's all," he said smoothly.

Her mouth tilted into a smile and she continued walking. "You, on the other hand, remind me of the classics. You walked into Myers' office like you had your own background music. I could have sworn I heard some Barry White playing somewhere."

She looked him over quickly, her eyes lingering on his. "I'll bet you've smashed more than a few hearts since you've been in this world, haven't you?"

Lucas was sure he had. "I wouldn't know. I never got the feedback."

"Okay. I didn't come down with yesterday's rain, though."

"Uh-huh. You probably broke a few hearts of your own."

Nick threw his words right back at him. "I wouldn't know. I never got the feedback."

Lucas was looking at her intently, wondering what her story was. Was she married? What about kids? Was there some miniature Nicole running about somewhere? He wondered who held her heart.

"What are you thinking about?" Nick asked.

He wanted to tell her he was thinking about running his fingers through her hair, but he didn't. "Nothing."

"I don't believe you. You look like you're always thinking about something. What's your story, Lucas?"

"Don't you read the papers? It was in there."

The words fell out of his mouth sharper than he'd intended. He didn't try to fix it. Nick looked momentarily thrown off-guard by his reaction and the drop of acid in his voice.

"That was insensitive. I should have put more thought into that question."

Lucas averted his eyes as they walked into the liquor store. "Uh-huh."

She stopped in front of the Merlot shelf. Nicole seemed indecisive, and Lucas took it as an opportunity to move closer to her. He stood just behind her and leaned in. He could smell her hair. It was definitely strawberries.

"I'm no good at wine," she said, shifting her weight to one foot.

Her back touched Lucas' chest and she bounced off him like he'd shocked her. She turned to face him, and their eyes locked. Lucas decided to see how Nicole felt about his machismo. He took another step forward until they were almost touching. Nick swallowed hard and searched his eyes, but she didn't fall back. Lucas had been totally aware of his own drawing power for a long time. He flexed on her, but just a little. He looked down at her through his eyelashes and touched her arm. A tiny frown creased her brow as she tilted her head back. Lucas smiled down at her enticingly… and reached behind her to take down a bottle of wine. He held it out to her.

Karma II

"This one." He said, quietly. Nicole kept looking at him, then seemed to fight being flustered. She'd thought he was going to kiss her, and it was clear to both of them, she was going to let him. She really did frown when Lucas' smile became slightly cocky. She snatched the bottle from him and walked away without a word.

Lucas swallowed the laugh that threatened to escape from him. He hadn't really meant to taunt her like that, but something in him felt he had to. Nicole appeared at the end of the aisle, holding the wine in one hand, and a bottle of Sapphire gin in the other.

"Are you just going to stand there, basking in the glow of your own masculinity, or are you gonna help me buy this liquor? I thought martinis would be nice."

"I don't drink gin." He went into the scotch aisle and picked up a bottle of single malt. He turned and Nicole was standing at his elbow, giving him the evil eye.

"I guess that did a lot for your ego."

Lucas smiled down at her engagingly. "My ego's fine. What did it do for you?"

The look he gave her was potent. Nick blinked and cast her eyes away with lightning speed. A blush crept over her face as those kissable lips poked out, helplessly. Lucas stared at her with an arrogant astuteness that suggested he was the one in control, that he was cognizant of his own allure, and he was in full command of it.

"Stop staring at me," she muttered, and turned on her heel.

Nick went back into the wine aisle, set the gin between her feet, and picked up a bottle of vermouth. They paid for the liquor and left the store. Nick didn't speak to him until they were almost back at Leah's.

Karma II

Nick pursed her lips and gave him a very dark look. "I was only trying to get to know you better, Lucas. You didn't have to catch me off guard like that," she said, quietly.

Lucas knew he played her, embarrassed her on purpose, but she was so opinionated, and talked so tough, he'd wanted to see if she had any softness to her. She wasn't wearing that little imperious, smarmy smile now. Her lip was poked out like a child's.

"I apologize," he said, sincerely.

She rang for the elevator without looking at him. "Apology accepted."

They rode up in silence. He leaned with one shoulder against the wall and looked at his boots. He smiled to himself.

"What are you smiling about?"

He looked up and gave her a dose of her own medicine. "Stop staring at me."

She shook her head and got off the elevator. "I knew

you were difficult."

Lucas laughed. "You're not so easy yourself." They stopped in front of Leah's door and Nick grinned.

"Five dollars says they were feeling each other up."

"No bet."

"Why not?"

"I don't like to lose."

Nick laughed and rang the doorbell. She looked at him appreciatively. "You're not as bad as I thought you'd be. A little full of yourself, though."

"Thanks," he said with a heavy dose of sarcasm.

Leah opened the door, wiping her hands on a towel. "It's about time. You took forever."

She took the bag Nick was carrying and headed back to the kitchen. Noah was at the stove, deftly sautéing onions and garlic. He glanced at Leah as she took the gin out of the bag.

"I hope that's for you and Nick."

Lucas sat at the breakfast bar. Leah ignored him and spoke to Nick. "Martinis?"

"I thought that would be nice."

Noah winced and looked at Lucas. "Please, tell me you got scotch in that bag."

Lucas laughed and produced the bottle of Glenlivet.

"That's why you my boy. Hit me," Noah said cheerfully.

He stepped away from the stove and lit a cigarette. He motioned to Leah, "I'm done. You take over."

Noah sat down next to Lucas and Lucas poured them each a drink, while Leah put an ashtray in front of Noah and started mixing martinis. Lucas looked at Noah, asking an unspoken question. Noah stuck his cigarette in his mouth to hide his smile. Lucas sipped his drink to hide his. He would have lost that bet.

They went on to have a pretty pleasant evening. Nick's lasagna was well worth the wait, and both women were great company, although inclined to be argumentative and in a constant power struggle with Lucas and Noah. They ate, drank and played spades, laughing a lot, like they'd all known each other a long time.

At times, though, the tension in the air was so thick, you could cut it with a knife. Not serious tension. Sexual tension. Leah wanted Noah so badly, every time he touched her, she looked like she was going to have an orgasm. Noah didn't help matters much. Practically everything he said to her was a double-entendre. It was different between Lucas and Nick. He spent a lot of time watching her, admiring her considerable beauty and the graceful way she moved. She stole long looks at him when she thought he was preoccupied.

Lucas had a feeling that if he reached out and touched her, she turn into a silky little puddle of something warm, sweet and wet… something… He had a sudden, unbelievably vivid scenario play out in his head. A vision of him spreading velvety, cinnamon colored thighs, and putting his mouth on her. He imagined she tasted like those damned strawberries she smelled like. He shook his head and gave up his seat on that daydream.

Noah was looking at him with unabashed merriment. He laughed out loud. "Damn, Luke. Where'd you go just then?"

Lucas started the car and pulled out. "Nowhere. I was just thinking."

"Thinkin' hard, huh? That tuck your lips in, frown your face up, concentrated thinkin'. Shit, man, what was you thinkin' about?"

Lucas laughed. "Fuck you, Noah."

Noah laughed, too. "Fuck you back, Luke."

Noah leaned back into his seat. "Kinda like Nick, don't you?"

"She got my attention."

He was surprised someone had finally managed to ease Justine out of the forefront of his mind. Lucas found himself thinking more about Nicole. He thought he was capable of losing hours just kissing her and smelling her hair. It started to rain again. Lucas put his wipers on and continued to think about Nicole.

Karma II

Chapter Four

Just like old times

Karma II

Noah rang Nadine's doorbell and braced himself. He never knew what mood he'd find his ex-wife in. Raine was on the honor roll at her school, taking a special trip to Washington. Noah had to come up with his half of the money. He figured he'd stop by before he went to work and get it out of the way. He had a meeting with Myers and Griffin this morning, and being late was not an option.

Noah was about to start banging on the door when Nadine opened it. As always, Noah felt a pang of regret when he saw her. She regarded him coolly in all her beautiful, glowing splendor. She'd put highlights in her hair and they made her even more radiant. She pursed her perfect mouth, raised a perfect eyebrow, and wrinkled her perfect nose. She stared at him with huge and gorgeous brown eyes.

"I know you weren't about to start banging on my

door, Noah."

She was on low seethe. Nadine was eternally angry with him. She held the door open and he stepped inside. Noah looked down at her and smiled optimistically.

"Good morning, Nadine. How are you?"

She rolled her eyes at him. "Fantastic."

Noah smiled. "That's nice. I'm feelin' pretty good, myself."

Nadine sucked her teeth. "Hurray for you."

He gave Nadine the check. "Here. I promised Raine I'd drop it by this mornin'."

Nadine plucked it out of his hand and stuck it in the pocket of her jeans. "At least you keep your promises to Raine."

They'd been divorced for almost four years and Nadine was still pissed.

He turned to go. "You're welcome, Nadine."

"Our children tell me Lissette's always at your house. What's up with that, Noah?"

He looked back at her as icily as she was looking at him. "Did they tell you that, or was it more like an inquisition?"

"I don't pick our kids' brains."

"Sure you don't." Noah opened the door, Nadine pushed it closed and leaned her back against it.

"Anything you want to tell me, Noah?"

He tilted his head and looked at her flatly. "Like what?"

"Does she live there?"

Noah thought about lying, then figured, what was the point? "Right now, yeah. Yeah, she does."

Nadine frowned. "What do you mean, right now? Is she getting her apartment painted?"

"Nah. She's pregnant." Not in a million years would Noah have expected the reaction he got from Nadine.

"What?" The word fell out of her mouth like a stone.

"You heard me."

Nadine's bottom lip trembled and she slid down the door and put her face in her hands. She crumpled to the floor and started to sob so harshly, she sounded like she was braying. Noah stared down at her with his mouth hanging open in complete shock. Noah tentatively put a hand on her shoulder. What the fuck was this?

"Nadine?" She shocked him even more by latching onto him. She threw her arms around his neck like she was drowning.

"God, Noah, you were put on this earth to hurt me!"

Noah pried her arms from his neck. What the fuck was this?

"Nadine-"

"You've done a lot of horrible things to me, Noah, but you just topped yourself. How could you do this to me?"

Noah looked at her as if she was crazy. "Alright. Now you're scarin' me. What's goin' on?"

She looked at him angrily. "You are such a bastard!"

"What did I do? *You* divorced *me*, Nadine. I moved on. Just like you did with that guy, Walter."

"You moved on right after we got married! You never even tried to control yourself, and it's obvious you're still out of control now!"

Noah blinked. "Outta control?"

Nadine started ticking his shortcomings off on her fingers. "Smoking, drinking, lying, hanging out until all hours, whoring with that goddamn Lucas! You took everything from me, Noah."

Noah's head went back in disbelief. "*I* took everything from *you*?"

She sniffed and wiped her eyes. "Everything."

Noah looked around, expansively. "Correct me if I'm wrong, but didn't you get everything? I mean, you got the house, the car, the kids, and a healthy chunk of my paycheck. What did I get? I got the right to take shit off you for the rest of my life 'cause I screwed up. That's what I got!"

"That's bullshit! You're an asshole, Noah."

Noah stared at her. "I don't have time for this. I gotta go."

He started to get to his feet, but Nadine grabbed his hand.

"You never even wore your ring," she whispered. "I have a million and one reasons to hate you, Noah, and I do. On the other hand, I have a million other reasons to love you, and I still do."

Noah frowned and looked away. Nadine put her hand on his face and turned him back to face her. "I was the one you married, Noah. I guess I was really a fool to think I'd be the only one to have your babies, or the only one to want to."

She smiled at him. A tear fell from each of her beautiful eyes.

"Nadine,"

"Shut up, Noah," she said, hoarsely.

Karma II

Noah narrowed his eyes and was about to come back at her, but she silenced him by locking her lips firmly over his. Noah's tongue was instantly in her mouth, eagerly exploring all the sweet and sugary places he thought he'd never taste again. She was awakening feelings in him that had lain dormant for a long time. Shit! This was Nadine. Nadine rose to her knees. Noah rose with her. She pushed his coat off his shoulders and pulled his shirt out of his pants. Their fingers found the buttons on their shirts at the same time and fumbled them open, hurriedly. They were still kissing with all the hunger and passion of going so long without even a taste of each other. Noah reached behind her and helped her out of her bra. Nadine pulled gently away from him, and ran her hands familiarly over his bare chest. She looked at his body as if she were remembering, and he did the same to her. Noah looked down at Nadine's small flawless breasts, the nipples like chocolate kisses.

"What are we doin', Nadine?" His hands glided over

her silky body until they settled on her breasts.

"Complicating things." She replied and kissed his neck. Her hands dropped to his waist and tugged at his belt impatiently. "Noah, help me." She said, urgently.

He didn't know why this was happening, but there was absolutely no way he was passing up the chance to be this close to Nadine again. "Okay," he said, and unbuckled his belt. Nadine's nimble fingers unbuttoned his pants and pulled his zipper down. She sighed as her hand curled around him warmly. Nadine kissed him again and Noah moaned. She let go of him and stood up, abruptly, and started moving toward the bedroom.

"Come on," she said over her shoulder. Nadine started removing the rest of her clothing as she walked. By the time Noah joined her, they were both naked. Nadine reached out for him, and Noah surprised himself by stepping away.

"Listen to me, Nadine. You gotta be sure this is what you want. If you're not sure, I don't wanna do this."

She sat on the bed. "This is exactly what I want. Stop pretending you're afraid of me."

Noah smiled. "I ain't afraid of you, sweetheart."

Nadine returned his smile, pushed herself back, and parted her legs.

"Good, then get in this bed and break me down like you used to."

Noah went to work on her. He had the experience of knowing her body as well as he knew his own. Within minutes, she was quivering and running her hands through his hair. Her thighs caressed his face as she started to groan and her body jerked in short spasms. Her fingers curled in his hair and she gently tugged him up.

"Noah. Noah. Come up, baby. Come up."

Noah came up slowly and a bit against his will. He could have eaten her alive. He kissed her flat belly and worked his way up. She placed a hand on either side of his face and grinned at him.

He smiled. "What?"

Nadine kissed him lightly and dropped one of her hands. She took hold of him and guided him to the bullseye.

"Go ahead, Noah. Give it to me like you used to. Make me call you Daddy."

He went in and it was like they'd never been apart. It was all still there. The same heat, the same intensity, the same passion. Their bodies moved and rocked with each other in fiery extravagance. As they rode the crest of that first big wave, Nadine dug her heels in and started sighing. Noah smiled at the accustomed response and moved faster and deeper. Nadine opened her eyes and looked at him. Noah could tell from that one look that she loved him like she always did. Her lips parted and she started shaking, pulsating and throbbing around him hotly. Nadine wrapped herself around him like a python and started screaming. He exhaled shakily, starting to succumb to the hot thrill that was spreading through him. He smiled down at her fiercely, with a carnal air of domination and played their old game.

"Whose is it?" He whispered, harshly. A look of rebellion flitted over Nadine's face.

Noah growled deep in his throat and went all the way in, grinding hard. Nadine began to groan and tightened herself around him. She was hot and wet and slippery snug. That hot thrill was growing and he knew he couldn't hold out much longer. Noah clenched his teeth.

"I said, whose is it, Nadine?"

She put her lips against the corner of his mouth, and gushed over him in hot spasms. She screamed and started to whimper.

"It's yours, okay? Daddy, you know it's yours."

"Damn, right. Oh God!"

He couldn't hold back anymore. He thrust himself into her hard and deep and erupted like a volcano. He slammed into her over and over like he was trying to nail her to the bed. He kissed her deeply to keep from screaming her name, vaguely aware that Nadine was coming again, all over him. He couldn't stop. He hammered her relentlessly, until he was empty and he collapsed on top of her, breathing hard and kissing her face. Nadine.

They lay there together, their bodies entwined, until the tremors were over. Instead of jumping up and leaving, he held onto her. He didn't know if he'd ever get a chance to have her like this again. Nadine clung to him, her head on his chest, and her arm firmly around his waist. She purred with satisfaction, snuggled into him, and put her thigh across his hips. He hated to break this up, but he had to.

"Nadine?"

"Hmmm?"

"Nadine… I really hate to do this, but I gotta go."

She nodded and lifted her pretty head. "I know. Go to work. I'm not mad. I'm satisfied."

Noah stood up. "So what was this for?"

Nadine got up and walked over to him. "I wanted to see if you still loved me."

"Shit, all you had to do was ask. What do you wanna know that for? "

He knew he had to go, but he couldn't keep his hands off her. He pulled her to him, his hands on her back just above her hips. He kissed her forehead, the tip of her nose, and lingered on her lips.

"What do you want from me?"

Nadine turned on her heel and went into the bathroom. Noah was right behind her. She handed him a towel.

"You should shower before you go to work. Can't have you walking around smelling like sex."

"Is that what it was?"

He hated the question the minute it left his mouth. It made him feel and sound very vulnerable. Nadine being the lady she was, didn't dawdle on his weak moment. She smiled at him and put her hand on his chest, backing him up toward the shower.

"I'm not going to talk to you about this right now, Noah."

"Fine. When?" He asked the question in a flat voice, but it came out a little whiny, even to him. Shit. Noah turned the water on as Nadine moved into his peripheral vision.

"You okay?"

He stepped under the spray and closed his eyes, willing his swagger back. "Yup."

"I'm going to pour us a cup of coffee. I'll see you in the kitchen."

She closed the door firmly behind her and left Noah standing there with a puzzled look on his face. This shit was getting weirder by the second. Nadine was acting like they'd never gone through that nasty divorce. Just yesterday she'd been as cold as ice. Hell, she'd been cold right up until the moment he'd told her Liz was pregnant. He finished his shower.

Karma II

Noah walked down the hall, into the sunny kitchen, and started to put his clothes back on. He pulled up his shorts and put on his shirt. They didn't speak as he slipped on his pants and stepped into his shoes. He buttoned his shirt and pulled his collar up. Noah was about to put on his tie when Nadine took it out of his hand and put it around his neck. She started to tie it like she used to. When she was done, she turned his collar down and smoothed his shirt. Nadine stepped back to admire her work.

"You look really handsome, Noah."

"Gee, thanks."

"Well, it's true. Don't you want your coffee?"

"I'm already pushin' it. Can't. Sorry."

"You mad at me, Lover?"

She hadn't called him that in six years. He clipped his badge next to his phone and slipped into his overcoat. Noah turned to her, not quite angry.

"You listen to me, Nadine. I don't know what all this

shit is about, but you and me gotta talk, and right now, I don't have time. There's too much shit floatin' around, and I don't need you runnin' hot and cold on me, see?"

She put her hand over her mouth and smothered a laugh.

"You know, when you get all upset and agitated, you sound like Edward G. Robinson in Little Caesar."

Noah looked at her in exasperation. Was she actually laughing at him?

"What?" He stuck a Dunhill in his mouth and picked up his car keys. "This is some bullshit. I gotta go."

She put her hand on his shoulder , stood on her tiptoes, and gave him an intimate kiss on the cheek.

"I love you, Noah. Have a good, safe day."

Noah hadn't expected her to say that. He really hadn't expected to feel like he'd just been kicked in the stomach, by her saying that. He kissed the top of her head and stuck his cigarette back in his mouth.

"I'll call you." Nadine smiled and patted his ass playfully.

"You better." Noah walked briskly to his car and got in. He looked over at Nadine, and she blew him a kiss before she closed the door. Oh shit. What had he done?

Chapter Five

More bust than buy

Lucas and Noah sat in an unmarked, watching Nick and Leah in the Corolla parked on the other side of the street. It was 25 degrees outside. Yet here they were, looking to bust some lazy-ass, low level street dealer, who was obviously afraid of the fucking cold. Noah took a sip of his coffee and lit a cigarette.

"I got problems, Luke." Lucas looked over at him and saw a look on Noah's face he hadn't seen in ages. Worry.

"No, what's wrong, man? You alright?" Noah shook his head and sighed.

"I got myself into a situation."

"What situation?"

Noah sighed again. "I told Nadine about Liz. I told her she's pregnant."

Lucas looked at him. "What did you do that for?"

"She was fuckin' with me at the time. Guess I just

wanted to piss her off."

Lucas smiled. "I bet it worked."

"I don't know…"

"What do you mean, you don't know?"

"Some weird shit jumped off, Luke."

"Weird like what?" Noah stared at Lucas for a second, then he laughed dryly.

"Well, she fuckin' freaked out. Started cryin' and shit. That was the last thing I expected outta Nadine, Luke, that kinda knocked me off guard, you know?"

Lucas waited for Noah to go on.

"She started sayin' how hurt she was, and how I'm an asshole and a fuck-up, and how I never took our marriage seriously. Then she said she loved me and she was a fool to think she was the only woman that would ever want my babies. Then… she started with that cryin' shit again, Luke. Damn."

Noah looked out the window and put his hand over his mouth. He wasn't used to seeing Noah this visibly upset over a woman. As a matter of fact, the last time he saw him in this particular mood, it had been over the same woman. Nadine.

Karma II

"So, what happened?"

Noah laughed that same little untickled, dry laugh. "You ain't stupid. She told me she wanted me to break her down like I used to."

Lucas smiled. "And of course, you did."

Noah laughed with a bit more mirth in his voice.

"Shit, you know I did."

Lucas stayed quiet. Noah hit the dashboard with his fist.

"It was like I never fuckin' left. It was Nadine, Luke."

He didn't have to ask Noah if he was still in love with Nadine. That was something he was certain of.

"Nadine wants you back?"

Noah shrugged. "I don't know, but if she didn't, I don't

think she ever would've let me touch her."

"Yeah, but does she want you back so Liz can't have you?"

"The thought crossed my mind."

"Yeah, Noah. Looks like you've got yourself a situation." Noah glanced at him and smirked.

"No shit, Luke. She laid it on me and I bitched right up. Got all whiny... sounded like I was beggin'."

Lucas laughed. "Damn, No. I don't know if I can believe that shit."

"I didn't believe it, either. Took me a minute to get my swagger back. By the way, don't be laughin' at me, Luke. I didn't laugh at you when you were runnin' behind Justine with your tongue hangin' out."

That was true.

"Sorry, No." He looked him in the eye, "What you gonna do, man?"

Noah laughed like a scoundrel and nodded toward the Corolla.

"I'm gonna be able to tell you what color panties Leah's wearin' by the end of the night."

"You're crazy, Noah."

"I got my mind made up."

Lucas looked at his old friend long and hard. "Are you that curious, or are you on self-destruct? What about Liz and Nadine? You gotta keep this shit in perspective."

"I got it in perspective. Right now, Liz is bein' a battle axe and I think Nadine may be on her way to winnin' the Bitch of the Year award. I'm gonna do what I wanna do. I tell you all the time, I am who I am. Noah don't change. If it ain't Leah, it'll be somebody else. At least I'm honest with myself."

"Uh-huh. You get points for that. What was it you said to me, once? I admire the cold bastard in you."

Noah laughed. "Good, cause I learned that shit from your cold ass."

"Fuck you, Noah."

"Fuck you back, Luke."

Again the lapse into an easy, comfortable, silence. He knew trying to talk Noah out of getting involved with Leah would be a wasted effort. Noah had a hard, hard head. If you told him there was a hole in his path, he'd break his neck stepping into it. Lucas was his friend, though. Whatever happened, he'd be there for him. He perpetually had Noah's back.

A white Acura pulled up next to the Corolla. Nicole rolled down her window and exchanged a bit of conversation with whoever was inside. The Acura pulled off and parked a few cars up the block from the Corolla. Lucas watched as the driver's door opened and Leah got out. Nicole got out on the other side. Lucas looked at Noah.

"We got activity."

"That figures. I was just gettin' comfortable." Nicole walked over to Leah and folded her arms across her chest against the cold. Nicole dropped something and bent to pick it up. Lucas winced. He hadn't seen an ass that perfect in a long time.

Karma II

"I'm gonna tell Nick you got a huge crush on her, Luke," Noah said.

Lucas didn't answer him. He ran his hand over his beard and admired the shape of her thighs and the way the light from the street lamp caught her hair.

"Lucas?"

"Yeah, No?" Noah leaned toward him.

"What you gonna do, man?"

"Nothing right now."

They'd been having lunch the other day and Leah had said something about some guy named Keith. Nick had an adverse reaction to the mention of his name. Later on, Noah asked Leah who he was and she'd confided that Keith Childs was Nicole's very recent ex-boyfriend and roommate. She told Noah, even though they'd broken up, Keith had been dragging his feet when it came to vacating the apartment.

Lucas wondered what Nicole had seen in Keith. Lucas

doubted Keith had turned into a nice guy. Maybe he'd worked real hard to get her. Lucas didn't think he'd have to work that hard. There was definitely more than a spark between him and Nicole. She was more than likely hanging back because of Childs. Lucas was leery for a lot of reasons. Keith Childs wasn't that high on his list. Fuck him. He cared about Nicole, though, and he didn't want to deal with her straight out of a bad relationship. Lucas had never in his life been a rebound guy, and he wasn't about to start now.

He also wasn't sure if he was ready to deal that hard again. Nicole had the potential to break down the comfort zone he'd carefully put up around himself since Justine. He wasn't in a rush, and he wasn't going anywhere. He knew it would happen sooner or later.

"What do you mean not now?" Noah asked.

"She doesn't need me pushin' up on her right now. Right now, she's gotta deal with Childs." Noah grunted.

"Guess you got a point. I'm glad she's through with him. That guy's a turd, bro. I was glad to scrape my knuckles up on his ass."

Lucas looked out at Leah and Nicole, waiting in the cold for whoever was in the Acura. He nodded at Noah.

"Let's start movin'. Radio in."

Noah radioed to backup that they were moving. They got out of the car inconspicuously, and started walking at a leisurely pace toward Nicole and Leah. It was taking the occupants of the Acura a little longer than a minute to get out. Noah gave Lucas a quizzical look.

"What do you think is takin' 'em so long?" Lucas stared up the block.

"Don't know. Be ready to move."

Noah put the cigarette he was about to light back in the pack. The driver and passenger finally got out. A third man exited from the back seat. The first man was tall and rangy, the second, shorter and thicker. The third was big. Tall and heavy, but he was a kid. You could tell from here, which made it more likely his companions were kids, too. They rolled up on Leah and Nicole like hawks, talking loud and bigging themselves up like ballers.

Lucas and Noah started walking again, not too slow, not too fast. The tall rangy one took the liberty of putting his fingers in Nicole's ponytail.

"Damn, baby, is this real? You a fine muthafucka. I'll give you your eightball free if you suck my dick."

Lucas looked at Noah. "That one's mine."

Noah chuckled. "I figured."

Nicole moved away from him and spoke to Leah. "Let's just get our stuff and go."

Leah sucked her teeth and put her hand on her hip. "Aight. I ain't pullin' out no money 'til I know I ain't wastin' my time. Y'all must think we stupid."

The big one stepped to her. "You got a lotta mouth on you. I think I'm gonna put your little young ass in the car and make you earn your shit."

The second guy held his hand up. "Chill, man. How much you want, baby?" He said to Nicole.

She stuck her hand in her pocket and pulled out two hundred dollars.

"Give her what she wants."

He turned back to Nicole. "My shit is good, baby, don't try and use it all at once. I want you to come back."

The big one handed over the drugs. Lucas and Noah started walking fast. Nicole looked up and saw them coming. She turned to the one that took the money.

"Thank you, baby."

Lucas and Noah were 30 feet away. They started running, badges displayed prominently, hands on their weapons.

"Police! Freeze!" Noah yelled.

The tall one and the shorter one broke and ran in separate directions. The big one panicked and tried to push through Nicole and Leah. Lucas heard Leah shout at him.

"Oh, hell, no! Get your fat ass down!"

Lucas figured they were too close for him to get away. The tall one was flying, but Lucas wasn't worried because he was damn fast himself. He saw him reach into his coat. Something glinted. Lucas promptly closed the distance. He didn't give him the chance to pull anything on him. His feet left the ground and he tackled him hard. So hard and so fast, the kid skidded down the block about 10 feet, screaming, with Lucas on his back.

"Shit! Shit!" Lucas growled as he felt the skin leave the heel of his hand. It burned like hell, but it was nothing compared to what this kid was howling about. Lucas put his knee in his back and put his cuffs on him. He paused to look at his palm. The flesh was so shocked, it hadn't really started to bleed yet, just tiny dots of red.

Lucas pulled him up with his good hand. The tall guy was bleeding. He'd skidded down the street on the left side of his face.

"Where's the gun?" He gave a cursory inspection of the perp's coat and the surrounding area.

"Where's the fucking gun?"

"I threw it. I don't know where it is!"

"Fuck!" Lucas took off his radio and told his back up the situation. Lost weapon. Some grade school kid could find it and shoot his little sister's face off with it. Asshole.

"I-I didn't do nothin'," Lucas pulled down on the cuffs. The kid yelped.

"Shut up! You have the right to remain silent…"

He read him his rights to him and waited for back up. He declined a ride and walked back to Noah, Nicole, and Leah. They were waiting for him with a senior officer. Lucas' hand was dripping blood now. The senior took one look and called for EMS. Noah was smoking a Dunhill. He patted Lucas on the back.

"Hurt yourself?" He grinned.

"Just a little road burn. You get your guy?"

Noah laughed with his usual sarcasm. "Do bears shit in the woods?"

Karma II

Chapter Six

Chivalry lives

Karma II

It had been a long day, and Nick was tired. All she wanted was a long bath and a date with some rum raisin Häagen Dazs. They'd been doing buy-and-busts all week, and the routine of it was exhausting.

Nick let herself into her dark apartment and took off her coat. She was halfway across the living room when she noticed light spilling out of the bedroom. She was not in the mood for this, not Keith and his bullshit. She reluctantly walked into the bedroom. Keith was at the closet, taking things out and packing them in a large cardboard box. Nick cleared her throat.

"What are you doing here this late?"

Keith looked at her ominously. "Just thought I'd come by and get my shit. You left me enough voicemails begging me to do it."

Nick stared back at him with just as much animosity.

"I shouldn't have to ask you to vacate the premises more than once. You should have just left and took all your crap when I asked you to."

"I did leave."

"Really? Looks like you're still here. By the way, make this your last trip, and I want my key before you leave. I don't want you traipsing in and out of here whenever you feel like it."

"Why? You got some other nigga creepin' up in here already?"

"What do you care?"

"I don't."

Nick had enough. "Fuck you, Keith. Hurry up and get out."

He dropped the sweater he was holding in the box without folding it. He was in front of her in three quick strides. He put his hand under her chin and tilted her head up.

"You need to check your tone of voice and your choice of words. You must've forgotten who you're talking to."

She knocked his hand away. "You're trippin'. Don't touch me. Get your shit and go before I-"

He grabbed her arm. "Before you what? Call the cops? Now that's funny, Nicky."

She tried to wrench her arm away from him, but he tightened his grip.

"What's the matter, Nicky? You don't want me to touch you? You got somebody else touching you? Huh?"

Nick had never been disgusted by Keith before, but his current behavior spawned a feeling of revulsion in her so strong, she was suddenly struck with a sick feeling deep in her stomach. "Get off!"

She tried to pull free again and Keith grabbed her other arm. Furious, Nick stomped his instep and pushed him away from her with a shoulder to the chest. When she turned to get away from him, he snatched her up by the back of her shirt so hard, she felt the hooks in her bra

Karma II

rip, and the first two buttons of her shirt popped off. Her eyes flew open in instantaneous fear and astonishment. He slammed her into the wall, knocking the wind out of her.

"You want to fight, Nicky? Let's fight then!" He hollered at her.

A ripple of terror went up Nick's spine. Who was this? She instinctively pulled her shirt together with one hand, and tried to use her other forearm to push him aside. Keith pushed her back and grabbed the front of her shirt, pulling down fiercely and popping all the remaining buttons.

"Don't get modest on me now, Nicky. I saw 'em already."

The word 'rape' popped into Nick's mind like a flashing neon sign. She felt extremely vulnerable with her breasts exposed through her ruined shirt. She dodged left, then right and slipped past him. Nick ran out of the bedroom, but Keith grabbed her in the hallway and knocked her down. She hit the floor like a brick, her chin bounced up and she bit her tongue. Nick scrabbled onto her back and Keith was on her before she could react. His fist connected with her mouth like a concrete slab and she tasted blood. He grabbed a fistful of her hair and pulled her up.

"You don't talk to me any kind of way you want to! I never thought I'd have to teach you!"

Nick couldn't believe this was Keith. She'd never been this scared before, or this angry. Nick gritted her teeth and brought her knee up as hard as she could into his groin. It was enough to get him off of her. She moved backward, got to her feet and pulled her gun.

"You son of a bitch! I should shoot your ass right now!"

She backed away from him and hastily grabbed her coat. Keith got to his feet and Nick leveled her gun.

"I want you out of here! You stay away from me, or I'll get your ass in so much trouble, you'll wish you were dead."

Keith laughed and looked at her arrogantly. "You

pulled your gun on me?"

Nick opened the door with a shaky hand. "Yeah, and I'll shoot your ass with it. Get your shit and get out. Don't be here when I get back."

She paused and licked blood off her rapidly swelling lip. Her voice trembled.

"You dirty bastard."

She stepped into the hallway and slammed the door behind her. Her gun was still in her hand and she was shaking uncontrollably. Nick put her gun back in its holster with trembling hands and put on her coat. She realized, with a jolt, that her wallet and her keys were still in the apartment. Nick felt for her cell phone and found it still clipped to her belt. She took the elevator to the lobby and hesitated. What was she going to do? Her sister lived in Boston, her parents had retired to Florida, and she couldn't even check into a hotel because her wallet was upstairs. She didn't want to bother Leah.

Karma II

Nick stepped out into the night. All the rest of her friends were either married, conveniently at work, or otherwise occupied. She tried Leah anyway and got her voicemail. Dammit! That only left one other person. She walked into the store on the corner, so she'd be visible to other people in case Keith wanted to come start some more shit.

Nick looked at her watch. It was 8:30. Maybe she'd catch him before he got up to something. He was the absolute last person she wanted to call. Nick scrolled through her phone and pressed send. He picked up on the third ring.

"What's up?" He'd surprised her by even answering.

"Lucas, it's Nick."

"I know."

"I have a problem."

"Talk to me."

"Do you think you could come get me?"

"Where are you?" She told him quickly.

"Be there as soon as I can."

"Thank you, Lucas."

"You're welcome."

She went into the store and stood just inside the doors. She knew she looked terrible. This was not the way she wanted Lucas to see her. She ran her tongue along her teeth. Keith hadn't knocked anything loose... the bastard.

Ten minutes later, a black Mercedes S500 pulled up on the other side of the street. Lucas got out and activated his alarm. He still had on the clothes he'd worn to work, a black Nautica sweater, jeans and a pair of black Timberland boots. He wasn't wearing a coat, even though it was still winter. He looked both ways and headed calmly across the street with that cool-ass, confident stride he had. The diamond in his ear glittered once as he looked at his watch. It had taken him exactly 20 minutes to get to her. He opened the door and stepped inside, staring down at her, his face totally serious. Everything changed in that moment. He was singularly the most appealing man she'd ever met. He was way, way, past handsome. He was sexy as hell. He was also kind, courageous, and there for her in 20 minutes, no questions asked. Very gently, he took her hand away from her mouth. He looked sad and angry at the same time.

Karma II

"Where is he?"

"I left him in my apartment."

"Where's that?" Nick took one look at him and knew his intention.

"I'm not telling you. Right now, you don't need to know."

"Alright. Come with me." They walked to the car in silence.

"Lucas?"

He glanced at her. "Yeah?"

She was suddenly very embarrassed, and more than a little nervous.

"Um, it was nice of you to come and get me. I know

you didn't have to."

He put his left hand on the wheel and took her hand with his right. He gave it a very comforting squeeze and didn't let it go.

"Glad you called. You're safe with me."

Nick nodded. "I know."

"Where do you want to go?" She shrugged.

"I really don't have anywhere to go. I left all my stuff up in that apartment."

"You want me to get you a hotel room?"

Nick looked over at him. "I kind of don't want to be alone."

That small dimple appeared in his right cheek, a flash of his pretty white teeth there in the dark. "I don't want you to be. I'll take you to my place and make you some tea."

Nick frowned. "Tea? Don't you have something stronger?"

"You better believe I got something stronger."

Nick didn't just assume he was talking about liquor. She felt something ticklish flutter in her belly, and covered his hand with both of hers. They didn't speak again until they got to his place. Nick followed him up the steps of a lovely old brownstone and tried not to smile as a cold wind rushed up the street and his teeth chattered involuntarily. Maybe the cold was his kryptonite.

"Where's your coat?" She asked.

"In the closet." He'd been in such a hurry to get to her that he'd left it. That was chivalry. He opened the door, stepped inside, and hit the lights. Nick tried hard to keep her swollen mouth from dropping open. She'd expected him to have an apartment in the brownstone, but

his front door opened into a great room. Living room, dining area, gigantic kitchen, all in one huge open space. It was tastefully decorated in deep rich colors that gave it a masculine feeling. Comfortable and homey. It was obviously expensive, too. There was some nice artwork on the walls, and in one spot, a black baby grand.

Karma II

"Wow." She said.

"Take your coat?"

Her hands moved to unbutton it and she froze. She turned to him, slightly mortified. "Um...I...no. That's okay."

He frowned. "Why?"

"You wouldn't happen to have a shirt I could borrow, would you?"

"What did he do?"

"He tried to intimidate me. He almost ripped my shirt off."

Lucas stared at her a long time. "Come with me."

She followed him upstairs. There was a big bedroom to the left, what looked like an office, and stairs leading to an upper level. A bathroom was at the top of the stairs. Lucas went to his right, to the master suite. It was huge and inviting. The bed was a king sized sleigh bed, the walls a little darker than cream. French doors stood before a small balcony. There was a fireplace in a small sitting area, to the right of the master bath. Lucas opened two double doors and walked into his closet. His clothes were hung up meticulously. Suits, shirts, ties, jeans sweaters, shoes - everything had its own place. He opened a drawer in a cabinet and handed her a pair of sapphire blue pajamas.

Karma II

"You can take a shower or a bath if you want. I'll wait for you downstairs."

Nick nodded and he walked out and left her alone in his bedroom. She peeked at his dresser. There were a few framed photos along the bottom of the mirror. An older couple dressed very nicely standing in front of this house. A man that absolutely had to be his father. A woman in a frame that looked like it had fallen, the glass of the frame was cracked across the middle. Whoever she was, she was very pretty, and he looked like her, too. Lucas' Marine photo. Young with no hair on his face. Very handsome. Him and Noah in their dress blues. Two little kids that looked like Noah. Last picture. Caramel skin, huge sparkling brown eyes. Her hair cascading over her shoulders. She was smiling like she was thinking of him. Justine Greer.

Nick had been shocked when she'd been murdered. She'd watched her on the news all the time. It felt strange standing here looking at her picture. She took one last look at the picture and went into the bathroom.

She showered quickly and ended up in dire need of a hair brush. She put on the pajamas, glad they had a drawstring. She drew it tight and wrapped her damp hair in a towel. Her bottom lip was busted, swollen and bruised. The bruise covered half her chin. She went to the stairs and paused. Lucas appeared at the bottom of the stairs as she stood there in her hesitation. He looked up at her and she felt something she knew she shouldn't be feeling. At that moment, she wanted him to touch her more than she wanted anything in the world.

"You okay?"

Nick found herself stammering. "I... I... could use a hair brush. Um... do you have one?"

He came up and disappeared into the bathroom. He came out with one still in its package. He went into his bedroom, and emerged with a soft, sable-colored throw and a pair of socks. Nick followed him back downstairs. There were two glasses on the coffee table and a bottle of single malt. Nick sat in the corner of the sofa, away from him. He smiled and slid over to her. He placed the cover over her lap and put the socks on her feet himself. He popped the brush out of the package and handed it to her. Nick took the towel off her head and started to brush her hair out.

Lucas poured two fingers of scotch into each glass. He turned toward her, and watched her intently. Lucas was watching her so intensely, she looked away. When she finished with her hair, he handed her the scotch and got up. He went into the kitchen and returned with some ice in a plastic bag.

Karma II

"Best I could do."

She smiled nervously and put it to her swollen lip. He sat and took a sip of his drink. Nick removed the ice pack and turned her drink up. It burned, but it felt good. She closed her eyes. When she opened them, she had a fresh drink, and Lucas was still looking at her.

"Whenever you're ready." He said quietly.

Nick laughed tensely, took a sip this time, and looked around.

"So… are you rich, or what?"

He smiled at her and shrugged. "I'm alright."

"Nice place."

"It's okay."

"Thanks again for this. I owe you one."

"Anytime, and you don't owe me anything."

She nodded and looked around, discovering she really wanted to get to know Lucas Cain better. Lucas Cain was not who she'd thought he was. He was being for her in a little over an hour what Keith hadn't managed in almost three years, and he was doing it well. Something felt warm in her, and it wasn't the alcohol. Lucas Cain, whether he realized it or not, had just kindled a fire. She wondered how it could be that Lucas was managing, in his quiet way, to make her have this strong stirring in her after everything she'd gone through with Keith.

Karma II

She was bitterly disappointed in Keith. After tonight, it seemed she'd spent three years with a stranger. He'd never actually put his hands on her. Right? Obviously wrong. That observation in itself hurt like hell. Nick had never been a big crier, but she felt the unwelcome sting of hot bitter tears in her eyes. She was appalled that she was about to cry in front of Lucas, but it was too huge to hold back. Her breath hitched in her throat. Lucas put his drink down like this was what he'd been waiting so patiently for. He seemed totally prepared to deal with her. She dropped the ice and put her face in her hands. Nick was dismayed that it didn't come silently. She sobbed harshly and that soon turned into a high pitched keening. She felt Lucas slide over to her. He put his hand on her back and she dissolved. Lucas put his arms around her and held her head to his chest. Nick cried until she couldn't cry anymore. Her tears finally slowed, then stopped. Nick could feel his heart beating in his well formed chest.

Lucas was pleasantly warm, and again, he smelled so subtly, wonderfully, good. Nick put her hand on his hard flat stomach. She felt the muscles there, rock solid, beneath his sweater. She hugged him gratefully. His arms closed tighter around her as he hugged her back. This was nice. He spoke to the top of her head.

"Better now?"

She nodded. "I'm glad you came and got me."

"Me, too." He loosened his grip on her, and Nick was a little disappointed.

"Feel like eating?" he asked. She was tired, but she was also famished.

"Yeah. I guess all that crying made me hungry."

"Good. I'll make you a steak." They went into the kitchen and he took two New York strips out of the fridge.

"Let me do that. You've been nice enough for one night.

Besides, your hand is still hurt." Nick said, nudging him out of the way.

"Go right ahead." His kitchen was enormous with a center island and Viking appliances. The range had a grill. Nick turned it on with child-like enthusiasm.

"I love your kitchen."

"You cook?"

"I went to school to be a chef."

"Yeah?"

"Yeah, I did. I went to Juilliard, too, for a while. Voice and piano. "

He smiled a little as he looked at her. "I have a piano. Maybe one day you'll sing for me."

Karma II

"After what you did for me, whenever you want it just let me know."

He looked at her with intense deliberation. Nick looked back at him, aware that her words could be taken in more than one way.

"I sure will."

He was standing unjustifiably close to her. An inch or two more, he'd be in her way. Nick didn't mind. She wanted him right where he was. He looked at her with a steady, even, watchfulness. Nick wondered what made him look at people like that. Was it because of his job, or was it innately in him? She was leaning toward the latter. Lucas was enigmatic. There were a million things she wanted to ask him. She put her hand on his bicep and leaned over to get the olive oil. Okay, it was a cheap excuse to put her hand on him, but he was slightly in her way. Lucas didn't budge, but his arm flexed under her hand. She glanced at him and he looked amused. Nick put the steaks on the grill and looked over her shoulder at him.

"What's going on in that gorgeous head of yours, Lucas?"

He looked surprised at her flat out compliment. He laughed.

"Gorgeous?"

"Just stating an obvious fact. What was going through your mind while you were watching me like that?" She opened the refrigerator and gathered the makings for a salad.

"When are you going to answer my question?"

"I was thinking a lot of things."

"Like what?"

"Like, why are you a cop?"

"Ultimately? My father was a cop and he didn't have any sons. My sister's a cop in Boston. Why did you become one?"

"I get bored easy. Being a cop's a lot of things, but one thing it's not is boring."

Karma II

"What else were you thinking?" She was taken aback when he reached out and touched the bruise on her face with the back of his fingers.

"I was thinkin', if I see Keith, I'm gonna hurt him."

"Okay. What else?" She asked, a tremor in her voice.

He smiled that soft little smile. "I'd rather not say."

He held her gaze for a moment longer, then dropped his hand. Just like that he walked out of the room. That was the second time he'd done that. She turned the steaks and put her hands on her hips. She didn't blame him for not following through. Tonight had been crazy. Keith put his hands on her, she'd put Lucas in a precarious position, and she probably looked like shit. She'd been though a lot today. Lucas probably didn't want to put her through any more.

"Your cell phone was ringing," he said.

Nick jumped. He was standing right behind her. She hadn't even heard her come back. She reached for her phone, but he put it on the counter.

Karma II

"You look angry. Why?"

She didn't realize she was still frowning. "It's nothing."

He moved closer. "It's something."

She backed up. "It's you."

He tilted his head and leaned toward her. "What did I do?"

"Nothing." He touched her hair and she looked back up at him.

"Then I guess I have to do something."

"Maybe you should."

He put his hands in her hair and kissed the bruise on her chin with such tenderness it brought tears to her eyes. His lips were soft and his kiss was light. Lucas kissed her puffy bottom lip delicately, with the same tenderness. Nick put her hand on his face. His beard was surprisingly soft. Lucas slipped his tongue into her mouth and her knees went weak. He didn't shove his tongue down her throat aggressively, like she'd grown used to. He kissed her like he thought about every wonderful, delicious move he made. Like he was making love to her mouth. Nick had never been kissed like that before. He withdrew his irresistible tongue from her and kissed her softly, fully on the lips. She felt like he'd just taken her to the moon and back, and all he'd done was kiss her.

"I really felt like we had to get that out of the way."

She smiled at him. He was so much more than she gave him credit for.

"You know what?" She asked, breaking the spell and reaching into the cabinet for two plates.

"What?" She put a steak on each plate and turned off the grill.

"I like you very much." She said matter of factly.

He smiled. "Well, that's good, 'cause I like you, too." They got the salad and the steaks, went into the dining area, and sat down to eat.

Nick noticed that Lucas was usually a pretty quiet guy, but he was talking to her. They didn't get into anything too heavy until the meal was over.

"I really don't want to go back to that apartment."

"So don't."

"I have to, Lucas. I live there."

"You don't have to."

"Yes, I do. In case you didn't hear me, I live there." She snapped at him.

He raised an eyebrow. "I heard what you said, Nicole. I'm not deaf," he said quietly.

Her head snapped back a bit. He'd just checked her without raising his voice. God, she liked him.

"Sorry, I'm a little stressed out." There was a hint of sarcasm in her voice.

He smiled that small, beautiful, close mouthed smile. "It's okay. You're worried about finding another place to stay?"

"Yeah, I am. I guess I could convince Leah to let me

73

Karma II

stay with her for a minute, but then, what am I gonna do with all my stuff? I've got a lot of stuff, Lucas."

"I have a solution if you want it."

"I'm listening."

"I have another brownstone with an empty apartment. If you want it, it's yours." Her eyes widened.

"You have another brownstone? You are rich, aren't you?"

"Let's just say I ain't starvin'. Do you want it?"

"Where is it?"

"Down the block." Nick smiled.

"Thanks for the offer."

"It's not a problem. If you want, you can stay here until it's finished."

She stared hard at him as she digested his offer. Wow.

"That's a big intrusion, Lucas. Really, all I needed was a ride. I can't ask you to do that." He got up and sat in the chair to her left and took her hand in his.

Karma II

"Look, Nicole, let's be real. You needed more than a ride," he said, pointedly. "It's no intrusion. Right now, you need a little help. I can give it to you. Take it."

His long strong fingers were closed around hers protectively. His thumb grazed the back of hers. A thrill went through her like she'd been dipped in bubbles. He'd said he could give to her. Told her to take it. She decided she wanted it very much.

"You're being very nice to me, Lucas."

"I don't mind."

Nick gathered the dishes and went into the kitchen. Lucas helped her load the dishwasher.

"I have to go get my clothes and my car."

"I'll take you in the morning."

"I hope he's not still there."

"It doesn't matter. I'll be there with you."

Nick's cell phone rang. It startled her. She already knew who it was from the ringtone.

Lucas was eyeing her with the same calm fortitude she

was starting to like so much.

"Aren't you gonna get that?"

"No. That's Keith."

"Pick it up. Let's see what he's got to say."

Nick answered her phone with major reluctance. "What do you want, Keith?"

"Is that the way you talk to me, Nicky? I'm like the comedian now, right? I get no respect."

"You don't deserve any."

"Don't be mean, it doesn't become you. Why'd you leave? We were talking."

"If you were talking, your fucking fist sure had a lot to say."

"I thought I told you not to talk to me like that. Don't make me have to tell you again." That was it. Who did he think he was?

"Fuck you, Keith! I told you, you put your hand on me again, I'm shooting you! You'll be in the fucking morgue! I'm not afraid of your cowardly ass!"

He laughed. "You looked pretty scared when you left. We need to talk. I've decided I don't want to leave."

"Fine, then. Stay. I'm coming to get my stuff tomorrow. Please don't be there."

"I'm not going to let you dictate to me what to do with my time, Nicky."

"Suit yourself. Just don't be there tomorrow." She hung up.

Her phone rang before she put it down. She returned it to the counter without answering.

"You okay?"

She nodded. "I think I hate him."

"That's a strong word. Don't let him know he makes you so upset. It just encourages his behavior."

Lucas led her upstairs to the bedroom closest to his, turned on the bedside lamp, and turned down the covers.

"I'm right next door if you need me. I'll see you in the morning."

"Okay. Goodnight, Lucas. Thanks for everything."

"You're welcome. 'Night," He said and left the room.

She slipped into bed and lay there in the dark, trying to fall asleep.

Chapter Seven

And stay away

Leah took a sip of her coffee. She couldn't believe Keith had punched Nick like that. Leah had never really liked Keith, but she never thought he would have gone there. She was trying to convince Nick to get an order of protection. Noah said she didn't need one. He'd said if Keith laid another hand on Nick, Keith's ass would need one.

Lucas, as usual, stayed silent, even though Leah could tell he'd love to put his foot in Keith's ass. Leah offered Nick her spare bedroom, but Nick told her she was okay where she was. Nick was in no hurry to get away from Lucas and all his fineness. Leah could tell she was falling for him, hard. She wasn't so sure that was such a good idea on the heels of her relationship with Keith, but she didn't have a bad word to say about Lucas.

She could certainly understand Nick's attraction to

him. He was an extraordinarily handsome man, and he was nice to her.

"Thinkin' 'bout me?" Noah asked, walking into the office.

Leah looked up and her heart stuttered like it usually did when faced with the overwhelming drawing power of Noah Ramsey. He was outrageously fine.

"What makes you ask that?"

He sat on the corner of her desk. "You were smiling."

"Every smile I have is not about you, Noah."

His face lit up with a sparkling, mischievous grin. "Why not?"

Leah smiled back just as brightly. "Believe it or not, the world doesn't spin just because you're in it."

He threw those beautiful grey eyes on her. "Somethin' I said?"

Leah smiled and sat back. The look he gave her was glancing, but appreciative.

"Nope. Actually, I was thinking about Lucas. He's going out of his way to be nice to Nick."

"Yeah. Luke's a prince."

"Now that he's suffered a little, right?"

Noah stared at her for a moment. "What do you mean?"

Leah crossed her legs. Noah watched this move with great appreciation, too. He was, not so subtly, lecherous. Leah loved it.

"Justine Greer must've taken a lot out of him."

His clear grey eyes grew a bit darker and he stood up and went to his own desk. He sat back in his chair and stared, pensively, out the window. Leah admired him silently. His skin was the exact color of tea with a splash of milk. His dark brows knitted toward each other. His right hand half hid his just right lips as the sun shone on his curly head. She wanted him very badly, but she was terrified of Noah Ramsey. Noah turned away from the window and locked his eyes on her.

"Come here." Very sexy, and she didn't think it was

intentional.

She got up and perched herself on the corner of his desk like he'd sat on hers. He surprised her by placing one of his hands above each of her knees.

"Listen to me, we're not gonna discuss Lucas like that, okay?"

He paused and let his strong hands trail up her thighs. "I know Nick's going through a hard time. If he wants to help her, fall back and let him. Don't speculate about my friend. Leave his past where it belongs."

He continued to lightly rub her thighs. Leah leaned back, propping herself up on her splayed fingers, as Noah stood up. He'd stepped between her legs and put a hand down on either side of her before she could think about what he was doing.

"I was only saying that, maybe, you should worry about your own business, lady."

His lips lightly brushed hers. It was heaven, but she pushed him back.

"Noah, you need to chill out."

Karma II

"Why?" He smiled at her wickedly as his hands settled back on her thighs. It took a strong woman to resist Noah. He was as handsome as sin, and sex rolled off him in waves. Leah summoned up some inner strength and firmly pushed him away.

"Noah, stop. You can't be all up on me like this in here."

He threw his hands up in defeat, but kept that wicked grin.

"Fine. When?" Noah laughed softly and sat in his chair. Leah frowned at him.

"What's so funny?"

"You are."

"Don't you have a girlfriend somewhere?" She asked.

Noah ignored the question.

"You should just give up, Leah."

"What does she look like?"

"It's just a matter of time."

"Is there more than one?"

"You know you want to."

"You're dangerous, Noah." He winked at her.

"I know it."

He was looking at her with a high level of confidence. It was just a matter of time. Noah made her woozy. She knew there had to be at least one woman lurking around somewhere. Maybe more than one. After all, she was discovering the fact that Noah Ramsey was fairly easy to fall in love with. Leah knew that getting involved with Noah would be like getting on your knees and begging to get your feelings hurt. He didn't know it, but she'd admired him for years. She wasn't jumping into bed with him like some ho just because he asked her to. She looked over at him. He had a cigarette dangling from the corner of his mouth, and he was looking noisily through his desk. Noah sat back in frustration, frowning like a kid who'd just lost his favorite toy.

Karma II

"I threw your ashtray in the garbage."

"What did you do that for?"

"You should stop smoking. You're killing yourself." He looked down at her with an unhappy little smirk.

"You're killin' me, Leah. I'm tellin' you, between all this sexual frustration, and you throwin' my shit away, you're killin' me. I'm goin' to smoke a cigarette."

He plucked his lighter off his desk and started out the door. As he was walking out, Lucas and Nick were walking in. He greeted Nick and clapped Lucas on his shoulder, turning him around.

"What's up, bro? Take a walk with your boy." Nick entered the room, smiling contagiously.

"What's got you so happy this morning, or do I have to ask?"

Nick hung up her coat and sat at her desk, leaning back in her chair. Leah couldn't remember the last time she'd seen Nick smile so radiantly. Leah's eyes lit up with sudden astonishment.

"Nick, did you sleep with Lucas?" Nick dropped her eyes and her smile became tiny, but it was still there.

"No. No, I didn't."

"No? Then why are you smiling like that? I don't believe you."

"You might as well, because it's true."

"Then why do you look so happy?"

"Because I woke up this morning and Keith wasn't there, but Lucas was. I was wrong about Lucas."

"How so?"

"I took one look at Lucas Cain and made a bunch of snap judgments about him. I had it in my mind that he was a bad boy, full of his own swagger. I thought he was arrogant and superficial and selfish. I mistook his quietness as aloofness and conceit, when all that's not really true at all."

Leah smiled. "That's funny. I kinda always thought he was a little quietly conceited, myself."

Nick put her feet on her desk. "Even if he was, who could blame him? He's fucking gorgeous. I think he's just not a big talker. When he has something to say, he does, but I think Lucas is a people watcher. An observer. He absorbs things."

"Yeah, your kids will probably be real smart. Cute, too."

"I was just admiring the man he is," Nick said, matter of factly.

"You falling for Lucas, Nick?"

"Me trying not to have feelings for Lucas would be like trying to stand up in an avalanche, Leah."

"Wow. That's deep, kid."

"Yeah, I-"

Nick was cut off by Noah and Lucas' return. She swung her feet off her desk and stopped talking abruptly. They were laughing at something Noah had said.

81

Karma II

"Feel better?" Leah asked Noah.

He smiled at her charmingly. "A hundred percent, no thanks to you."

The door opened and in walked Keith Childs in all his handsome fabulousness. He smiled his dimply smile, with his perfect white teeth. He looked first at Lucas, then at Noah.

"Well, well. If it ain't the pretty boys! Long time no see."

His eyes fell on Nick. "I need to talk to you, my love."

Leah glanced at Lucas. He was leaning back in his chair, his body language was relaxed, but his eyes were locked intently on Nick. If she'd said the word, Leah was sure Lucas would be all over Keith's ass in a heartbeat. She looked at Noah. He was leaning forward, one hand on his desk, like he wouldn't mind jumping over it. Nick stood up calmly.

"What are you doing here?" She asked with a sigh.

Keith smiled at her and moved closer. Nick took a step back.

"Like I said, I need to talk to you. May I have a moment?"

"If you want to talk to me, go ahead." Keith's eyes passed over them again and settled back on Nick.

"Alone."

"You've got to be kidding me. Say what you've got to say and get out of here."

He rolled up on her and grabbed her arm. Leah saw Lucas and Noah move forward in her peripheral vision. Leah popped out of her own seat in outrage. No, he wasn't trying to flex on her in here! Anger flashed in Nick's eyes as she tried to pull away. Leah was closer that Lucas and Noah. She was at Nick's side and stepping between them before Keith could make his next move.

"Oh, hell no! You better get your angry, woman-beating ass up out of here! What the fuck is wrong with you, rollin' up in here like this?"

Keith put his finger in Leah's face.

"Back up and mind your business."

Leah slapped his hand out of her face indignantly. Keith reacted by shoving her hard. Leah collided with Nick, almost knocking both of them down. Leah didn't even see Lucas coming. When she looked up, he was right there, standing in front of Keith.

"Get out." He said, in a quiet controlled voice.

Keith smirked and sized him up. "What you gonna do, Cain? You and your pretty friend gonna try and break me up?"

"That's the second time you said that. What's up, bro? You got a crush on me?" Noah said, stepping up behind Lucas.

Keith frowned at him. "You need to fall back, son, you don't want none of this."

Noah's face broke into a grin and his eyes glittered darkly. "Ain't nobody scared of your punk ass, man. I been waitin' years to fuck you up again."

Karma II

Keith's anger startled Leah. He tried to brush past Lucas to get at Noah, but Lucas was between them and held his ground. Keith reached for Noah over Lucas' shoulder, and Lucas grabbed the front of Keith's coat and started backing him up toward the door. Noah was at Lucas' back, baiting Keith.

"Oh, you wanna fight? Please let him go, Luke!"

When Lucas got Keith to the door, that's when he decided he wanted to fight Lucas instead of Noah. He pushed away from Lucas and threw an overhand right at his face. Lucas dodged him skillfully and the blow glanced off his shoulder. Keith immediately threw a left, followed by another right. Lucas bobbed and weaved as Noah opened the door. Lucas hit Keith in the throat with his right elbow, effectively cutting off his air supply, and used both hands to knock him out the door. Keith lost his balance and skidded out the door on his ass. He got to his feet less than graciously, as people in the hall turned to stare and snicker. Lucas wasn't even breathing hard.

"I'm gonna get you back for this shit, Cain."

Lucas smiled tightly. "Can't wait."

Nick appeared at Lucas' side. "You shouldn't do this, Keith. You're making a fool of yourself."

He looked like he wanted to lay hands on her, but both Lucas and Noah closed in on her protectively. He looked at Lucas with eyes full of malice, but directed his question to Nick.

"This your new boyfriend?"

"If you don't leave me alone, I'm going start putting this shit on paper."

He stared at her for a moment, then turned his attention back to Lucas. "I'm gonna get you back."

Lucas looked bored. "You're repeating yourself." He said, and walked away from him.

Noah smiled at Keith with ersatz sympathy. "This definitely ain't a good look for you, bro." He said and slammed the door in his face.

Chapter Eight

Under pressure

Noah thought he was still dreaming. He was lying on his stomach with his head resting on his arms. Somewhere people were yelling. Two women. He opened one eye slowly and listened.

"I knew you were going to try and hem him up like this! It's the oldest trick in the book!"

"Don't be coming in my house, yelling at me! If Noah wanted you, he'd still be with you!"

"You don't know what happened between me and my husband! I hope you don't think he'll be marrying your conniving ass!"

Noah sat up in alarm. What the hell was Nadine doing here?

"Shit!" He muttered, hurrying out of the room and running down the stairs. He got to them just before they came to blows.

"Whoa! What's goin' on? Liz?" Liz put her hand lightly on the slight bump of her belly, and her eyes filled with tears.

"She came over here, calling me names and making insinuations. She said I set you up so you'd marry me."

Noah looked at Nadine.

"Well, she did. Don't fall for her bullshit, Noah. You've been around enough to know that's the oldest trick in the book. Don't you let her take advantage of you!"

"I'm not taking advantage of Noah! Get over it! Noah's not you husband anymore, Nadine!"

"Maybe not, but he won't be marrying you. You're a whore with an agenda."

Noah put a hand on her arm. "Whoa, Nadine, wait a minute-"

"Noah! You're gonna let this bitch call me a whore?"

They both closed in on him.

"You are a whore!"

"Say it again, I'll kick your ass!"

Noah pushed them apart. "Alright! Cut this shit out! I'm not havin' this!"

They fell silent and stared at him. Noah stared back, at Nadine in particular. He knew she hadn't told Liz he'd slept with her, because things were still relatively calm.

"Listen to me. I gotta go to work. This shit is ridiculous, wakin' a man up outta his sleep with some bullshit."

He put on his sternest face, even though he was about to break into a cold sweat. He didn't like this shit at all. He didn't need his women meeting up.

"Liz, go to work," He paused and looked at Nadine. "Nadine, you do the same. Leave first."

Her eyes passed over his naked chest possessively.

"Okay, Noah. I'll see you later."

He looked at her with barely concealed hostility. "You bet. Have a nice day."

Nadine walked to the door. She stopped and looked at Liz. "Honey, you know the real reason Noah will never marry you?"

Noah froze. Oh, shit. He wanted Nadine to leave.

"He doesn't love you like that, sweetie. Noah's not my husband because of decisions I made. If I'd have left it up to him, we'd still be married."

She turned her eyes to Noah, and he looked back at her darkly.

"Don't be too mad at me, sugar, I just told her the truth, and you know it."

She slipped out the front door without looking back. He looked around for his smokes, found them, and lit one. Fuck what Liz had to say on this one. He inhaled deeply, blew out the smoke, and looked at Liz through narrowed eyes.

"Was she telling me the truth, Noah?"

"Nope." He answered, with no hesitation.

"Noah?"

"What?" He sounded annoyed.

"Nadine sounds like she wants you back. Are you going?"

Karma II

"Nadine's talkin' out the side of her mouth. She's just mad 'cause you're pregnant."

Liz regarded him thoughtfully

"Are you going back?"

"I'm goin' to work, Liz. Don't let Nadine upset you."

"It's a little late for that."

"There's no weight behind what she says."

"I'll bet that there is. I love you, Noah."

"Yeah, me too."

Liz looked up at him with sad eyes. "Don't leave me, Noah."

Oh, Jesus Christ! He tried a different approach. "You better go to work, before I take you upstairs."

He kissed her neck, amorously. That got a giggle out of her.

"Okay, alright, I'm going." She gave him a peck on the lips and left.

Noah put his cigarette out and stared into space. This shit was getting a little too serious for him. He went upstairs, took a shower, and dressed for work. Bad scene, very bad scene. He put on his coat, picked up his car keys, and hurried out of the house. He felt better at once. Noah started up the Caddy, and was pulling out, when his cell phone rang.

"Yeah?"

"Hi, Daddy." Nadine almost sang in his ear, talking very sweetly, like she used to.

Noah got goose bumps in spite of himself. "What's up with the shit you pulled, Nadine?"

"Was Liz upset?"

"Stop playin', Nadine. This shit ain't cute."

"Did you get in trouble?" Noah laughed.

"Stop, Nadine. That was just wrong."

"If it was, why are you laughing?"

"What's the deal, Nadine? Liz bein' pregnant got you that pissed off?"

"She's trying to trap you, Noah."

Noah frowned. "Why are you so worried about me? You told me once, you wished I was dead. You change your mind?"

"You want the truth?"

"Of course."

"Then I'll give it to you. Yes, I'm pissed about Liz. It's killing me that she's having your baby."

"Why? *You* divorced *me*. What the hell is going on with you? Clue me in. Please."

"I can't talk to you about stuff like this over the phone, Daddy. What are you doing for dinner?"

Noah was quiet. A million things were going through his mind.

"Are you brooding? Why are you so quiet?"

"You want me back all of a sudden?"

This time Nadine was silent.

"Or do you just not want me with Liz? Which one,

88

Karma II

Nadine?"

"You flatter yourself, Noah."

"Yeah, and you play mind games. I gotta go to work."

"What about dinner?"

"It ain't lookin' real good right now."

"Don't be mad."

Noah hung up on her. Fucking Nadine. She was trying to play him, and Liz was being ridiculously needy. He didn't want to be bothered with either one of their asses right now. If Nadine wanted him back, how could he just leave Liz? What did Nadine really want him back for? Maybe she just wanted to get even with him for cheating on her. After the shit he'd seen Lucas go through with Justine, it wasn't a stretch. Women were capable of revenge that made strong men cry like babies. Maybe Liz was trying to set him up. Maybe Nadine was plotting revenge. Maybe they didn't know him as well as they thought they did.

"Sittin' around anticipatin' my next move. Fuck both of y'all." He mumbled to himself.

Karma II

He walked into the office and found Leah sitting alone with a bagel and coffee, browsing through the newspaper.

"Hey, Noah." He hung up his coat and looked at her sitting there in her tight lilac blouse and her tight jeans.

"You okay?" Leah asked, standing up and looking concerned.

Noah nodded. "I'm cool."

She frowned. "Something wrong?"

Knowing he was most likely making things a lot worse, Noah walked over to Leah and kissed her. Really kissed her. He caught her off guard, and her inner freak popped out. Her hands went under his sweater and over his body lightly with her fingernails. He grunted softly and accepted it as invitation to do the same. His hands slipped under her shirt and his fingertips toyed with her breasts. Leah moaned and pushed herself into him. That created a problem. She noticed and palmed him with her right hand. He laughed and moved her hand.

"Wait a minute." Leah shook her head, as if to clear it, and stepped away.

She sat at her desk and looked at him in angry confusion. "Why did you do that?" She asked.

"Do what? Move your hand?"

"Why do you always roll up on me like that? That's not right, Noah."

Noah sat at his own desk. He felt a little guilty, but not really. "What's not right?"

Leah looked at him sharply as Lucas walked in.

"Good morning, Lucas." She said, her eyes still on Noah.

"Morning, Leah." He gave Noah dap, sat at his desk, and took the lid off his coffee.

"What's your private life like, Noah?"

Lucas swung his head in her direction with a look of surprise. Noah smiled at her.

"Where are you goin' with this?"

"I'm not a ho, and I don't do one night stands, so what's up, Noah? I don't go a step further until you tell me what's up with you."

Lucas raised an eyebrow and gave Noah an 'I told you so' look. Noah shrugged.

"Nothin'. Ain't nothin' up."

Lucas stood up with his coffee.

"Where are you going?" Leah asked.

Lucas laughed quietly and moved to the door. "Looks like you two need a moment. I'm giving it to you."

"Like you won't know what's going on anyway. You might as well sit down."

He shook his head. "No thanks." Lucas left the room, closing the door behind him.

"I don't know what you want from me, Noah."

He smiled his most engaging smile. "Sure you do."

"Yeah, but is that all?"

Noah looked at his desk. What was with all these women and their feelings? What about his feelings? Right now he was feeling like he needed a distraction, and Leah wasn't playing along. It made him a little angry and bit more determined to break her down.

"What do you want from me, Leah? " He stood up, well aware of how she felt about him and also of how handsome he was.

He knew her point of weakness. He stared at her, and withdrew completely. "I'm not promisin' you anything. I'll just leave you alone."

She stood, too, wrapping her arms around herself, protectively. "I didn't say all that."

Noah tucked a cigarette in his mouth and put his hand on the doorknob. She looked worried and attempted to back pedal. "Noah, don't be mad."

He smirked. That was the second time he'd heard that today.

"Who's mad?"

"Noah, wait, I don't want you to get the wrong idea."

He smiled at her, but his eyes were serious. "And I don't want you to get the wrong idea, sweetie.."

"We need to talk."

"About what?" He walked away.

She called his name and he smiled. Noah left the building to go have his smoke. He had deftly turned the tables on her. He found Lucas on the steps. He took a sip of his coffee as Noah lit his cigarette.

"Noah, what the fuck are you doing, man?"

"Well, shit, nothin' yet."

"You need to stop and think, No. You only think you got a situation now."

"Luke, you don't know the half. I woke up this mornin' to Liz and Nadine downstairs screamin' at each other."

Lucas sipped his coffee. "Serious? That's not good."

"Nadine says Liz is tryin' to trap me."

"Well, she is. She definitely played her ace, No. If you

open your eyes, you can see that yourself."

Noah frowned at him. "My eyes are open."

Lucas looked at him. "Okay, No. I see you're in one of your moods, so anything I say to you right now is gonna go in one ear, and right out the other. I will say this, though, Nadine is your Achilles' heel, and you know it. You need to resolve that shit before you get into anything else. I get the feeling she's fuckin' with you because she knows you still love her. Don't be weak and let her play you."

Noah nodded and flicked the ash off his Dunhill. "I told Leah I was gonna leave her alone."

Lucas laughed out loud. "This is me, Noah. You can't piss on my head and tell me it's only rain. I'm pretty sure you just switched it up on her, changed your approach, to make it not look like you're pimpin' her too hard. Come on, Noah, I know you."

Noah smiled and threw his smoke down. "Never could fool your ass."

Lucas smiled, too. "Nope." He looked down the steps. "Here comes Griff."

Griffin jogged up the steps to them. He'd changed since they'd gotten to know him better, dropping all his stiff formalities. Lucas eyed him warily.

"Damn, Cain. You're a slow brother to thaw. Put it behind you already."

Lucas smirked. "It's behind me."

Noah laughed, knowing his old pal well. "He's like a dog with a bone, Griff."

Griff smiled. "Nick and Leah here?"

"They're here." Lucas answered.

"Good. I need all of you in the office in about," he paused to look at his watch, "Say, 15 minutes."

Lucas frowned. "You ready to move?"

"Tell you real soon. See you guys inside." They watched him walk into the building, then Lucas looked at Noah seriously.

"You ready for this, No?"

Noah looked back just as serious. "You know me, Luke. I'm always ready. I'll make it do what it do."

"No doubt. You need to simplify your life, bro. Now's not the time to have a gang of women raisin' up on you, too. You don't need that type of pressure, man. I'm tellin' you."

Lucas was very clearly worried about him. He smiled to lighten the mood.

"I don't walk with shit like that, Luke. I got no pressure."

Lucas looked back at him. He looked for so long that Noah turned his eyes away.

"Yeah, okay, Noah. Remember one thing."

"What's that?"

Lucas looked him in the eye. "Pressure busts pipes."

93

Karma II

Chapter Nine

Moving on

Lucas was a little worried about his boy. Noah was the type of guy that usually didn't let shit like this bother him, but Lucas knew that Liz's pregnancy and Nadine's new interest in him were seriously stressing him out. He could understand Noah needing a diversion, but he didn't think he'd find it in Leah. He hadn't even slept with her and she already looked at him like she loved him. She looked up when they entered the room. Noah sat down and gave her the gray stare. Noah was flexing on her, hard.

"Good morning," Nick said, walking in holding a cardboard tray with four coffees. "I got coffee."

They all spoke to her in unison. Leah got up and helped her. Nick was wearing a cherry red blouse tucked into a pair of jeans. Lucas looked away to keep from staring.

"Here you go. Black, one sugar."

Nick put the coffee on his desk and smiled down at

him. Lucas' heart fluttered in his chest. "Thank you."

"You're always welcome."

He watched her walk away. It was an enjoyable experience. Griff walked in with Myers, two other detectives and one Fed. Lucas recognized them immediately. Tony Colletti, Nate Dombrowski, and Victor Calderone. Tony was the Fed. Myers took a seat on Leah's desk.

"Good morning, my elite unit of narcs. Here's your backup, I'm sure you all know each other. Say hello."

These were guys you wanted to have your back. Nick and Leah obviously knew them, too. Griff clapped his hands together and called the meeting to order.

"Alright, people. I'm glad you're all familiar with one another. We have some information we'd like to share, and we're ready to make a move. We've got two informants, I'm pleased to announce."

"Who are they?" Nick asked, taking a sip of her coffee.

"Well, one of them came to us like a gift from God."

Noah sat up. "Don't leave us hangin'. Who is it?"

Griff paused for effect. "Tate's baby momma, Tamiko Brewster."

Tony's eyebrows went up. "He must've really pissed her off for her to give him up."

Griff nodded. "Beyond pissed. It didn't take much of a nudge. She wants his ass swinging in the wind."

"Who's the other one?"

"Oscar Tirado." Myers said, smiling with satisfaction. He had everyone's full attention.

"Oscar Tirado? How'd you get Old Scratch to snitch?" Lucas asked.

Griff looked at them hard. "He got some serious guarantees of clemency from way up.

Believe it."

Lucas sat back in his chair. Shit! Oscar Tirado. Fucking criminal, nefarious, bastard, with a goddamn detective's badge. Well, not anymore. He'd been Upstate for the past two years. He looked at Griff.

"What did they promise him?"

Griff looked back, and chose his answer carefully. "I'm not at liberty to say."

Noah tapped his lighter on his desk. "That's some bullshit, Griff."

Nate laughed.

"What are they gonna do? Let him out?"

"They can't. Tirado was responsible for the deaths of three cops," Leah said.

Lucas laughed without humor. "Yeah, they can, Leah. It's called commuting his sentence."

Myers stood up. "Enough about Tirado, already. We're going in. We'll start out with surveillance. We want you all to participate, but once we send you in, surveillance will go exclusively to Dombrowski, Calderon, and Colletti."

He paused and looked at them all like they were his children. "Your back up will have back up. We want you in and out as quickly as possible."

"You sound scared, Boss." Noah said.

"Not scared, Ramsey. Cautious. Very cautious."

They went over the preliminaries, and then Myers informed them that he was giving them the next couple of days off. Lucas, Noah, Nick, and Leah wound up in their office at the end of the day, staring at one another. When Leah mentioned she was a little nervous about the sting, Lucas and Noah were pretty unrelenting. In order to relax, they decided to have dinner together at an upscale soul food place in downtown Brooklyn.

Leah rolled her eyes at Lucas through the whole meal. He weighed the pros and cons of ignoring it, or addressing it. He was leaning toward addressing it. As they put their coats on and prepared to leave, Nick touched his arm.

"Lucas?" She was looking at him so sternly, he almost smiled.

"What?"

Nick frowned. "I know your mother didn't teach you

to answer people like that."

He did smile then. "I probably forgot most of what my mother ever taught me."

"That's not a very nice thing to say."

He laughed. "It's a very true thing to say."

"You need to smooth things over with Leah."

"Is that so?"

Nick smiled. "I'd appreciate it."

He walked up on her and tilted his head. "You would, huh?"

Nick tried to smother her smile and regain her stern attitude, but it didn't work.

"I would."

"I'll do it."

She was unable to keep the grin off her face. "Thank you, Lucas."

He didn't quite dare move any closer, he'd be all over her.

"You're welcome." He gave her his keys and went to talk to Leah. Noah was talking to her at the corner. Leah was looking at him with soft eyes and a reluctant smile.

"Noah, you mind if I pull Leah away from you for a minute?"

"Yeah, you could do that, but bring her right back. I wasn't done."

Leah looked at Lucas and took a totally funky posture. She folded her arms across her chest and shifted her weight to one hip. "You ready to make a fool out of me again?"

"That wasn't my intention. I apologize if that's how I made you feel. Sincerely."

"I guess you don't ever get scared."

"Everybody does, but you know as well as I do that you can't go into this like that. It'll freeze you up."

She relaxed her posture. "I guess you're right. Your delivery sucked, though."

"Sorry. You gonna be alright?"

"I'm a professional, if I have any qualms in the future,

I'll just keep them to myself."

"Don't feel like that, Leah. You know exactly what I'm saying to you, so stop being stubborn."

She studied his face for a moment and smiled. "Okay. Alright, we're cool, Lucas."

"You sure?"

"Yeah, we're cool. Did Nick ask you to say you're sorry?"

Lucas smiled. "I was gonna do it anyway."

Leah looked at him slyly. "What's going on between you two?"

Lucas laughed. "We're friends, Leah. Just like you and me."

"Uh-uh. Not like you and me. Me and Noah, maybe."

Lucas kept his smile. "Goodnight, Leah."

"Goodnight, Lucas. Tell your 'friend' I'll call her tomorrow."

"You got it." He said goodnight to Noah and walked to the car.

"Everything okay?" Nick asked.

"It's okay."

"Leah's a damned good detective, Lucas. I'd trust her with my life. Just like you trust Noah."

"Uh-huh." Lucas was never worried with Noah. He couldn't even imagine not having Noah have his back. They never really mentioned shit like being scared, though. It was like invoking weakness. When you were weak, you made mistakes, and mistakes get you killed. He said as much to Nick now. Nick didn't comment until they got inside.

"You know what your problem is, Lucas?" She asked, following him into the kitchen. Lucas took a bottle of water out of the fridge. He smiled to himself.

"I didn't know I had one." He twisted the cap off his water and took a sip.

Nick started to take the pins out of her hair. "Your problem is, you're not used to working this close with women. You're used to it being some exclusive boy's club."

"You're paranoid."

She shook her hair loose and it fell around her shoulders. Lucas caught his breath and instantly wanted to plunge his hands into it.

"What am I paranoid about?"

"You feel like you always have to prove yourself and outshine the men you're working with. That's paranoid."

Nick hooked her thumbs into the pockets of her jeans and smiled at him invitingly. "That's not true."

He smiled back. She was making the hairs at the nape of his neck stand up.

"What's not true?" He asked.

"I don't think you have a problem with me because I'm a woman, do you?"

"Nope. I don't have a problem at all."

He looked at her standing there in her red blouse and her blue jeans and was suddenly very interested to know what she looked like without them. Nicole was looking at him like she was waiting for him to make a move. Lucas was hesitating because he felt conflicted. He knew he'd failed Justine terribly. He never wanted to hurt anyone else the way he'd hurt her. Nicole had enough going on in her life. She wouldn't let him off the hook, however. She looked at him with those big, beautiful dark eyes and moved in close.

"I was waiting for you to kiss me, but you seem to have something on your mind. Do you want to share it with me?"

"Not really. I'm good."

She tilted her head and smiled up at him. "I don't buy that. You've got issues, Lucas Cain. I have a feeling I know what they are, but I'm not touching that with a 10 foot pole."

Nicole had a habit of running her mouth. Everything coming out without her taking a breath. It irritated the hell out of Noah, but Lucas found it oddly endearing.

"If it makes you feel any better, I have issues, too. Well, maybe not issues, but stuff. You're not by yourself, Lucas. You looked so sad just then. I know sometimes things   seem so."

He stifled her by putting his hands in her luscious mane of hair and putting his mouth close to hers.

"Yeah, I do have issues. You're a big one."

He started kissing her sweet mouth. Softly at first, savoring the feel of her full, pouty lips against his. He slipped his tongue into her mouth. Her mouth was delectable, and she knew how to kiss him back. She made his skin tingle and his knees weak. She put her arms around his neck and pressed her body into his. Lucas returned her heat, and they stood, tasting each other in his kitchen for a long time. He wanted to take her upstairs and put her in his bed. Lucas was more aroused than he'd let himself be in a long time. He stopped kissing her and put his forehead against hers. They were both breathless. She was driving him crazy.

"Lucas?" Speaking seemed to break the spell.

"Yeah?"

"Let's go upstairs."

Nick turned and walked out of the room. He sighed and ran a hand over his beard. He wanted her. Being indecisive was new to him, but he'd learned the hard way to be a bit more discerning when it came to women and their feelings. He waited a moment longer to push back the impetuousness that came with desire. He went upstairs.

The shower was running in the bathroom in the hall. He went into his own bathroom and stepped into the shower. Lucas was in no way new to the game. He knew it was going down, and it was going down tonight. Neither one of them could escape the velocity of the inevitable. He sincerely hoped he was a better man. He took the diamond out of his ear and felt a tug at his heart. There wasn't room for both Justine and Nicole to share the same space. He looked at the diamond that had once been Justine's engagement ring and closed his fist around it. He was surprised at how much it still hurt.

He went back into the bedroom. He picked up Justine's picture, but didn't look at it. Lucas opened the top drawer and put the picture in it. He put the diamond on top of it and pushed the drawer shut, just as Nicole knocked on the door.

"Come in."

She walked in, still dewy from her shower, wearing a short white robe. She was beautiful. Her eyes flitted over the dresser.

"You okay?" He smiled.

"Never better." She looked slightly uncomfortable.

"I know what you did, Lucas. You didn't have to do that."

He looked at her, seriously. "Yeah, Nicole, I did."

"I mean, I know that you'll probably always-"

He pulled her to him. "You talk too much."

Karma II

He pulled the belt on her robe and it fell open. Lucas lowered his eyes and pushed the robe off her shoulders. It landed in a puddle at her pretty feet. His eyes took her in, from her graceful collarbones, to the tips of her full round breasts. Her waist was small and her shapely hips curved away from it. Nicole raised her hand. Her fingers traced the outline of his tattoo, pausing over the mostly hidden scar in the middle.

"Is this where she shot you?"

"Yes."

"It's not too soon. Life is short and unpromised. We have to live in the moment."

Her hand fell to his towel. Lucas looked down at her with a smile.

"I can do that."

She smiled back and pulled on the towel, but didn't let it go. "I'm a hard woman to please."

"Is that so?"

"So I've been told. I've never had a man take me there."

He decided to play with her, glad things were lighter and not so serious.

"Where?"

She put her hand on her hip. "To the damn movies, Lucas. Don't be difficult. You know what I mean."

He moved closer to her, her nipples brushed against him and she gasped.

"What makes you think I can?"

"I didn't say you could."

"I don't think I believe what you said."

"Well, it's true."

Lucas looked her over and bit his bottom lip. "Then we gotta fix that."

She looked at him coyly. "And you're the man, right?"

"Absolutely."

Nicole removed his towel at last and stepped back. She looked at him the way he'd looked at her. She touched his stomach and let her fingers trace the ripples of muscle there. He shuddered involuntarily and was instantly at attention. Lucas was done playing around. He kissed her, hard. His hands traveled down her back and over the soft swell of her hips. He backed her up to the bed and pulled her gently down with him. He had her on her back, still kissing her, her fingers in his hair.

Lucas' lips blazed a sweltering path down her neck, until they found her breasts. He flicked his tongue over her nipple and she moaned. He smiled and started playing with her, nipping and tweaking and lightly using his teeth. Nicole was breathing hard and biting her bottom lip.

His hand drifted over her body and he dipped his finger into her sweetness. She sighed and arched her back. He lingered there, stroking her masterfully until she was slippery. His mouth left her breast and resumed its fiery downward trail. When he got to her navel, he changed

103

Karma II

position and put his hands under her sumptuous ass. He parted her satiny thighs with his face, feeling his own heat rising.

He pulled her to the edge of the bed and put his mouth on her. She whimpered and pushed up on her elbows. Lucas went to work on that hard, but soft, little pearl. He went at it like he had all the time in the world, but with a studied precision. He lifted her hips and applied a little pressure. She threw her head back and her body tensed.

"Oh! God, Lucas... oh!"

Nick was still trembling when he started in. She gasped as he inched his way. She was a lot tighter than he'd expected. He closed his eyes and tucked his lips in to hold back a growl. Her tightness and wetness and the fact that her body was still pulsating were working against him. Lucas had never in his life been a two minute brother, but if he didn't take a moment to get control, that was exactly how it was going down. He didn't have a choice, he started pulling out, but Nicole put her hands on his ass and forced him back in.

The growl he'd managed to hold back exploded from his throat. Nicole pushed him in further and moved her hips slowly up and down. Lucas froze.

"Stop! Wait a minute!"

He was not going out like this. He pulled out and raised up off of her. He was almost panting, his heart was slamming in his chest. Nicole started giggling and his eyes flew open. She put her hands over her mouth. Lucas, now regaining some of his composure, raised an eyebrow.

"You laughing at me?"

She moved her hands, still grinning. "What happened, Lucas?" she asked, playfully.

He frowned at her, but couldn't quite stop the smile that touched his lips. It was kind of funny. "Nothing happened."

She looked amused. "You know, I thought you could bring it a little better than that. I thought you were the man,"

Lucas smiled and cut her off. "You talkin' shit to me?"

Nicole laughed. "I sure am."

Lucas was fine now. He'd gotten his confidence back. He reclaimed his swagger and glided back in. He started off slow, making up for the time he'd just lost. She put her hands on his waist.

"See? That's much better. That's nice." Lucas leaned back until he was on his knees, pulling her with him.

"Yeah? You think that's nice?" She met him move for move.

"Real nice."

It was nice. So nice, he kept her like that for a while. When she started to move faster, He raised her legs and pushed up. He watched her face as surprise washed over it. Her mouth popped open and goose bumps stood out on her flesh. Nicole cried out and turned her head like he'd struck her. As she started to come down, he jerked her onto his lap and held her close. They rocked together, oblivious of everything except each other. A warmth started to spread through his body as he felt her tensing up again. She pressed her body against his and went into a fast bounce, but Lucas put his hands on her hips and slowed her down so he could do most of the work. Nicole threw her head back, then forward. She shut her eyes and made a face like she was crying. She was drenching him. He laid her on her back and kept going. He went in all the way, grinding hard, while she made random little moans.

"Hey, hey, Nicole. Open your eyes," he whispered in her ear.

Her eyes fluttered open. Lucas smiled at her brashly, totally sure of himself. "Talk shit now," he said.

He tucked his bottom lip in and thrust himself into her, fast and deep. Nicole squealed and started coming hard. She closed up so tight around him, she pulled him into the vortex of her orgasm. He gritted his teeth and growled his

105

Karma II

way into erupting like a geyser. A tremendous thrust, then another, as Nicole rose to meet him. He was so spent, he almost collapsed on top of her. He tumbled onto his back, breathing like a racehorse.

"Jesus Christ!" He whispered.

He glanced at Nicole. She was smiling at him. Lucas felt a strange physical pull in his chest as he looked at her. Oh, God. He touched her and she was straddling him in a heartbeat. Lucas pushed himself up on the pillows and put his hands on her thighs. They looked at each other as Nicole leisurely ran her hands over his chest.

"You're a beautiful man, Lucas. Inside and out. You're probably the best man I've ever met."

"Thanks for the compliment, but I've got my share of flaws."

"I said you were beautiful, not flawless. Nobody's flawless, Lucas."

His hands moved over her bottom with great indulgence.

"You are," he said, holding her gaze.

"No, I'm not. Where's your earring?"

"I put it away."

She frowned. "Why'd you do that? Why didn't you just take it off?"

He looked at her hard and long, then decided to be honest with her.

"I had to. It was the diamond from her engagement ring," he said, softly. His eyes were focused somewhere around her navel.

"I don't know exactly what to say to you about her. I'm sorry it happened. Truly sorry. I know you loved her very much, and it's tragic. On the other hand..."

Lucas gave her butt an encouraging squeeze. "Go on."

She looked as if she were choosing her words very carefully.

"If things had gone the way they were supposed to...

you wouldn't be here with me now. I wouldn't have had a snowball's chance in hell with you, because you'd be in love with someone else. Married to her. I would never have had the chance to find out how wonderful you really are."

He stared at her. It was a weird moment. Nicole had just made him happy to know that they were eye to eye with their emotions, but it made him extremely sad to think that Justine had become a her in the conversation.

"Why are you frowning?"

"I was just thinking. That's all."

"Was I anywhere in there?"

"Uh-huh."

She kissed him again. Deeply and passionately. He pulled her down to where he was, and they lay there facing each other.

"What on earth are we doing, Lucas?" He kissed her forehead.

"Moving on."

Karma II

Chapter Ten

Sweetheart and all those things

Nick sat with Noah, in a black town car. They had their eyes on the Trinidad brothers' latest money laundering venture. They'd purchased a club in trendy Chelsea, and were just completing renovations. Noah sat in the driver's seat wearing a pair of dark shades. He had a Kangol turned backward on his head and a toothpick sticking out of his mouth.

Nick sat in the backseat like a passenger. She had a scarf tied around her head, homegirl style, and a black Yankees cap over that. Nick looked across the street. Leah was dressed similarly to her, with a scarf and cap, handing out those free daily newspapers that had so recently started to clutter up New York.

Two doors down from the club, Lucas stood next to a truck dressed in work clothes and a hard hat. Vic got out of the back of the truck and joined Lucas. They spoke, briefly, and Vic disappeared into the club. Lucas got into the driver's seat. Vic had just gone in to bug the place. Dombrowski and Colletti were in the back of a florist's van parked in front of the town car. Griff was in there with them. Noah was watching out the window. He leaned forward and folded his arms across the top of the steering wheel.

"Vic's in," he mumbled.

"Hopefully, without a hitch," she said.

"Let's hope so."

A silver Mercedes SUV pulled up in front of the club, trailed by a white Yukon. The windows were tinted so dark, they were almost opaque. Four big guys got out of the Yukon, obviously security. Two went to either side of the Mercedes, as one of them spoke into a cell phone. Noah and Nick both sat up a bit straighter. She glanced at Lucas, his head was tilted in that direction. Meanwhile, Leah was putting up a nice front, passing out those messy dailies while nonchalantly eyeing the vehicles.

Karma II

The back doors of the Mercedes swung open and a woman got out, helped by one of the big guys. She was a tiny thing, with delicate features. Her hair fell almost to her waist in a sleek black sheath. She was small, but nicely built, wearing a clingy red dress that showed off her figure, and an oversized Chanel bag slung over her shoulder. Noah lifted his chin and scratched his goatee.

"Now that's what I'm talkin' about." He said, in a low, sexy voice.

"You don't ever stop, do you, Noah?"

"I ain't shoppin', I'm just lookin'. Don't go gettin' tight on me, Nick."

Nick laughed. "Why would I do that?"

"Leah, maybe?"

Nick leaned forward and put her arm on the front seat like she was giving him directions. Looking at Noah, it was easy to see what Leah saw in him, with his café skin, piercing eyes and that thick, dark, curly hair.

"Well, since you brought her up…"

"What?" He asked with zero enthusiasm

"So what's the deal, Noah?" Do you have a wife and kids tucked away somewhere?"

"Nah, I'm not married. Got two kids, though."

"That's it?"

"Yeah, that's it. What kind of question was that?"

They watched as the woman across the street reached into her Chanel bag and pulled

out a fluffy little white dog. Noah laughed.

"I hope she doesn't carry that thing around all the time. Lucas is gonna get a little freaky."

Nick perked up. "Lucas is afraid of dogs? You're kidding me, right?"

"He ain't jumpin' on the table tryin' to get away, but he's got a real strong aversion." He paused and looked out the window. "Here's asshole number one."

Tate Trinidad exited the Mercedes dressed in cream-colored Armani. The front passenger door popped open and out stepped Troy.

"Asshole number two," Noah said.

Both men were about 5'10" or 5'11", not as tall as Lucas or Noah, but not short. They had burnished, coppery skin. Both had the standard issue beard and goatee, but that's where the similarities basically stopped. Tate was decked out in that cream Armani, and Troy was hip-hop to the core in a throwback jersey and True Religions. He wasn't wearing a lot of jewelry, but what he had on blinged hard. Tate wore his hair close to his head. Troy's was cornrowed straight back. Noah rolled his toothpick around in his mouth. He was smirking.

"What are you thinking?" Nick asked.

"I'm thinkin', I ain't impressed. I could kick both their asses at the same time."

Nick agreed. In a fair fight, he probably could. Nick watched as Troy leaned back into the car. When he emerged, he was tucking a gun into his waistband like he didn't care who saw him.

"Look at the balls on this guy." Noah said.

"I wouldn't sleep on him, Noah."

"Believe me, baby, Noah don't sleep on nobody."

Nick smiled. "I'm not your baby, Noah."

He turned and grinned at her. "What is it with you? So argumentative!"

Tate, Troy and Tamiko went into the club. Leah moved closer and Lucas got out of the truck. Ten minutes later, Victor emerged unscathed, escorted to the door by one of the Trinidad brothers' peons. His job was done. The two-way crackled to life.

"Vic's out, let's get out of here." Griff said from the back of the florist's van. "Leah, you walk away first. There's an unmarked waiting for you on the corner of 20th and 9th. Lucas, you and Vic move next. Noah, you're next. Wait three minutes and pull out. Drive slow, no hot-rodding. I heard about you. We'll bring up the rear. Alright, Leah. Move now."

Noah stuck a cigarette in his mouth and lit it. He turned his head, watching Leah walk away.

"Do you really like her, or do you just want to sleep with her?" Nick asked.

"Leah's a grown-ass woman, Nick."

Noah could be a real asshole sometimes. Difficult, too. She had no doubt that Noah had a lovely, sensitive side to him, but it was buried under at least three feet of cockiness, bullshit and bravado. Noah was built in layers. With Lucas, once you cracked the surface, he was like the deepest part of the ocean.

Nick looked at the back of Noah's curly head as he pulled into the lot for the unmarked cars. Noah parked and got out without a word. Nick was surprised he waited for her.

"You mad at me?" He asked with a grin.

It was hard staying pissed at Noah. "No. We're okay. You put me in my place."

"It ain't gotta be all that. As for me and Leah, I'll repeat what I said before. Leah's a grown-ass woman, and you got enough shit of your own going on to be mindin' other people's business."

"Shit like what?"

"Shit like Keith Childs." He stopped walking and looked at her. "Listen, I'm not sure just how close you and Luke are, because he's being incredibly close-mouthed about you, but I can tell you one thing, though."

"Yeah? What's that?"

"You need to get the situation with Childs under control. Lucas ain't gonna tolerate his ass for a heartbeat, and I got his back. So unless he don't mind getting' his ass kicked, tell him to cool out. You got me?"

He was dead serious.

"Got it, Noah."

He held her eyes a beat longer. "Good," he said, finally, and started walking again.

He held the door to the precinct open for her, and followed her inside.

"You don't really like me too much, do you, Noah?"

"You're real nice to look at, but you're not pliable enough for me. Oh, and you talk too much. Ask too many questions. Other than that, you're pure joy. I got no problem with you. Just stop pickin' on me."

"You got it, boss," she said with heavy sarcasm.

Noah looked at her funny and opened the door to their office. Griff was there, waiting with Myers, Leah, Nate, and Tony. They took a seat and Lucas and Vic walked in 10 minutes later. Nick tried to be subtle as she watched Lucas. He moved something in her that Keith couldn't touch. He threw his chocolate eyes on her and took them right off. That sweet little dimple appeared in his cheek, but he didn't quite smile. Lucas turned his back toward her, giving her a sexy view of his broad shoulders and the back of his gorgeous head.

Griff started talking. "That was perfect. Nice job.

Karma II

We're not going to keep you guys in here all day. Pretty soon you'll be in grave danger and your free time won't be your own," he said, lightly.

"Ha, ha! Very funny, Griff." Nate said. "I'm not laughin'. I got a wife and kids."

"Yeah, so do I." Vic added.

Noah put the icing on the cake and said it out loud. "I gotta tell you, Griff, that grave danger shit ain't all that enticin'. For real."

Griff looked at them all. "If we keep stressing how dangerous this is, it's because it is, Ramsey. We want you aware. We're not gonna stop saying it just because you're tired of hearing it. Dammit, it's something you need to know. Do I make myself clear?"

"Yes, sir." Noah answered immediately, and surprisingly, with no latent sarcasm.

Karma II

Myers stood and clapped his hands together. "Okay, you guys. The day is yours. We'll give you tomorrow off to spend with your families,"

He looked pointedly at Nate and Vic. "We'll see you back in this office Wednesday morning." He left the room with Griff.

"I ain't apologizin' 'cause I got a family," Nate mumbled.

"Yeah, me neither," Vic said, quietly.

"Seems to me like you guys are in the wrong profession, then." Tony said from his seat by the window.

"I still ain't apologizin'," Nate said again.

Lucas stood up and took his jacket off. "Then don't. Listen, you gotta let all this shit go and just do what we have to do. You can't spend that much time thinking about how scary this shit is, 'cause you'll be too shook to get the job done."

"I'm just sayin', I got a lot to lose. I got a family," Nate repeated.

"We all have a lot to lose. Come on, Nate, we been

through dangerous shit together. Don't let this sting intimidate you. You're a better cop than that," Vic clapped Nate on the shoulder.

"Thanks for the compliment, but I kinda dread havin' my nuts stuffed into the mouth of my severed head, with a happy sticker slapped on my forehead."

Tony laughed dryly. "Your nuts are safe at home with your wife and kids. Yours too, Vic."

"I'm gonna say one more thing, then I'm done," Lucas started, "If we see this, you think Myers and Griff don't? Why do you think they keep hitting us over the head with it?"

He looked at Noah. "I know you ain't scared, bro, but you see what I'm saying?"

Noah looked back at Lucas. "I hear you, Luke. I ain't scared of shit. I just hate repetition."

Nate shrugged. "I never said I was scared, but I ain't got no John Wayne Syndrome like you two guys."

"Yeah, fuckin' rock stars." Vic said under his breath.

One of Lucas' eyebrows went up and Noah leaned forward.

"What?" Lucas asked.

Vic looked at Lucas steadily. "Rock stars. Come on, Lucas, you know what everybody says about you and Noah."

There was a hint of something nasty in his tone.

"No, I don't. What do they say, Vic?" When Lucas didn't look away, Vic dropped his eyes.

Lucas spoke to Vic in a low, serious voice. "Don't stop now. Keep talking, Vic. I really want to know."

Vic remained silent. When Lucas looked at Nate, he looked at the floor "What do they say, Nate?"

"I don't know. I been cool a long time with all of you. I'm stayin' cool."

Tony stood up. "You want to know? I'll tell you. They say Myers lets you guys run wild and do whatever you want, and he sweeps all your bad shit under the rug and makes it disappear.

Especially that crap that followed Nine's bust. Everybody knows it didn't go down exactly like it did on paper."

Lucas leaned forward and smiled. "Oh, yeah? Then what happened? I mean, I was there, but if you think you know what really happened, I'd like to hear it."

Tony shrugged noncommittally. "I'm not getting confrontational with you, Lucas. You, me and Noah go way back. I know what kind of cops you are."

Noah finally spoke up. "Why is everybody always gettin' at us about that Bainbridge thing? We took Nine's ass down, which was a damn good bust, his woman, who was Justine's so-called best friend, couldn't stand it. She had some kinda grudge against Justine. She was also crazy, with a capital C. When she was subpoenaed to testify against him, Nine tried to make sure that didn't happen. He had some people start makin' threats against her. Simone flipped out and thought it was Justine. On New Year's Eve, Simone got a gunshot through her window while she was drinkin' and feelin' sorry for herself."

He paused and looked at Lucas. "She twisted it in her mind that it was Justine and she went over there and killed her. We caught her in the act and took her down. End of story. Three of Nine's people are serving time for harrassin' Simone in the first place. Stop rehashin' this shit."

Vic looked at Lucas. "What did she shoot you for?"

The skepticism in his voice was a bit thick. Lucas retained that small, tight smile, but his chocolate eyes sparkled with indignation.

"She shot me because I was going to kill her. She killed Justine right in front of me. My intent was to kill her, so she shot me."

Just like that the sparkle of anger left his eyes and was replaced with a look of sorrow and remembrance so deep, it hurt Nick's heart.

Vic looked remorseful. "Look, Lucas, I'm sorry

man."

Lucas stood up. "Fuck you, Vic." He said, and walked out of the room.

Nick and Noah were both on their feet at the same time. She wanted to rush to him, but Noah put a restraining hand on her arm.

"I'm going." She said, and wrested her arm away. Before she left, she turned and spoke to Vic. "I don't know what that was ultimately about, but you're a colossal asshole."

Nick slammed out the door. She looked around and saw Lucas step into the elevator. She hurried over and stuck her foot in the door just as it closed.

"Lucas?" She ventured.

"What?"

"Are you alright?"

"Not now, Nicole."

She handed him his coat. He took it but didn't put it on.

"Lucas, I just…"

He frowned at her. "I said not now."

The elevator opened and he walked out. Nick followed him out of the precinct.

Karma II

"Where are you going?" She ran to catch up to him and reached him as he got to his car. She moved between him and the door. "Don't run off like this, Lucas."

"I'm not running off. Move. I'll see you later."

Nick frowned. "Did you just tell me to move?"

The anger returned to his eyes. "Please move."

Nick stepped out of the way. Lucas got into his car and drove away without looking at her. The pain in his eyes had been incredible. She knew it must have been terrible for him. It was also plain to see he wasn't over Justine. She wanted very badly to wrap her arms around him and tell him everything would be alright. That he had someone new to love, if he was willing. Lucas wasn't ready. Hell, she probably wasn't quite ready herself.

"Where's Luke?" Noah asked over her shoulder. Leah was standing there with him.

"I don't know. He just left."

Noah put his hand on her back. "He'll be okay."

Leah looked up at him. "You're not going to look for him?"

"You just gotta understand, Nick, that shit was hard. Just leave him alone. He'll be alright. He ain't made of glass."

Nick nodded. "Thanks, Noah."

"Don't mention it."

Leah gave her a supportive peck on the cheek and walked off with Noah. Nick got into her Altima and drove to Brooklyn. Lucas wasn't there when she let herself in. She spent the rest of the day keeping busy. By seven, he still wasn't home. At eight, he still hadn't made an appearance. Nick went upstairs and took a shower. She walked out of the bathroom brushing her hair.

"Nicole?" Lucas startled her so bad, she dropped her hair brush.

Karma II

"Lucas! Shit, you scared me."

She reached past him and flicked on the light. A great wave of relief washed over her when she looked at him and saw that he was okay, then she instantly felt stupid. What had she thought he was going to do? Jump off a bridge or shoot himself in the head because of something Vic said?

"I didn't mean to scare you. I just wanted to apologize."

"Apologize for what?"

"I was rude to you."

"Yes, you were."

"You were worried about me."

She nodded. "Yes, I was. Very worried."

"Don't worry about me."

"I can't help it."

He kissed her palm. "Why not?"

"Because I care about you." She replied.

"You do?"

He pulled her into his arms. Lucas was effectively

crushing her with his masculinity, his handsomeness and his personality. She felt like she wanted to step inside of him.

"Very much."

He lightly kissed the corner of her mouth. "Oh, yeah?"

He held her closer. As delightful as it was to be held by Lucas like that, he also left her feeling tremendously vulnerable.

"Lucas…"

"Yes?"

To hell with it. She was letting him in on her feelings. If she told him how she felt, the worse thing he could possibly do was walk away.

"Lucas, I have to be honest with you. Is that okay?"

She half expected for him to tense up and move away, but he stayed right where he was and didn't flinch.

"It's okay." He kissed her forehead and gave her an encouraging squeeze. He smiled suddenly. He was gorgeous. "I think we need to talk."

Before she could answer, Lucas led her into his bedroom and switched on the lights. He sat on the bed and motioned for her to sit beside him.

"What's on your mind, Nicole?"

"You're about the only person I know that calls me Nicole."

"That is your name." He touched her hair again." He smiled that sweet little closed mouth smile she favored. "What did you want to say to me?" He asked, leaning back on one elbow, and placing his hand on her thigh.

Nick smiled. "I've got some really serious feelings for you. I mean, at first thought it was a crush, but these feelings aren't going away. The more I get to know you, the more I like you. I've never met a man like you."

Lucas was looking at her steadily. "I haven't always been the way I am now."

"I believe you."

"You probably wouldn't have wanted to know me then."

"Probably not." They shared a laugh.

"I got a couple of questions for you, Nicole."

"Go ahead."

"What makes you think you'll scare me away? What makes you think you're the only one catchin' feelings, and what makes you think this is just for the moment?"

"So you're saying this isn't one-sided?"

"Yeah, I am."

"I'm not real sure you're ready, Lucas."

He looked at her with a fair amount of uncertainty. "I'm not real sure you are either."

"Do you want to see where this is going?"

He laughed. "I hadn't planned on going anywhere."

"What about days like today? What about when you get hit in the face with... Justine? God, Lucas, you must think about her all the time."

Something sad passed over his eyes, but he didn't hold onto it. "I used to, but lately I've had a damn good reason not to. As far as days like today go, I just have to deal with it. Grief is never easy or simple, and it lasts a long time."

Nick sighed heavily. Lucas looked her in the eye. "Nicole?"

Nick felt a stab of jealousy that was so intense, it almost took her breath away. She was shocked and ashamed at the unexpected emotion.

"Yes?"

"Do you want me to lie to you, or tell you the truth?"

"You know the answer to that."

"If I told you I was over her, I'd be straight up lying to you. She's gone, though, and she's not coming back. I realize that. I also realize I'm still here."

"Yeah, you are." Nick agreed. Irritation and jealousy tinged her words.

Lucas smiled at her patiently. "I see how you feel."

"You do, huh?"

He laughed his low, mellow laugh. "Yeah, I do. I don't want you to think you have to compete with her."

"That's debatable, Lucas. You can't even say her name."

"Justine." He said it without so much as blinking. "Her name was Justine Greer, and I'm trying to put her in a place where I can deal with her, so I can deal with your beautiful, contrary, complicated ass. I want to try with you. I think about you all the time. I dream about you at night and I fantasize about you during the day. I have to see what's up with this thing between me and you. You woke me up, Nicole."

Nick stood up. She pushed off her boy shorts and pulled the camisole over her head. Lucas stood, too, wearing a hint of a smile.

"Oh, it's like that?" He asked. Lucas pulled his sweater over his head and started loosening his belt. Nick put her hands on her hips and tossed her head, throwing her hair over her shoulder.

"After what you just said to me, all this is officially and immediately available to you. You may lease with an option to buy."

"Lease with an option to buy, huh?"

"It's just an option. I'd offer you a test drive, but you've already had one." Nick smiled as she pulled his zipper down and slipped her hand inside. "You're an excellent driver, by the way."

Her hand glided back and forth as she worked his clothing down with her free hand. He was like a rock. Lucas bent his head to kiss her and she dodged him, teasingly.

"A little eager, aren't you?"

Lucas looked momentarily puzzled, then he smiled and frowned at once. "Oh… I get it. You're playing with me."

Nick laughed. "You're not used to being teased, Lucas?"

He surprised her by picking her up and dropping her unceremoniously on the bed. Lucas kissed her hard and deep. "No, I'm not, and I'm done talking."

Lucas started making love to her with slow and tender care. She'd never gotten out of anyone's bed so completely satisfied. Lucas worked his magic and she felt the warm tingle, then the heavy throb as she slammed her way into her orgasm. Her toes curled and her back arched reflexively as she put her hands in his hair and ground her hips against his. He was getting at her from an angle, applying direct pressure along the soft roof of her femininity. Nick was still in the middle of the first orgasm when the second one barreled in on its heels, hitting her like she'd been jolted with electricity. She cried out and gritted her teeth as Lucas expertly worked that small tender spot she'd heard so much about. She screamed his name so loud her throat hurt, as she lost control, he persisted with his steady, gentle pumping and she kept coming. He had her, and she kept making small whimpering sounds.

Lucas slipped his hands under her shoulders and started thrusting slow and deep, pulling himself into her, still working that spot. He had her in such a heightened state of pleasure, she felt like he was killing her. Slaying her.

"God, Lucas! Don't stop. Please don't stop."

He didn't. He worked until she was exhausted, with tears spilling out the corners of her eyes. He kissed them away and put his tongue in her mouth, kissing her deep and picking up his pace. She was in love with him. Lucas Cain. She knew he'd be the love of her life. He made everyone else pale in comparison. Nick twined her legs around his and put her arms around him. She held him as tight as she could and kissed him back. He started moaning, then he growled deep in his throat. She smiled, loving that growl. It was sexy as hell. He started pounding into her, quick and hard.

"Nicole... damn, girl... what are you doing to me?" He

asked the question, breathlessly, and went over the brink, like he was trying to hold back, but his passion wouldn't let him. He came hard. He went in all the way, grinding so hard, he was almost pushing her off the bed.

He slowed to a gradual stop, then pulled her into her arms, kissing her. She was overwhelmed by the depth of what she felt for him.

Nick remembered teasing him about breaking women's hearts and realized she'd placed herself in the slippery position of having the same thing done to her. Lucas was lying on his back with her head on his chest. When he spoke, he startled her.

"What are you thinking about?" He asked, running his fingers through her hair.

She sat up and looked down at him lying there with his hand behind his head. "I was hoping you don't hurt me."

He looked surprised. "Why would I do that?"

"Because you can."

He sat up, too. "Why would I want to? You afraid of me, Nicole? Who do you think I am?"

Lucas leaned forward and spoke into her ear. There was an edge of agitation in his voice. "Who, Nicole? Who do you think I am? I'm not the same guy you've heard so much about. Life has a way of changing people and teaching them a little humility."

"Is that what it taught you?"

"Damn straight. I spent the last couple of years making up for every dirty deed I ever did, and for every time I just didn't give a damn."

Nick smiled. "I couldn't imagine you not giving a damn, Lucas."

"Well, I didn't."

Nick made a face at him. "You and Noah out there getting your mack on, huh?"

"All I'm saying is, women were never a problem for me, and I took it for granted, and I wasn't always nice. What goes around, comes around, and you have to pay

Karma II

what you owe."

"You think that everything that happened was karma, don't you?"

His voice lost that edge. "Yeah, I do."

She climbed into his lap, facing him, and wrapped her arms around him. "You couldn't have been that bad."

"Yeah, sweetheart, I was pretty bad. Did some things. I mean, I loved somebody enough to marry her, but still, I did some things."

When she tried to look at him, he averted his eyes and concentrated on caressing her thighs. Nick frowned. What had he done to Justine?

"Lucas."

He stopped rubbing and looked at her. "I don't want to talk about it. That's a conversation for another time." His hands drifted up her body until his thumbs found her nipples. "I don't want to talk anymore. I just want to be with you, sweetheart."

He kissed her tenderly and leaned back on the pillows. Nick stayed on top and slipped him back in. They started moving slowly.

"Lucas?"

He put his hands on her hips. "Hmm?"

"Did you just call me sweetheart?"

"Yeah. Sweetheart, darling, baby, honey, you're all those things."

"Really? I wasn't sure you cared."

"Oh, most definitely. I care, Nicole. I care a lot." He rolled her over on her back and showed her just how much.

Chapter Eleven

Revenge is all sweet

Keith Childs sat behind the wheel of a rented Chrysler in the parking lot of Midtown South, wondering if what he was doing was really called stalking. Fucking Nicky. Women didn't walk away from Keith Childs. He left them. The thing was, he hadn't planned on leaving Nicky. He'd worked too hard to get her.

When Keith met Nicky, he'd had an instant crush on her. She'd avoided him like the plague because his lecherous reputation was common knowledge. He'd finally convinced her to go out with him and she'd quickly informed him that she wasn't looking to be a conquest. Nicky had really made him work for it. It took him the better part of three months to sleep with her, and when he did, he decided he didn't just want to hit it and split. She was a pleasure to look at, she could do amazing things in the kitchen and the sex was off the chain. He purposely took her off the market by convincing her to live with him.

Keith was happy with the arrangement. He had a beautiful piece of ass, and he still had the freedom to do whatever else he wanted because he wasn't bound by a piece of paper. Nicky, on the other hand, wasn't quite that satisfied. Keith stayed stubbornly resistant. No way was he letting some bitch tie him down. He didn't give a fuck how fine she was. The more pressure she put on him, the more he showed her she needed to kill that noise, that her ass was expendable. He'd act like the shit was over until she calmed her ass down. Nicky had been a bit too independent and strong willed when he'd met her. He'd meant to break her will. But now it was crystal clear Nicky didn't want his ass coming home.

He drummed his fingers on the steering wheel impatiently. He'd been sitting here through two hours of shift changes and he hadn't seen her yet. From what he could judge from the last time he saw her, she was either moving on or giving it some damned serious thought. It was probably that fucking Cain. Something was definitely going on there, or maybe it was that goddamned snarky-assed Ramsey. He was pretty sure one of them was trying to put the mack down on her. Either way, he'd never be a cheerleader for either one of them.

Keith had known those two clowns since the academy. To him, Ramsey was still the same slick, loud-mouthed, shit talking asshole he'd always been, and Cain was still the same arrogant, condescending, aloof motherfucker, who seemed to think he sat on a throne above everybody else.

They both looked just about the same, too. Like they'd made some kind of goddamned deal with the devil. He remembered, with a smile, being sick of Ramsey's pretty face and his smart mouth. He remembered he'd made up some story and told the sergeant Ramsey was padding his overtime. Someone told Ramsey it was him that had put

Karma II

the bug in the sergeant's ear.

Ramsey had surprised him by coming down on him like a hammer. He'd snuck him, old school, in the locker room. No words. He'd just started whipping his ass. That yellow nigga hit hard, too. It took five other officers to break that shit up.

Keith was considering getting a cup of coffee when Nicky walked out of the precinct with Leah. He felt a twinge of regret for punching her in the face, but he wasn't really sorry he'd done it. She'd deserved it. He moved to get out of the car, but stopped himself when he saw Ramsey and Cain walking toward the two women. Ramsey was grinning. He said something to Leah and kind of rolled up on her. Keith zeroed in on Nicky. She laughed at the two of them as Cain showed the world one of his infrequent smiles and gave Ramsey dap.

Ramsey walked away and got into a white Escalade, Cain went a few cars down and opened the door to a black S500. Damn! That was big pimpin'. They were living a bit larger than he was, at least larger than he was willing to risk showing. Nicky and Leah got into Nicky's Altima.

Karma II

Keith waited until they left the lot and started his tail. Their first stop was the Whole Foods down in Chelsea. He watched them from a distance as Nicky picked up a few staples, all the while having an animated conversation with Leah that included a lot of girlish giggling. He wondered what the fuck was so funny. He also wondered how she was managing to look so goddamned happy without him.

She dropped Leah off in Sunset Park and got back on the parkway. Nicky got off in Carroll Gardens and drove to a street lined with brownstones. If she was living here, her rent had to be crazy. Nicky got out and jogged up the steps of one of the brownstones, opened the door with her key, and disappeared inside. She came back a couple of minutes later in a pair of shorts and a T-shirt.

Keith was frowning hard. Something was very wrong with this picture. The front door swung open and out stepped Lucas Cain, moving fast and pulling a T-shirt over his naked chest. Keith's mouth dropped open. He watched with horrified disbelief as Cain started taking bags from her.

"What's all this?" Cain asked.

Nicky looked up at him, beaming. "I'm gonna make you a really nice dinner," she said as she dangled a Victoria's Secret bag in front of him, "and then I'm gonna give you a really nice dessert."

Cain smiled at her. "Is that so?"

Keith grimaced as he felt the bile rise up in his throat.

"You hungry?" She asked, coyly.

"I'm starving." Her hand slipped up to his neck and she pulled him down for a quick kiss.

Keith's eyes narrowed and he stared at them coldly. This motherfucker was fucking his woman! He reached into his jacket, and was pulling his gun out of its holster when someone tapped on the roof of his car. Keith's head whipped around in that direction as he let go of his gun. A slim, middle aged Asian man was standing there looking slightly irritated.

Karma II

"Excuse me, sir, but could you pull your car up so I can park in front of my house?"

Keith smiled at him. "Sorry about that. Sure, no problem."

The man looked him over warily. "No big deal. Do you need some help?"

"Nah. Actually, I think some chick just ran a game on me." The Asian guy looked sympathetic.

"Yeah? How so?"

"I think she gave me the wrong address. Can you believe that shit?"

The guy nodded. "Sure can."

Keith laughed good naturedly. "Oh, well. Anyway, sorry about that."

He put his windows up and turned the key in the ignition. Cain was holding the front door open for Nicky.

He looked toward the sound of Keith's engine turning over as she went inside. Keith ducked down and fiddled with the knob on the radio. When he looked back up, they had gone inside.

He couldn't believe Nicky had left him for Lucas Cain, of all people. He wanted to kick the door in and shoot them both. He laughed ruefully. At least it wasn't Ramsey's big mouthed ass. So Nicky was living with Cain. They were both going to pay for this shit. He felt every cozy feeling he'd ever felt for Nicky falling away from him, like leaves from a dead tree.

Keith hadn't noticed Cain's Mercedes parked in front of her car before. He left the motor running and got out of his car. Keith looked around surreptitiously and took his house keys out of his pocket. Starting at the front end, he dug a deep furrow into Cain's paint job. He scraped his keys over the trunk and continued up the other side. Keith smiled. Cain was going to shit a brick when he saw it.

He pulled away, knowing that keying Cain's car was a bitch thing to do, but that was more than likely what Cain would think. He'd think some bitch did it. It was a small thing, but it was a start.

Karma II

Chapter Twelve

I want you back

Nadine stood at the living room window waiting patiently for Noah to bring their children home. She was wearing a short filmy halter dress that she knew Noah would love, but she didn't want the kids looking at her funny. Maybe the spike-heeled sandals were a bit much.

She was kicking them off when she heard Noah's Caddy screech to a halt. Some things never changed. Noah was still driving like a lunatic. Nadine opened the front door and watched the kids get out, Raine with her long black ponytail and skinny nine-year-old body, and Noah Jr., looking like his father, was all frowned-up and bickering with his sister.

"You always get your way! I wanted to see Spiderman."

Raine turned her nose up at him. "So what? Shrek was good."

"Shrek is for kids."

"Well, what do you think you are? You're a kid, too."

Noah Jr. had just turned 11, and it was a chore convincing him he wasn't an adult.

"Yeah, I'm a lot older than you, dummy."

Noah got out of the truck, just as frowned-up as his son. Nadine's heart fluttered helplessly. He looked very annoyed. Raine ran to him and put her arms around his waist, playing daddy's girl.

"Daddy, Noah called me a dummy."

"Yeah, I heard. Don't make me have to snatch you up, boy."

"Mom! We're home!" Raine called out.

"How was the movie?" She asked. Noah Jr. was still scowling.

"It sucked! I wanted to see Spiderman, but Daddy made us go see a freakin' cartoon, 'cause that's what Raine wanted. Freakin' baby!"

Karma II

Noah looked at him like he was crazy. "Who you talkin' to, Noah? I guess you gonna start cussin' next, huh? Apologize to your mother and your sister, then carry your little narrow ass to your room before I fold you up, son."

Noah Jr. was instantly chastised. He hung his head, said he was sorry, and started for his room.

"Hey, Noah?" He called to his son.

"Yes, Daddy?"

"Come give your old man a goodnight kiss." He returned and gave Noah a hug and a kiss on the cheek. Noah kissed him back and slipped a twenty into his son's pocket. "Love you, son. Now go to your room."

Noah Jr. left, looking happier. Noah turned to Raine. "Next time he calls the shots, okay? Goodnight, baby girl."

"Okay. Goodnight, Daddy."

He gave her a hug and a kiss and told her he loved her.

"Don't I get any money?" She asked, looking

cheated.

Noah smiled at her. "You better get outta here. Go to bed."

She sucked her teeth and flounced off to her room. Noah took his wallet out and handed Nadine a twenty.

"That's for her little jealous ass." He tucked his wallet back into his pocket and took his time looking her over. "You're lookin' quite lickable this evenin'. You been somewhere foolin' around with some guy?"

His tone was light, but the flicker in his gorgeous eyes implied he wouldn't appreciate it if she had been.

Nadine laughed. She'd never stood on ceremony with Noah. "No. I put this dress on for you, Noah. I was hoping you'd find me lickable. I wouldn't mind fooling around with you."

Noah started to smile, but didn't. Nadine smiled at him. She knew how Noah felt about her. Nadine moved closer to him.

"Cat got your tongue, Lover?" She asked.

"Nadine, I don't know what you want from me." He said, shaking his head.

"Yes, you do."

"Don't do this, Nadine."

"Don't do what? Don't want my husband back?"

He frowned down at her. "What did you say to me?"

"You heard me." She answered, and moved to kiss him.

Noah forced her arms down and moved away from her. Then he got angry. He stuck an accusatory finger in her face. "You tryin' to play me, Nadine?"

"I have never tried to play you a day in my life, Noah, and I'm not going to start now."

He frowned, but most of the anger was out of his face. Nadine smiled as he started that goddamned head shaking again. He was fighting with himself, deciding what move he was going to make.

"Okay, Nadine, exactly when was it that you lost

133

Karma II

your mind?"

"I haven't lost my mind. Come sit down."

She tried to take his hand, but he wouldn't let her. The anger bounced back into his handsome face.

"Hell, no. I ain't stupid. See you later, Nadine."

He put a cigarette between his lips and walked out the door. Nadine followed him. She knew Noah very well. Now was not the time to relent. That little show of bravado was covering his vulnerability. When Noah felt weak he got angry. He opened the door on the driver's side and Nadine touched his arm.

"Noah, come on, talk to me." He removed his Dunhill and looked down at her feet.

"Go back in the house and put some shoes on."

She ignored him and hopped up into the driver's seat. "I'm not letting you leave until you talk to me."

He screwed his face up. He was adorable. "Stop, Nadine. Get outta my car."

Nadine was sideways in the front seat, facing him. She hitched her skirt up and parted her legs. Noah looked at her and sighed in resignation as he put his hands on her thighs.

"You know you ain't right. You really ain't right."

"Yes, I am." She whispered.

Noah's hands tightened on her thighs. He was looking at her with a mixture of regret, sadness and uncertainty. "Nadine, you know I… I mean, you-"

She cut him off by pulling his belt loose and pulling down his zipper. Nadine put her hand in his pants and pulled him out, hard and ready. Noah was always ready. That was it. He leaned down and started kissing her forcefully and urgently, while his hands pushed her dress up to her waist. He made her panties disappear like a magician. He pulled her off the seat to meet him, palming her ass in his hands and took the plunge. Nadine cried out in exhilaration, but also in shock. She'd planned on getting Noah to make love to her, but hell, not in the driveway. He was moving faster.

than usual, but that was most likely due to their outdoor situation. It didn't stop her from climaxing. It crashed down on her prematurely and pointed her toes. Noah grunted. The force of it almost pushed him out. He was smiling at her wickedly. She smiled back and he started talking shit to her.

"You sure you want me back, Nadine, or do you just want this? Hmm? Answer me, Nadine."

She put her hands in his silky, curly hair and ran her fingers through it. She closed her eyes and gritted her teeth. He felt so good. Nobody was Noah.

"I want both. I love you, Noah."

When she said that, he paused, then started sliding in long and slow. All the way in,

like she liked it. Nadine felt herself start to throb again.

"Say my name, Nadine." He kissed her quickly.

Say it? Hell, she shouted it. "Noah! Oh, Noah! Don't even ask, Daddy. You know it's yours."

"Alright, then." Hard and deep. Hard and deep.

Nadine knew she was a screamer, so did Noah. When he took her back there again, he covered her mouth with his to stifle her. He almost dropped her when he started coming, too, but it was more delightful when Noah didn't miss a beat. He held her weight with his arms and kept grinding into her. He was filling her up. He slowed to a stop whispering her name in her ear. When he was done he kissed her with one of his long delicious kisses. He seemed very reluctant to let her go, but eventually he released her. Nadine was unnerved by the sudden loss of contact.

Noah stood up and started to get himself together. Nadine pulled her dress down and looked around for her underwear. She looked up when she heard him finally light his cigarette.

"Where are my panties?"

Noah squinted at her through the smoke. "In my pocket."

"Can I have them back?"

He gave her a genuine smile and looked down at her. "Nope. Not a chance."

Nadine shrugged. "Fine. Keep them."

"I planned on it."

"I meant what I said earlier, Noah."

He stuck his Dunhill back in his mouth and feigned ignorance.

"About what?" He was annoying her, but she was still enjoying him.

"Stop playing games. I want you to come home."

He flicked his cigarette on the ground and stared at her. "Come home? You're really kiddin' me, right?"

"I couldn't be any more serious. Let's work this out, Noah. Come home."

He continued to stare at her. "It's a little late. What do you want me back for? So Liz can't have me? That's what this is all about."

Karma II

Nadine pursed her lips. She really didn't want to hear about Liz and her situation. She didn't want to think about anybody else having Noah's babies. She'd love Noah Ramsey until the day she died. If Noah had only been able to keep his pants up, he'd have been the best husband she could have asked for, and the best father for their kids. Instead, Noah stayed on that long winding road of whoring he'd always been on. Even though Noah loved her, and Nadine knew that to be true, he'd never been faithful to her.

She knew in her bones Noah hadn't changed. It was plain to see that he was still cheating, even if it was with her. Nadine was just about certain, if Noah came back, it would be the same thing all over again. She still loved him and wanted him just as much as she had when she first saw those wonderful gray eyes. The possibility of him settling down and having a family with someone else was killing her.

She was willing to deal with this baby business and prepare herself for almost definite future infidelity, rather than see him building a life with some other woman. Fuck

Lissette. Nadine wasn't going to let her have Noah without a fight, and Nadine was willing to fight dirty. She nodded at Noah.

"You're right. This is all about what's going on between you and Lissette. She's trying to take my spot."

Noah laughed and lit another cigarette. "You vacated your spot, Nadine."

"That was a mistake. I want it back."

Noah raised his eyebrows. "Is that so? A mistake, huh? You divorced me, Nadine. What about Liz? How can you ask me to come be with you, when Liz is carrying my baby?"

Nadine slipped her arms around his waist. "Are you in love with me, Noah?"

He kissed her softly on the lips. "Yes."

He kissed her again. A long sweet kiss like he used to. The sadness had returned to his eyes. "I can't leave Liz."

"Yes, you can."

He frowned at her. "I won't."

Nadine's hands stole under his shirt. She ran her fingernails lightly over the muscles in his stomach, and grazed her teeth over his bottom lip. A low sound of pleasure rumbled in his chest. Just like that, he was ready again. She never should have divorced him. They should have gotten counseling or whatever it took, but they never should have divorced. She'd been wrong.

Karma II

"You will, Noah. If not now, sooner or later, you will, because you don't love her. You love me."

He started kissing her again and Nadine put her arms around his neck. Noah's hands slipped to her hips and he pushed himself against her insistently.

"I gotta go, Nadine."

She laughed softly in his ear. "Then go. Stop dry humping me."

"I can't." He said, starting to pull her dress up.

"We can take this inside, you know."

He pressed against her like steel, and shook his head.

"Nah, baby, let's do it right here, come on."

Noah was bad, but he was thrilling her and giving her goose bumps. He put his hand under her dress and touched her with his middle finger. Nadine gasped and reached for his zipper. She had him in her palm, about to guide him in, when she heard a young voice.

"Daddy! You still here?"

They both froze and turned toward the open window. Noah Jr. was standing there grinning back at them. Nadine started grinning herself. It was impossible for him to see more than her head from where he was standing. Instead of guiding Noah in, she started slowly moving her hand up and down. Noah closed his eyes and swallowed hard. Noah Jr. was unrelenting.

"Daddy, is Mom out there with you?"

Noah's eyes flew open in irritation as he looked toward the window. "Boy, didn't I tell you to carry your ass to bed? Don't make me come in there and take my belt off!" He yelled at him.

Karma II

"Mom? What are y'all doin'?"

"Talking, Noah. Go to bed."

"About what? Y'all makin' up?"

"Go to bed, Noah!" Noah snapped at him. The light in the kitchen winked out quickly, but Nadine let go of Noah all the same. He blew air out through his teeth and dropped his head. Nadine put her fingers in his hair and kissed his temple.

"He's still there." She whispered.

Noah brushed his lips against hers but didn't linger. He straightened up and discreetly fixed his clothes. He looked at the window, scowling. "Bad-ass kid." He mumbled.

Nadine laughed as she and Noah traded places. "I'm sorry." She said.

Noah smirked. "No, you're not. You like seeing me suffer. Gotta go, Nadine."

"I know."

Nadine stood just inside his open door. He smiled

down at her. Nadine was captivated by that smile.

"Look at you. You don't want me to go, do you?"

"No. I never want you to leave."

His smile faltered. "Shit, Nadine. You really want me back?"

She laughed. "That's all I've been saying for the past hour."

He stared down at her. "That's some serious shit, Nadine."

"Yes, it is."

"I gotta see how I feel about that."

She frowned. "What do you mean?"

"I mean, you ain't the only person walkin' around here with feelings. This ain't the Nadine Ramsey Show, you hear what I'm sayin' to you? A decision like that affects other people."

"The kids would be ecstatic."

"Yeah, okay. Liz wouldn't."

The words 'Fuck Liz' almost flew out of her mouth before she could stop them. He leaned down and kissed her.

139

Karma II

"I'll call you tomorrow."

"Okay." Nadine stepped out of the way and let him close his door.

"Goodnight, Noah."

"Night, Nadine."

She watched him drive away. Nadine went inside, set the alarm, and went into the bedroom. She took off the dress and put on her nightgown. She got into bed on Noah's old side and put her head on his former pillow. She put her hands on her stomach and smiled to herself. Noah was coming home. It wouldn't be long now.

Chapter Thirteen

Home sweet home

Noah sat in his Escalade, parked in his own driveway, smoking. So, Nadine wanted him back. He wanted to go, too. He loved her. The day she told him she wanted a divorce had been one of the darkest days of his life. He knew he'd caused everything himself. Noah knew she loved him, too. Maybe he'd just expected her to always be there. When she'd told him to leave, he'd gotten a lot wilder. Fine, Nadine. Now he really could do whatever he wanted. He'd gone crazy, had no restraint.

Then he'd met Liz. Noah had never completely stopped what he was doing, but Liz had slowed him down a lot, and gotten him off a sure path to self-destruction. He tucked his cigarette in the corner of his mouth and slumped in his seat. He cared about Liz and loved her in his own way, but he sure didn't feel the same way about her that he felt about Nadine.

Noah sighed and got out of his truck. This shit was getting complicated. His mind danced on Leah. He'd been uncharacteristically restrained and indecisive when it came to her. He'd been in quite a few touchy situations with her, but he hadn't knocked her off yet. Shit, now he really didn't know if it was a good idea to pile that on his plate. He stepped on his cigarette and entered the house through the kitchen door.

He went upstairs, directly to the bathroom. He stripped off his clothes and stepped into the shower. Noah turned the water on full blast and stepped under it, lathering up quickly and removing all traces of Nadine. He washed his face and his hair, even under his fingernails. Liz was like a fucking bloodhound. He stepped out just as quickly and toweled off. He walked down the hall and entered the bedroom. Noah slipped into bed beside Liz, who had her back to him. Noah lay on his back, putting one arm behind his head and the other on his stomach. He was lying there enjoying the silence when Liz abruptly turned over to face him.

Karma II

"How was the movie?"

"It was okay."

"What did you see?"

Noah yawned expansively. He wasn't in the mood for the third degree. "Shrek."

Liz mover closer to him. Noah opened the eye closest to her.

"How are the kids?"

"They're okay."

"What took you so long?" She asked, curling her hand around his manhood.

Noah opened his other eye. Her grip was a touch too firm. "So long for what?" He came back at her, in a voice that was a touch too tight.

"To come home to me." Liz sat up, putting her weight on her elbow. Her other hand stayed where it was. "What happened? Did you get dirty?"

Noah frowned. His hand drifted down until he had her

by the wrist.

"What're you talkin' about, Liz?" He asked, carefully.

"You must have gotten pretty dirty or something. You took a shower the minute you got in here. What's up with that, Papi?"

Noah kept frowning. What was up with these women calling him Daddy? Shit, he had two kids. He was on the road to getting seriously irritated, but he decided to take the off ramp.

"I take a shower first thing most of the time, sweetie." Oops.

That didn't come out like sugar. It had the bitter bite of sarcasm. Noah tightened his grip on her wrist and moved his other hand from behind his head.

"Yeah, I noticed," She replied, with sarcasm just as thick. "What's going on, Noah?"

"What're you talkin' about?" He repeated.

"You stuck on the same question?" She asked, with heat in her voice.

"Depends, you stuck on the same bullshit?" He calmly slid his thumb between the base of her thumb and the first bone in her wrist.

"Were you with your kids, or were you with their mother?"

"You're trippin', Liz."

"No, I'm not." She sat all the way up and tightened her grip.

Noah remained calm, though his grip tightened also. "I'm just gonna say this once and I'm gonna be nice about it. I really think it would be in your best interest to take your hand off me in such an aggressive manner, sweetie."

Liz flipped out, but Noah anticipated it. She started cursing in Spanish and screaming at him. "To hell with you, Noah! You're screwing her and I know it!"

She tried to make a fist, but Noah closed down on her wrist like a vise. Liz yelped in pain and he forced her as gently as he could onto her back.

"You tryin' to hurt me, Liz?"

Her free hand connected with his jaw and Noah was surprised she'd hit him so hard. He grabbed her other wrist and effectively restrained her.

"You cut it out, Liz! Stop!"

Another stream of Spanish curses. She couldn't use her hands, so she started kicking at him. Noah got up, switched on the lights, and started getting dressed. He was tightening his belt in his jeans when Liz stood up. Noah raised an eyebrow.

"Don't you come at me, Liz. I don't know what your problem is, but I can tell you, I ain't havin' it."

He looked at her. She was so angry she couldn't stand still, shifting from one foot to the other, curling and uncurling her fists.

"Where are you going in the middle of the night, Noah? You better not leave this house! You better not!"

Noah couldn't stop himself from laughing.

Karma II

"I'm a grown-ass man, Liz, you don't tell me what I better not do," He paused and looked at the small bump of her stomach. "You need to calm down before you hurt yourself."

Liz put a protective hand on her belly. She kept shifting her weight and her nightgown swirled around her mocha colored thighs, prettily. Liz ran her other hand through her tousled hair and actually bared her teeth at him. Noah found her very attractive at that odd moment. He smirked and put a light sweater over his head. Okay, it was time to bounce before things got weirder and more out of hand.

"I'm takin' a little time out, sweetie. I'll be back. Don't burn the house down while I'm gone." He turned and left the room.

"Don't you leave, Noah. I'm serious."

When he got to the door, she grabbed his arm. "Don't go." She said.

He looked down at her. "I'm tired of you goin' berserk.

You been this way since you got pregnant."

"No. I've been this way since your ex-wife rolled up on me in my own house."

Noah opened the door and put one foot outside. "It's my house." He said under his breath.

He pulled the door shut behind him and got into his truck. He was two blocks away when he realized he didn't know where he was going. Noah pulled over and leaned back in his seat and lit a Dunhill. Shit. He looked at his watch. It was kind of late to hit Lucas. His mind bounced on Leah, but ricocheted right back off. Bad idea. Just digging the hole deeper.

He pulled out, took the Harlem River Drive and got off at the Polo Grounds. He got out of his truck and put the alarm on, even though he wasn't worried about anybody fucking with it. It was rough up here, but this was where he was from. Everybody knew him, and he'd had crazy respect since he was a kid. His older brother Junior had been a big deal, back in the day, and not in a bad way. Junior had been a young, handsome, over-achieving, church going guy. He was active in his community, captain of the football team, and valedictorian of his senior class. He had a scholarship to Stanford.

Karma II

As usual, as Noah entered his old building, his eyes dropped to the spot where Junior fell after taking two bullets to the head. Unsolved murder. Noah paused to say hello and chit chat with a couple of guys he grew up with. He also took the time to pass a couple of words with a few others, who always hung outside drinking and bullshitting like they got paid for it. They were as constant as the light posts on the corner. He rode the elevator to the eighth floor and rang the bell twice before using his key. He didn't want Big John going for his baseball bat. His mother came out of the kitchen to greet him.

"Hi, baby. It's good to see you. What brings you here this time of the night? The kids alright?"

Noah bent and kissed the cheek of the long suffering,

but still beautiful, Anita Ramsey. She was a tall, slim woman with smooth amber skin and sparkling gray eyes. Her hair held a generous amount of silver, and she wore it woven into a French braid that hung to the middle of her back. She hugged her son and kissed him back.

"Hey, Mama. Everybody's cool. Pop home?"

"Last time I checked," She turned her head and yelled over her shoulder. "John! Your son is here!"

"Which one?" Big John called out.

"Noah." There were three of them. Noah, Drew and Emery. He didn't know who the hell he thought it was. Emery was in Iraq, and Drew was teaching at Howard.

"You hungry, son?"

"Nah, Mama. I'm good."

His father entered the room wearing a faded pair of jeans and a white wife beater. He half scowled, half grinned at his son, and it was easy to see what Noah would probably look like in the next 30 years. He had the same café coloring, he was tall with a still athletic build and they had the same hair, though John's once raven curls were peppered with silver. The only big difference in them was their eyes. John's were a deep dark brown, and Noah's were gray, like his mother's.

"Hey, boy! What the hell you doin' here so late? Your old lady throw your ass out?" He sat down at the kitchen table, laughing at him in his deep raspy voice.

Like he had since he was a kid, his father reminded Noah of a handsome pirate. He felt a sudden wave of deep affection for him. He sat across from him and lit a cigarette.

"No, Pop. I left by my own free will."

His father frowned at him. "What? Ain't that your spot?"

"I didn't leave, leave. I just got out 'cause she was trippin'."

Big John helped himself to one of his smokes, while Anita made herself scarce. "What you got that gal stayin'

Karma II

with you for anyway?"

John asked with a raised eyebrow. Noah looked at him and momentarily felt like he was 12 years old again. He'd been putting off mentioning Liz's pregnancy because he knew what Big John was going to say. John got up and went into the living room. He returned with a bottle of Chivas Regal and put it down. He took two glasses out of the cabinet and reclaimed his seat.

"You look miserable. What's the problem, son?" John asked, pouring two short drinks.

Noah sighed and took a sip. "I got problems, Pop."

"How big?"

"Pretty big," Noah met his steady gaze. "Liz is pregnant."

"Damn, boy. What did you do that for?"

"Wasn't my fault, Pop. She stopped takin' her pills."

"I don't believe you just said that ignorant shit. I been tellin' you since you was young not to count on no woman for no shit like that. You a goddamned fool, Noah."

"Yeah, well, it gets worse. I told Nadine."

Karma II

His father sat back in his chair and started shaking his head in disapproval. "What the hell did you do that for?"

It was the same question Lucas had asked him. Why had he told her? Because she was getting on his nerves? To dig into her a little bit? Just to hurt her? He should have kept his big mouth shut, then maybe he wouldn't have all these problems. Then again, if he hadn't said anything, he'd probably never know Nadine wanted him back. On the other hand, maybe she only wanted him back so she could fuck him over. After all, she did owe him one. Or two. Or three.

"I don't really know why I told her. I just did."

"To be so bright, you really do some stupid shit. What happened, boy?" John was looking at him like he was an asshole.

Noah didn't appreciate that, but it was what he'd come here for. He rehashed Nadine's reaction, and conveniently left out the fact that they'd slept together, but John was no fool.

"So, Nadine went crazy on you, huh?"

"Yup. Said I was put on this earth to hurt her, some shit like that."

John shrugged. "Well, you were. You're a man. All women think that. What else happened?"

John poured another drink and sat back in his chair, looking at him shrewdly. Noah went back to staring at the table and not answering. "You didn't sleep with her, did you?"

Noah winced. "I-"

John cut him off by banging his fist on the table. "I'll be damned! Boy, what's wrong with you? Did you protect yourself, or did you slide your dumb ass up in there with nothin'?"

Noah dropped his head. Oh shit. "I-"

John interrupted him again. "Nothin', right? Boy, are you crazy?"

148

Karma II

Noah closed his eyes and slid down in his seat. "Shit."

"Yeah. Shit, son. What the hell is wrong with you?"

"It was Nadine, Pop."

"Humph, I know that was your wife and all, but what would make you go in there blind like that? That gal got an ass made of gold?"

Noah opened his eyes and smiled a little. "No, Pop, platinum. Like I said, it was Nadine. I didn't even think about it. For real. I don't think Nadine would play me dirty like that."

"What makes you so sure? Shit, when you was married to her, you did whatever the hell you wanted. That was playin' her dirty. What makes you think she ain't tryin' to get pregnant too, and play her baby against Liz's baby? Maybe she just wants to get some revenge for all the whorin' you did while y'all was married. Plottin' and schemin'. Women love revenge, son. You can ask your boy Lucas about that."

He didn't need to ask Lucas shit. He'd seen firsthand the devastation that shit could cause. "The damage is done. I can't take it back."

"That's the truth," John stated, simply. "I understand about Nadine," he added, with sympathy.

Noah was surprised. "You do?"

"I sure do. You always loved that gal. You goin' back to her?"

"I can't."

John smiled. "You a grown-ass man. You can do whatever you want."

"I can't leave Liz like that. That ain't right, Pop."

Big John took a sip of his drink. "Oh. Now you got some morals, huh?"

Noah looked at him sourly. "I got plenty morals."

John looked at his son steadily. "Yeah, you do, son. Maybe sometimes they get misplaced. Sometimes they go out the window altogether. 'Specially where a woman's concerned. Some of that's my fault. Watchin' me not do right by your mother probably made you think that was the proper way to treat a woman. It ain't."

Noah could count on one hand the number of times John had taken an apologetic tone with him. He looked at his father with some concern. "You feelin' alright, Pop?"

He nodded and looked back at Noah fondly. "I feel fine, boy. I just wish I'd taught you different about women. Maybe you wouldn't be in the position you're in now, but hell, back when you boys were growin' up, I didn't know shit myself. I just told you what I was always told, which was to basically get all the ass you could possibly get and worry about everything else later."

"You had a change of heart?" He asked.

Big John stared into his glass and didn't answer him right away. Noah really looked at his father for the first time in a long time. He noticed the crow's feet at his eyes, and the creases in his forehead. He saw how gray he'd

Karma II

really gone. Big John was getting old.

"I think when your mother got sick, I saw what an asshole I'd been to her, and I was sorry, because like you said, son, I couldn't take it back. I thought she was gonna die and I'd never get the chance to make it up to her."

Anita had a nasty bout with breast cancer five years ago. They thought they were going to lose her because it had been so aggressive. She'd ended up having a double mastectomy and a long course of chemotherapy. She'd scared the shit out of everybody, but so far it hadn't come back.

"I made a deal. I said if He let her pull through, I'd do my best to change."

Noah smiled. "You found God, Pop?"

John laughed. "No, son, He found me. You may never see my ass in the Amen Corner, but He let me know He was there."

They laughed together. Anita drug her boys to church with her every Sunday, but Big John stayed away like he'd catch fire if he walked through the doors.

"Let me tell you somethin', Noah, sometimes He makes you sit back and decide what's more important, you hear me? I had to decide between all my other women and your mother. I chose your mother. You gotta decide, too, son. You gotta choose Liz or Nadine. You can't have 'em both. He ain't gonna let you. Sooner or later, somethin' will happen and you'll be assed out with at least one of them, if not both. Best bet is to just choose. Nadine, Liz, or neither one. You gotta do it before it becomes a situation you can't control. Hell, it's probably already too late. Do it now, son."

Noah shook his head. "I can't leave Liz."

"'Cause she's pregnant?"

"Uh-huh."

John looked at him directly. "What if Nadine is, too?"

Noah put his elbows on the table and his face in his

hands. Nadine wouldn't do that to him. Shit, would she? Sure did seem like she was trying. She would have let him hit her twice in one night if his son hadn't saved his weak ass like a Saint Bernard. His hands slid slowly down his face.

"Jesus." He whispered.

Big John nodded. "Yeah, son. Jesus."

He stood up, came around the table, and laid a hand on his son's shoulder and gave it a squeeze. "I can't make no decisions for you, son, but I can try to be there for you if you need me. I believe you done made a mess." He said in his Louisiana twang.

Noah smiled. "Mayhap I did, Paw." He twanged back.

John pushed him in the head, playfully. "Don't be mockin' me, boy. You stayin' tonight?"

Noah stood up, too. "Guess so, Pop."

"Come on, then."

He walked Noah down to the spare bedroom and said goodnight. Noah sat on the side of the bed and took his cell phone out. She answered on the second ring.

"Noah?"

"Nadine, listen, you're not tryin' to hem me up, are you?"

"Hem you up? What are you talking about, Noah?"

"You still on the pill, Nadine?"

"What? Oh, you think I'm trying to get pregnant so I can steal you away from your little side dish."

"She ain't a side dish," Noah said absently. "Are you?"

Nadine laughed into the phone. "Really? What is she then? A distraction?"

Noah was starting to get angry. He stood up. "Answer the question, Nadine."

"No. You answer the question, Noah."

He started pacing. "Answer the fuckin' question. You're pissin' me off."

"You honestly think I would do that to you, Noah?"

"Given the circumstances, yeah, I think you would."

"For your information, I'm still on the pill, but if that's how you feel about it, let me remind you that condoms are readily available at just about every store on the street. Better yet, if you kept your dick in your pants, you couldn't get anybody pregnant. "

He laughed at her, spitefully. "It was in my pants until you pulled it out."

"If you were here now, I'd do it again. Stop being an ass, Noah, and come home."

"Who you talkin' to, Nadine?"

She laughed. "I'm talking to you, Lover. Go ahead and be angry. You're just frustrated because things are so complicated."

Noah held the phone away from his ear and looked at it. Nadine was either totally sincere or her ass had gone crazy. His mind flashed back to Liz trying to scratch his balls off, then to Nadine perched in his driver's seat with her legs parted.

"Both of y'all are fuckin' nuts."

"What did you say?"

"Gotta go." He said and ended the call.

He left the room and headed for the front door. His father surprised him in the hall by stepping into his way. "Where you goin', boy? Thought you was stayin' the night."

"Changed my mind, Pop."

Big John looked at him knowingly. "Don't go makin' things worse, son. I can just about read your mind."

Noah opened the door and stepped out. "Thanks, Pop. I'll call you later."

"Okay. You a grown man. I'm done dishin' out advice. I'll be here if you need me."

"Thanks, Pop. See ya."

Chapter Fourteen

Complication can be fun

Leah was just turning over when the sound of her doorbell woke her up. She looked at the clock. Two in the morning. Who in the hell was this? She slid her feet into her slippers and went to the door.

"Who is it?" She asked in a strong voice.

"Noah."

Her eyes flew wide, and her mouth popped open. Oh shit! What the hell was he doing here at this hour of the night? She looked down at herself in her short white cotton nightgown and ran back to her bedroom for her robe. Noah was ringing the bell again when she got back.

"I'm coming!" She called out, fluffing her hair with her fingers.

Leah opened the door. Noah was standing with his shoulder against the frame, about to ring the bell again. He looked down and smiled his sexy smirk at her.

"Sorry I woke you up." Leah tightened the belt on her robe, flustered by him.

"It's okay. Are you alright?"

"I'll live." He said, simply.

"It's two in the morning, Noah."

He looked a bit remorseful. "I know. I'm sorry."

Noah ringing her doorbell at this hour was dangerous. He was like that apple in the Garden of Eden must have been. Impossibly beautiful, monumentally tempting, and most likely, incredibly delicious and satisfying. But just like that apple, taking a bite out of Noah probably came at one hell of a cost. The price of falling in love with him was, no doubt, like selling a small piece of your soul. She should know better, but Noah was extremely appealing, and she wanted him like someone dying of thirst just wants a cold drink of water. Leah smiled. He smiled back. He was waiting her out, letting her make up her mind, letting her choose. Noah was giving her the free will option like he was a goddamned vampire. She took it, holding the door open and stepping aside.

"Come in."

"Don't look so worried. I ain't gonna bite you."

Leah laughed. Not so much because what he said was funny, but at the irony of what had come out of his mouth and her own musings.

"If I thought you would, I wouldn't have let you in."

They stared at each other for a moment. Noah held her gaze so long she looked away. Leah felt her body heat rise like mercury in a thermometer.

"What are you doing here?" She asked.

He smiled. "I wanted to see you."

"Why?"

"I don't really know. I just did."

"I don't believe you. What happened? Your woman throw you out?"

His eyebrow went up, but he stayed quiet. Leah was about to speak again, but Noah surprised her by opening his mouth and telling her the truth.

"I don't think she's my woman anymore. I think maybe, now she's just my baby's mama."

She knew he had a woman. "You guys got kids together?"

"Not yet." Leah leaned away from him.

"Well, hell, are you planning to?"

He laughed, but he didn't seem too tickled. "She's incubatin'."

"What's up with you, Noah? If you got all that going on, why are you here? That's fucked up."

Noah stared at her. "Come on, Leah."

She stood up. She was so pissed, she wanted to hit him. "Come on, what? I don't appreciate-"

He stood up, too. "Don't appreciate what? I didn't make a move on you, Leah."

"You wanted to. What were you going to do? Get what you wanted and then leave me hanging, all twisted up in your bullshit?"

He looked at her pointedly. "Yeah, maybe you're right. Maybe I was, but I didn't. You and I both know, that if I wanted to bad enough, I would have had your legs in the air and my hands under your ass a long time ago."

Leah's mouth dropped open. He was unbelievably arrogant. He rolled up on her, but didn't touch her. She took a step back and he took one forward. She felt dizzy, like he was fucking up her equilibrium. Leah pushed him back as Noah looked down at her smugly.

"See? It could happen right now, but that's not why I came here."

"What did you come here for? You need to talk?"

He shrugged his nicely built shoulders. "Not really."

She smiled. "What's the matter, Noah? You need somebody to hold you?"

He looked at her noncommittally. "I don't know. Maybe."

She moved ahead of him and gently took his hand.

"Come on, then."

He raised his eyebrows in surprise, but he followed her into the bedroom. Noah watched her, pensively, as she slipped out of her robe and got into bed. Leah had never seen him hesitate before, usually, he was like a tiger. It charmed her.

"Get in. It's okay," she said, quietly.

Noah looked at her a moment longer, then sat on the bed and removed his shoes and pulled his sweater over his head. Leah thought it was funny that he would keep his pants on, but he did. Noah lay down and pulled her into his arms so that they were spooning. Her back was against his hard chest and her ass was planted securely against his manhood. He put his hand on her hip and pushed her short nightgown up until his hand was resting on her bare skin. Leah sighed and pushed against him. He was as hard as a rock. Noah's hand went under her nightgown and up to her breast. He put his hand on it, gently, and hugged her. Noah kissed her cheek and held on to her.

" Night, Leah."

Leah closed her eyes. He had no idea in the world how she felt about him. She wanted him to make love to her so bad, she felt swollen and ready to burst, but that was just the physical part. Her heart was so happy he was here, in her bed, she really didn't give a damn what brought him here. She wanted him any way she could get him, flaws and all. She knew she was probably making a huge and hurtful mistake, but she didn't care. She wanted her chance to love him, too.

Karma II

When she woke up, the sun was shining and Noah was teasing her left nipple with his thumb. She moaned with pleasure.

"Good. You're up."

He moved against her and she smiled. "I see you

are, too."

He laughed. "Yes, ma'am. Been up for hours."

She laughed, too.

"It ain't easy, sleepin' with you, Leah." He pushed her gown up

to her waist.

"It's not easy sleeping with you either."

Noah kissed her neck and she could tell he was smiling.

"Well... we're both awake, now."

Leah giggled and nodded. "Yeah, we are."

His hand drifted down to the top of her thigh. "Hey, Leah?"

"Yes?"

Noah spoke directly into her ear. "Why don't you open your legs for me, honey?"

It wasn't really a request. Her legs parted like he'd said the magic word. Noah dipped his first two fingers into the sweetest part of her, and his fingers came back wet and slippery. He laughed wickedly.

"That's real nice, baby. I like that."

Leah did, too. His touch was light, but he hit his target with each stroke. He had her trembling in short order. The whole while he was stroking her, he was grinding against her. Noah stood and got rid of the rest of his clothes. She smiled. Definitely no going back, now.

He whispered in her ear. "Turn over."

She rolled onto her back and Noah started kissing her. He had the most delectable lips. He raised up, suddenly, and got to his knees. Noah pushed her legs back and parted them smoothly. The sane part of her blew her head out of the clouds and knocked her back to reality. She put her hand on his chest and let her fingers trail over the light silky hair there.

"Wait a minute, Noah."

He smiled at her. "Relax. I got this."

He put a condom on without her having to ask.

157

Karma II

"Thanks."

"Don't mention it." He replied with his sexy smirk. Noah positioned his pillow beneath her hips and smiled his wicked smile again.

"This won't hurt a bit. I promise." Noah watched himself slide into her tantalizingly slow.

"*Aaahhh.*" He breathed softly, through slightly parted lips. Leah felt every inch of him go in. He felt so good, Leah had to close her eyes so he wouldn't see them roll up in the back of her head. He pulled out just as slowly. Her hips rose off the pillow as he went back in and started thrusting slow and deep. Noah brought his head back and fixed his lovely gray eyes on her, sliding in deep, then retreating, almost to the point of pulling out, creating a shockingly intense, almost lewd sensation. Leah grabbed his biceps and shouted his name.

He grinned at her, as her body started to spasm. "Oh, yeah, baby. That's nice. Look at you, comin' just for me."

Leah grinned back at him. She'd waited a long time for this. She intended to enjoy every minute of it. She flipped the script on him.

"Your turn." She said and sat up, pushing him down onto his back. Noah looked pleasantly surprised. He laughed and looked at her gamely.

"Okay, lady. Take your best shot."

Leah swung one leg over his hips and twined her fingers around his, holding his hands over his head. "Don't worry. I intend to. Noah, you have no idea how long I have wanted your beautiful ass."

He smiled at her cockily. "Yeah, I do."

"No, you don't." She tucked him back inside and it was on. They went at each other with an unbridled lust. Noah proved he could back up all the shit he talked. He was wild and unrestricted, playful and bawdy, while still managing to be skillfully meticulous in pleasing her. Leah would have lied to herself and said Noah had made love to her for hours, but she hadn't come down with yesterday's rain. It was what it was.

At the moment, the delectable Mr. Ramsey had her on her stomach, spread-eagled on the bed. He was on top of her with his face close to hers, dipping into her. Not too fast, not too slow. Driving her insane and talking dirty in her ear. Leah was loving it! She pushed back against him and closed her legs. Noah's breath got short real quick. He rose to his knees and held on to her hips, breathing harshly through his teeth.

"Ah, Leah… goddammit!" He went all the way in and found his way to satisfaction, grinding into her and making her come again. It was bliss. Leah didn't expect to be cuddled in the afterglow, and she wasn't, not exactly. Noah lay next to her, on his back and put his hand on her thigh.

"Noah?"

"Yeah?"

"Everything okay?"

He looked at her and smiled, charmingly. "Everything is most definitely not okay."

"Are you sorry?"

He laughed softly. "Nah. Then again, I'm not sorry for a lot of the shit I do. Why? Are you?"

Leah laughed, too, and sat up. "Hell, no! I told you, I waited a long time for that."

Noah got up and ran his hand through his hair. Leah sighed. He was so fine, it should have been illegal. He smiled again.

"Glad you liked it. Let's get dressed and I'll buy you breakfast."

Karma II

👑 👑 👑 👑 👑 👑 👑 👑 👑 👑 👑 👑 👑 👑 👑 👑

Noah drove them to a diner in Windsor Terrace. She took a bite of her pancakes and asked the question.

"So, what's going on with you, Noah?"

His eyebrows went up with practiced innocence. "Me?

Nothin'."

Leah sucked her teeth. "You're not telling me the truth. You're a goddamned liar."

Noah blinked at her and his eyes changed. She'd just pissed him off.

"Well?" She asked, pushing her plate away.

Noah wiped his mouth with a napkin and sat back, too, with his arms across the back of the booth. "Well what?"

"I need to know what's going on with you, Noah."

He shrugged and shook his head at the same time. "Why?"

She looked at him in disbelief. "Why? Did you just ask me why?"

"Yeah, I did. Don't go gettin' all funny on me, Leah."

"Getting funny on you?"

He looked around with great exaggeration, then back at her. "Is there an echo in here, or is it just me?"

Leah frowned. "Listen, it's pretty clear you've got a lot going on. Why don't you fill me in, so when some chick comes after me to kick my ass, I'll at least know why."

He stared at her, a bit resentfully, and kept silent.

"I'm waiting." Leah watched his face change from mild annoyance to thoughtful, then back to irritation.

"You know what? You wanna know what's goin' on? I'm gonna tell you. I got this woman I been seein' for a couple of years pregnant, and she's puttin' the screws to me to do right by her. I ain't doin' it. I ain't lettin' no woman pigeonhole me, understand?"

Leah looked back at him patiently. She wasn't into pigeonholing people and she'd basically heard this part before.

"I also have an ex-wife, who's doing her damndest to get me back ever since she found out."

Now, that was new, and she didn't care for it at all. "Really?"

He didn't answer her and he didn't smile.

"You didn't sleep with her, did you?"

"Course I did."

Instead of withdrawing, Leah leaned forward and put her hand on his forearm. "Noah, what the hell are you doing? Why did you come to me?"

His eyes dropped and he rubbed the back of her hand. "I can't really say."

Leah narrowed her eyes. "Are you trying to hurt me, Noah?"

He raised his eyes to meet hers. "I'm not tryin' to, but I probably will."

"What's that? Sorry in advance?"

Noah winced. "Ouch."

"Ouch, yes." Noah let go of her hand and sat back. She continued. "So, which one do you love? Your ex?"

Noah raised an eyebrow. "I'm takin' the fifth on that one, if you don't mind."

"I do, but I'm not going to try to force you to answer me. Besides, it doesn't matter much, anyway."

He frowned. "Huh?"

Karma II

"I said, it doesn't matter anyway. Somewhere deep inside, your mind is already made up. Just like my mind was made up the minute you rolled up on me in the parking lot."

He laughed. "I didn't roll up on you."

"Yes, you did. Don't worry. I loved it."

Noah smirked. "You did, huh? You're kinda different, Leah."

"How so?"

"I just told you a bunch of stuff that should have sent you screamin' in the other direction. You're still here."

"Guess I'm not the average woman." Noah looked doubtful.

"That remains to be seen," He looked at his watch. "I gotta go."

Leah tried real hard not to let the disappointment she felt touch her face as Noah put the money down for the check.

"You need a ride?" He asked, standing up. Leah followed him outside.

"No. I think I'll do some shopping."

Noah looked down at her. "Okay. Then I'll see you tomorrow."

She smiled. "Tomorrow it is." She turned and started to walk away.

"Hey, Leah?" Noah called after her. She turned and he was walking toward her, smiling. "Don't I at least get a handshake?"

Leah smiled back and offered him her hand. Noah took it and gave her a soft, non-intrusive kiss on the lips.

"See you later."

He walked away from her without looking back. Leah watched him get into his truck and drive away. Against her better judgment, she'd tossed her hat into the ring. Who knew? Maybe Noah would forsake his pregnant girlfriend and ignore the pleas of his ex-wife for her. Stranger things had happened.

Chapter Fourteen

Bitch behavior

"Did you know Noah's girlfriend is pregnant?" Nick asked Lucas.

Nick was eating strawberry yogurt out of a cup and he was drinking black coffee at the counter, thumbing through the newspaper. Lucas looked up from what he was doing.

"I'm not in that, Nicole."

Nick cocked her head to the side and gave him a smarmy look. "I know you knew, Lucas."

"I didn't say I didn't know. What I said was I'm not in that. How do you know, anyway? I know you didn't get that out of him."

"I didn't, but Leah did."

She ate the last of her yogurt and licked her spoon. He wished she hadn't done that. He wanted to take her back to bed, but they had to be at work in an hour. Damn.

"Noah told her."

Lucas frowned. What the hell was wrong with his boy? Giving up personal info wasn't the way Noah rolled. He had no doubt Noah had finally taken Leah to bed, telling her shit like that, but, why?

"What are you all frowned-up for?"

"Nothing. Just thinking." He looked at his watch. "Let's get out of here."

"What do you suppose Noah is thinking, screwing my friend and going home to his pregnant girlfriend? What's up with your boy?"

"I don't know. I can't speak for Noah."

Nick looked at him shrewdly and stepped out the door behind him. "You can't or you won't, honeybunch?"

"Both."

"You're such a man, Lucas."

He laughed. "I hope so."

He was about to say something slick when he stopped dead in his tracks. What the fuck? His eyes had to be playing tricks on him. He blinked twice. Nope. It was real.

"I don't believe this shit." He said quietly.

"Lucas, what-"

Lucas felt a pulse start to beat at his temples. "I don't fucking believe this shit!" He yelled and threw his keys at his ruined S500.

"Fuck!" He yelled, checking out the grooves dug so deep in the paint, he could see the gray body of the car. Who did this shit to his car? Who? He kicked the tire in disgust.

"Fuck." He said, and walked away. Nick tried to touch his arm, but he steered himself away from her. Lucas hadn't been so suddenly furious in a long time and it shocked his system. He was halfway up the block, breathing hard and telling himself it was only a car, when Nick did touch his arm.

"Calm down, Lucas."

He flipped on her without meaning to. "How you gonna tell me to calm down, Nicole? Don't you see my fuckin' car? Fuck calming down! Get away from me!"

Nick folded her arms across her chest and put her weight on one leg.

"I see your car, Lucas. I'm not going anywhere. You need me right now. Don't be rude. What's done is done. Call your mechanic. I'll trail you there and we'll take my car to work. Is that okay with you, or do you plan to bitch and moan about that, too?"

Lucas took his phone off his belt and stared at her until she walked away. She was trying to suppress a smile. He really failed to find the humor in this. His brand new car was fucked up. Stuff like that was usually a woman's work. Lucas ran a mental list of people that would be hating on him that hard.

Lucas had basically dropped off the player radar when he met Justine. He hadn't really been back out there since, minus a few random booty calls, until he got involved with Nick. Any woman that would trash his car like that would be harboring a very old grudge.

Karma II

Lucas parked his car and gave it over to his guy. Nick was wearing a small smile when he got into her car.

"What's funny?" He asked, frowning.

"You are. Believe me, I'm not laughing about your car. But you? You're funny."

Lucas wasn't in the mood to break out his secret decoder ring to have a conversation with her. "What are you talking about?"

"I'm talking about your reaction to all this."

"Uh-huh. What about it?"

"All that yelling and cursing. I haven't known you long, but I do know you well enough to say it really wasn't the car you were screaming about."

"Yeah? Then tell me what it was, Dr. Phil."

"I don't like sarcasm on you, it suits Noah better. Like I said, it's not about the car with you. It was no big deal for you to take it to your mechanic."

Nick paused dramatically and put her hand on his thigh. "You feel violated, Lucas."

He started laughing. "Yeah, okay. Violated."

"I'm serious. You feel violated. Like, how dare someone have the audacity to do some sneaky, cowardly shit like that to Lucas Cain?"

He laughed again. "I don't think of myself like that."

"That's bullshit. Your ego steps through the door long before you do."

"Long before, huh?"

Nick nodded enthusiastically. "Long before, but it's okay. It's very attractive. You keep it subtle. Anyway, somebody vandalizing your ride right in front of your home, where you lay your head, and where you have all you personal things made you feel vulnerable. You know I'm right."

"You like being right, don't you?"

Nick nodded and laughed. "Seriously, who do you think did it? Any idea?"

Lucas had thought about it. There was only one person he could think of that had promised him some sort of retribution. "Nah, not at all."

"Who do you think it is?"

"I'm not sure."

"Who?"

"Leave it alone, Nicole."

"You think, maybe, it was some chick you used to deal with?"

"I don't think it was a woman."

"No? Women usually do that sort of thing, you know."

"I'm aware of that, Nicole, but if it was a woman, I'd have to reach way back to find her, besides, that type of thing is emotional. It's done on impulse. I don't think any woman that upset with me could have stopped herself from acting on it for years. It was a man, and I'm almost one hundred percent sure of who it was."

They got out of the car and Nick looked at him. "You think it was Keith, don't you?"

"I'm leaning in that direction."

She blinked. "Are you mad at me?"

Lucas was furious, but not at her. It wasn't her fault her ex was some kind of maniac that was looking to get his jaw broken.

"No, but Keith's gonna get his ass kicked."

"What are we kickin' his ass for?" Noah asked, coming up behind them.

"His punk ass keyed my car."

Noah paused to light a Dunhill, and squinted at him through the smoke. "Yeah? Definite bitch behavior. Certainly needs his ass kicked. Mornin', Nick."

Nick looked at him funny. "Good morning, Noah. How was your weekend?"

Noah blew smoke out the side of his mouth and looked at her hard. "Full of fun. How was yours?"

Karma II

Lucas was getting tired of playing referee with these two. He turned to Nick. "See you upstairs."

Nick returned Noah's hard stare. You didn't have to be a genius to tell she didn't approve of Noah's escapades. You also didn't have to be a genius to tell Noah was in no mood to be judged. His eyes glinted and he smirked at her dangerously.

"What? You got somethin' to say to me?"

Nick stepped in his face. "You're being an asshole."

"I am? How so?"

Noah's eyes were like storm clouds. Lucas moved between them.

"See you upstairs, Nicole." He repeated.

Nick gave Noah another funky look and left.

"What's her problem?" Noah asked.

"She's worried about her friend, No, and I'm a little worried about mine. You okay?"

"Right as rain. What about you?" He answered with a

fair amount of sarcasm.

Lucas looked at him. "Come on, Noah. This is me. I ain't letting you off that easy. What are you doin'?"

Noah looked away. "It's not that bad."

"What did you sleep with Leah for?"

Noah smiled. "I told you I would."

"Maybe you shouldn't have done that. I hear she's got some serious feelings for you, bro."

Noah smirked. "The usual story, Luke? She think she's in love with me? She don't even know me like that."

Lucas shrugged. "Maybe she does."

"While we're on the subject, how does your woman feel about you? Y'all in love yet, or still screwin'?"

Lucas laughed. "Nicole's a nice lady."

Noah laughed, too, and looked at him slyly. "That ain't what I asked you, and at the risk of soundin' like a bitch, why you bein' so close mouthed and quiet about this shit? You ain't talkin' to me."

Lucas laughed. "I'm sorry, baby."

"Fuck you, Luke."

"Fuck you back. Seriously, No, I'm not rushing. I don't know if I love her yet. It's not like it was with Justine. It's a lot, quieter."

"Good. You need quieter. Hell, I could use a little quiet myself.

The shit I'm dealin' with is loud as hell."

Lucas looked at him with empathy. "You just gotta take a step back, Noah. You gotta decide what the most important thing is. Even if it's you."

"Pop just told me that. So, tell me, when will we be takin' your car out on Keith's ass?"

"Soon as he shows his face."

Noah grinned. "Can't wait."

They took the elevator to the office and weren't surprised to find Myers and Griff waiting for them. Griff looked at his watch.

"Mornin', fellas. Running a little late, huh?"

"Just a little," Noah said, sitting at his desk, "I'll bring you an apple, next time."

"Funny, Noah," Griff stood up and started right in. "I hope you guys enjoyed your time off. We're ready to move. Before you ask, Tony, Nate, and Vic are setting up and making sure your back-up is up to date and in proper order. You probably won't be seeing much of them from this point on."

Myers stood up. "Meet us downstairs in 20 minutes. We're going to the Hamptons."

He turned and looked pointedly at Noah. "Don't worry, Ramsey. I'm not gonna say it. By now, you already know."

He looked around the room. "I have personal affection for all of you. When the shit hits the fan, get out with no hesitation. Be careful. Today we have a rendezvous with Tamiko Brewster."

He gave them a grim smile and left the room with a stone-faced Griff. Nick stood up and wiped her hands on her jeans.

Karma II

"Lucas, I need to say a few things to you in private, if you don't mind."

Noah got up and grabbed his jacket. "Let's go, sweet cheeks."

Nick crossed the room and sat in Lucas' lap. Nick bent her head and kissed him with her soft sweet lips, then she put her arms around his neck and hugged him hard. Lucas hugged her back.

"I wish I'd met you a long time ago." She said softly.

Lucas didn't answer her, instead he took her hand and kissed her palm. "What's wrong?"

"Nothing. I love you very much, Lucas."

Lucas looked back at her. He knew she did, was sure of it, but it still felt odd to have someone else say those words to him after all this time. He was hit with an almost overwhelming feeling of nostalgia, and a dour sadness for things that would never be.

"I know that was really heavy, but I just needed to let you know how I feel. I'm sorry if you weren't ready."

Lucas was quick to try and rectify what she seemed to be taking as rejection. It wasn't. It was just that, in that moment, he'd missed Justine so clearly, he could almost smell her perfume.

"No, baby, don't feel like that."

He'd told Noah less than an hour ago, he wasn't sure he loved her. He wasn't surprised to find that he did. He loved everything about her, from her irrepressibly raging beauty, to her strange little idiosyncrasies. He did. To hell with it. Whatever would be, would be.

"I don't know how ready I am, Nicole, but I'm feeling like I love you, too. I can't help myself."

"You're not just saying that, are you?"

Lucas smiled. "No. I love you, Nicole. I do."

She smiled. He smiled, too. Lucas felt like he had a weight lifted off him, at the same time, he also felt the unmistakable tug of sadness that came with change. He'd just admitted Justine was truly gone. She had just been relegated to being a beautiful memory. He'd just moved on. The idea made him incredibly sad, but he kept it light for Nicole.

"Why are you crying?" He asked.

Nick laughed. "You just made me very happy."

"Good." They spent the next few minutes lost in each other, kissing. They were reluctant to stop, but the clock was ticking. He kissed her again.

"I'll be careful. You do likewise."

Nick smiled. "I will. We can't afford to lose each other now."

"Never that. Let's go."

He held her hand in the elevator and whispered sweet nothings in her ear. Once the doors were open, they regained their professional faces. Lucas looked down at her as they crossed the parking lot.

"You look like you've been crying." He said.

Nick glanced at him and smiled. "Tears of joy, honeybunch, but they don't have to know that."

"They may think you're scared."

She laughed. "I'm not."

He looked at her again. "You don't have to be, sweetheart. I got your back."

Karma II

Chapter Fifteen

Planning makes perfect

"What's got you so lit up?" Leah asked.

They were following Lucas, Noah, Griff and Myers to the Hamptons. Nick was driving.

"I'm going to marry, Lucas."

Leah's mouth fell open. "Are you serious? When did he ask you?"

"He didn't. I'm gonna ask him."

Leah stared back at her in open-mouthed silence. Nick laughed. "Stop looking at me like that."

Leah blurted out a stream of questions. "Are you sure? How do you know he's feeling you like that? When did you decide this shit? Why are you asking him, why don't you let him ask you, Nick? Shit, what about Keith's no good ass?"

Nick glanced at her, mildly annoyed. "Damn, Leah," she said, with her mouth turned down. "For your information, I am sure. I'm going to ask him because I think he's still a little too shell-shocked to ask me, and I think maybe, he'll say yes. If I wait for him to ask me, it may take forever. Oh, by the way, fuck Keith's no good ass. Hard, with no grease."

"Okay, fine, but I really think you're rushing things."

"I don't think I am."

"Yeah, you are. I know you're all caught up and trippin' over how wonderful you think Lucas is, but maybe you should take a little time out to remember that he's still getting over some pretty deep shit. So are you. Don't rush, girl. Let him come around to you."

She didn't look at Leah, because Leah was right, and Nick didn't want her to be. Even though Leah's words reeked of truth, Nick resented her for taking the bloom off her rose with such a humongous dose of reality. Nick hadn't been happy in a long time, and now that it seemed she'd finally found what she was looking for, and she wanted it. Now.

"Nick?"

She sucked her teeth.

"Never mind. Sorry I said anything."

Leah offered her a stick of gum. Nick took it, grudgingly.

"Don't be sorry. I'm glad you said something. You're my girl, Nick, and I want you to be happy, but I don't think you'll get what you want by pushing. I just don't want to see you make a huge mistake."

Nick let out a churlish little chuff of laughter. "Yeah, like you just did, right?"

Nick wasn't real pleased with herself for coming back at Leah like that, but she felt like her friend needed to take a look at her own situation before she started dishing out advice. Leah, as expected, bristled instantly.

"Oh, no, you didn't just say that crap to me."

"Yes, I did. Maybe I think you made a huge mistake, sleeping with Noah and all his nine million problems."

Karma II

"You know what, Nick? You and I are two different people. We don't want the same things."

"Really? Well, tell me what you want, Leah, and how you're gonna manage to get it out of Noah?"

"Stop trying to turn this back to me. I'm trying to talk you out of committing relationship suicide. Besides, I don't want anything more from Noah than what he's already doing. I just want him to be what he is, one helluva maintenance man."

Nick smiled. "Okay, I'll just bet he is, but you're lying. I know you want more."

Leah wasn't the only one who thought her friend was making bad choices. Nick thought the one Leah made about Noah was a monumental error.

"I can't ask him for anything more. I don't know whether he's got it to give. My eyes were wide open, Nick."

"You're gonna get hurt, Leah, and you don't have to be a psychic to see it."

"Maybe. Maybe not."

"Noah breaking your heart is practically a done deal."

Leah sighed. "You just don't like Noah."

"I do like Noah. He's cool, but you're my friend, Leah. Noah's got too much conflict in his life."

"Nick, it's my decision."

"Okay. Be careful with him, Leah."

"Yeah, Nick. You do the same, Miss Cart Before The Horse," Leah replied, sarcastically. Nick changed the subject and told Leah about Lucas' car.

"That sounds just like some sneaky shit he'd do. I hope Lucas beats his monkey ass."

"I'm sure he will."

Karma II

Lucas threw on his turn signal as he got off the exit

ramp. They turned onto a private road and entered a cul-de-sac. An enormous home loomed before them, maybe not as grand as some they'd passed, but it damn sure wasn't a shack, with its fountain and reflecting pool in the front courtyard, and the circular driveway. The mansion itself was a stately, tasteful Tudor, surrounded by tall oaks and a smattering of bayberries. The grounds were a riot of color, covered with simple, pretty flowers.

They followed Griff onto what could only be a discreet service road meant for the staff, to the rear of the property. Griff pulled to the rear and killed his engine.

Leah smiled. "What's this? Slave quarters?" She asked, snidely.

Nick laughed. "You've been hanging around Noah too much. Gotta be the guest house." A white Bentley was parked discretely close by.

"Here we go," Nick mumbled.

Karma II

They got out and joined everyone else as they approached the back of the house. That little white dog scurried out of the open French doors and started yipping. Tamiko Brewster stepped out behind it and scooped it up.

"Miss Brewster," Griff said with a nod.

Tamiko nodded back. "Let's get this over with."

She turned her back without acknowledging anyone else and went back inside. Nick disliked her instantly.

They went into the house. Tamiko was perched on the edge of a sofa that was wearing a dust cover like most of the furniture in the room. She petted her dog, absently. Griff and Myers joined her on the sofa. Nick and Leah shared an oversized ottoman, and Lucas and Noah sat last, taking the sofa across from her. She took her sunglasses off and looked at them appreciatively. A slow smile spread across her face. Her eyes were large, luminous, and exotically slanted, her teeth, small and pearly white. She pointed at Lucas and Noah with her sunglasses.

"Who are they?" She asked.

"Detective Cain and Detective Ramsey." Myers answered, then gestured toward Nick and Leah. "Detective Hardaway and Detective Wheeler."

Tamiko turned her attention to the ladies and looked them over like she was choosing servants. "Let's get it over with. I want to be done with this." She looked at Myers. "You're still going to give me clemency for handing you Tate and Troy?"

"The offer's still on the table."

"You hand us Draco, it's guaranteed." Griff interjected.

"Tate and Troy just stopped doing business with one of their chief coke broker's down in Venezuela. Troy just got back. He went down there and personally gave him a Columbian necktie for a substandard shipment. They're shopping around for another connection."

"Anyone in particular?" Griff asked.

"Not really. A lot of people are afraid of them, most others think they're too volatile to stay in business much longer," She paused and smiled at the irony of her next comment. "They think you guys are coming for them."

"We're not the only one's coming. Word on the street is Draco's made more than a few enemies." Lucas said, staring a hole through Ms. Brewster.

"What do you mean?" The dog trotted over to Noah and sprang into his lap. Nick suppressed a smile when cool-ass Lucas tightened up just the tiniest bit. Noah smiled and placed the dog back on the floor.

He turned his gray eyes on Tamiko. "He means, maybe it's a good idea for you to take matters into your own hands instead of lettin' some other guttersnipe lay in the cut for y'all and take you out. See what I'm sayin'?"

Her mouth popped open in shock. "You calling me a guttersnipe?"

Noah shrugged. "I don't know you, lady, but your baby's daddy is a definite piece of shit. Uncle Troy, too."

She looked as if she started to get angry, but then

177

Karma II

figured that was not the way to go with Noah. "Maybe you should just let them get taken out then."

Noah shook his head. "No can do."

"It's not like you people really care how they go down, as long as they do."

Nick leaned forward. "You said Troy just iced your supplier in Venezuela and you need to replace him?"

Tamiko looked at Nick like she was surprised she was speaking.

"Yes, that's what I said. Only I didn't suggest I was any part of that. I said they. They."

She repeated with emphasis. Nick didn't like her funky attitude and the way her upper lip had crept up at the corner.

"You're already implicated, sweetheart. You're cutting a deal. Don't forget it." Leah tossed the words at her snotty ass and took her down a notch.

"How much are you privy to the deal making? Does he let you in on the way things go down? How the money changes hands?" Nick asked.

She turned her nose up at Nick and uncrossed her legs. "I know everything. I keep his books."

Nope. Nick wasn't feeling this chick at all.

"Have you ever been part of the selection process?"

Tamiko looked over at Griff and Myers. Myers gave her an encouraging, sympathetic smile, that didn't quite meet his eyes.

"It's a little late for cold feet, Ms. Brewster. Go on, now. Tell us what we need to know." His voice was low and soothing, but his tone was dead serious and intentionally ominous. Talk, or your ass is going to jail.

"It's a little late for a lot of things, Captain, That's why I don't give a shit anymore." She raised her eyes to Nick's. "Yeah, I've got a part in the selection process. The broker they killed in Venezuela was my brother. I brought him in, and fucking Troy killed him. Tate authorized it. If you want to send me to jail, send me, but fuck them over first.

You don't know half of all the atrocious things those two have done. You should shoot their asses on sight."

Lucas stood and folded his arms across his chest. "I think you should let me and Noah go in and broker a shipment."

Myers rubbed his chin as Lucas looked at Noah to see what he thought about it. Noah nodded and put his arms across the back of the sofa.

"It's been done before, but it sounds like a plan. I think it would work."

Lucas passed his hand over his beard. "Cover story?" He asked, studying Noah.

"I don't know, Luke. The old standby always works. I think it'll work with these guys," He paused and smiled slow. "Hard cases have chinks in their armor, too."

Lucas nodded. "Yeah, big ones. Nobody's on their A game all the time."

Noah laughed. "Except us."

"Uh-huh."

Noah nodded. "Yeah, okay. We'll have Tamiko work us in, say I'm her drug dealin' cousin or some other bullshit like that."

He turned and winked at her, and Tamiko actually blushed. Leah sucked her teeth, a small sound in the big room, but it carried. Lucas' raised an eyebrow.

"Something wrong?" He asked.

Leah recovered nicely. "Just wondering where we fit in all this."

Noah's mouth turned up at the corner. "I'll let you be my girlfriend."

Nick looked at Lucas. "You need a girlfriend, too?"

Lucas looked like he was thinking about it when Tamiko spoke up.

"We have a stripper pole in the club," She said, cheerily.

Lucas frowned at her. "I don't think that's necessary." He looked at her hard and Tamiko drew back into her seat and pulled her dog with her.

"Tate needs a personal assistant," She said quietly.

"That's more like it." Lucas retorted, "I think you'd fit there, Nicole. It's a good spot." Noah nodded.

"Yeah, you could hear a lot bein' that close to him." Tamiko turned to Leah.

"Do you drive?" Leah looked at her sideways.

"Of course I do."

"Good, because Troy could use a driver. He runs his mouth like a faucet." She stopped and looked at Lucas and Noah. "You two are perfect. I'll set it up."

She stood and walked over to them, giving Noah a long once over. "Where are you from?"

Noah gave her an abbreviated version of her own inventory. "Harlem."

"That's not what I meant, but you're being obtuse on purpose. It's cool. I see you're a mutt like me. You look like you could actually be my cousin. I think Tate will go for it."

She turned to Lucas. "You're the serious one. You two must play very well off each other."

Griff finally spoke up. "So, Ms. Brewster, you think this is the absolute best course of action?"

"I do."

He looked at her doubtfully. "Like Detective Ramsey said, it has been done before. What makes you think it will work now?"

"Because the plan is simple. It will work, Agent Griffin. I think you've got the right people. Not some crusty old white dude with cop written all over him. No offense, Captain Myers."

Myers shrugged and seemed unfazed. "None taken. I know we've got the right people, and another advantage: We've got you."

"Precisely. When do you want to go in?"

"We'll introduce Hardaway first. Tell Tate you've found an assistant for him and she starts on Monday. Let Troy know he's got a new driver. Wheeler starts Monday, too. Cain and Ramsey will meet you for drinks on Tuesday."

"Alright, then. I guess this meeting is over." Tamiko watched them get into their respective cars. She paused at Griff's door.

"If Tate finds out, he's going to kill me slow."

Griff tried to give her reassurance. "Don't worry. You're in excellent hands."

"Famous last words." She got into that white Bentley and peeled out of there.

Nick turned to Leah. "I'm not feeling her tiny ass." Leah smiled and slid down in her seat.

"I'm sure she's still thinking about greasing up that stripper pole for you. The feeling's obviously mutual."

Karma II

Chapter Sixteen

Karma II

Noah to the rescue

Keith watched Nicky walk into Starbuck's early Friday morning. He had to get to work himself in an hour, but he didn't have far to go. He was Midtown North, they were Midtown South. He watched Nicky through the window and wondered when the fuck she'd started wearing her goddamned hair down to work. She probably wanted to look her best for that asshole, Cain. Keith snatched the door open and walked inside.

Nicky was standing at the counter with her iPod on, waiting for her order. Shit! She was wearing a fucking skirt! This wasn't the Nicky he knew, standing there, being so feminine during working hours. Fucking Lucas Cain had stepped in and stolen his woman. He rolled up on her and flicked one of her ear buds out. Nicky turned around to kick his ass.

"Good Morning, Nicky."

"What are you doing here, Keith? Leave me alone."

"What's wrong? You don't want that pussy, Lucas, to catch me talking to you?"

"You're the only pussy I see."

"What? What did you say to me?"

"You heard me. If he catches you here, he's gonna kick your ass."

Keith grabbed her arm "What? You got him fighting for you?"

She shrugged away from him. "I don't need Lucas to fight for me, but he would. He's already gonna beat your ass about his car."

Keith couldn't help but smile. "His car? What about it?"

Nicky looked at him blackly. "He knows it was you. Just leave us alone."

"Why? Do you love him?"

"I can let you know that I no longer love you."

"I can't believe you left me for that bastard."

Karma II

The barista handed her a cardboard tray with four coffees.

"I'm not discussing this with you. Stop stalking me."

She turned and walked out the door. Keith followed her. No, this bitch wasn't walking off to give that nigger his morning coffee. Keith flipped the tray out of her hand and coffee went everywhere. He grabbed her shoulders as he heard tires screech.

"It is my business! It's my business 'cause you belong to me! Do you fucking understand?"

Someone grabbed the back of his collar and pulled him away from her.

"That's enough, mad dog. Get your hands off her before I lock your ass up."

Keith staggered backward and recovered his balance. Noah was looking at him evenly, with his hand near his gun. Keith wasn't fucking with Noah. Noah would shoot you with no hesitation.

"I need to talk to you, Nicky. I'm sorry."

Noah smirked at him. "Then carry your sorry ass on. Go ahead, now. Take a little pride with you."

Keith looked at Noah. "You got this one," he said.

Noah smiled. "I get 'em all."

Karma II

Chapter Seventeen

Fight and flight

Noah pulled his truck up in front of Lucas' place and killed the engine. Keith was acting crazy, and he didn't want Lucas to get caught out there with his guard down. Keith was out of control, running around, bitching up cars and intimidating Nick with total disregard to the fact that he was a vice detective. What an asshole. He got out and rang the doorbell. Nick answered, looking shaken.

"Hey, Noah."

"You look like I'm the last person you want to see." He paused, and looked at her shrewdly. "Or maybe that would be Keith."

Nick looked at him worriedly. "You're not going to tell Lucas, are you?"

"That's why I'm here. Where is he?"

"He's in the shower."

"Go get him."

"Come on, Noah. Please. He doesn't need to know."

Noah stared at her. "He does need to know. Go get him."

Nick's lower lip dropped into a pout, but Noah didn't give a shit. "Get him," he repeated, "Or I'm goin' up."

"You don't have to tell him. I can handle Keith."

"I'm done foolin' around." He took his phone out and hit Lucas on speed dial. He picked up on the second ring.

"What's good?" He asked.

"Come downstairs." Noah answered and hung up.

Nick looked at him malignantly and sat down at the foot of the stairs. Noah put his hands in his pockets and waited patiently for Lucas. He came down in less time than Noah thought it would take. He stopped short at Nick's position on the stairs and assessed the situation.

"What happened?"

Karma II

Noah nodded toward Nick. "I had to peel Keith off Nick in Starbucks this mornin'. Thought you should know."

Lucas turned his attention from Noah to Nick. "Why am I just hearing about this?"

Nick put her face in her hands and didn't answer him.

"Nicole."

"It wasn't that serious, Lucas."

Lucas eyed her doubtfully, and ran a hand over his beard. "If Noah thought it wasn't that serious, he wouldn't be here.

What's going on?"

"Nothing's going on."

Noah rubbed his chin. "Yeah, nothin's goin' on. He just slapped the coffee out of her hand and snatched her up. Oh, by the way, he was screamin' at her that she belongs to him."

Lucas folded his arms across his chest and looked at Noah. "Keep talkin', No."

"I saw all this shit goin' down, and I jumped outta my truck and grabbed his ass off her. He backed off real quick. I think he thought I was gonna blast him."

"He just left? That's it?"

Noah nodded. "Scurried away like a rat."

"You okay?" Lucas asked Nick.

She nodded. "I'm fine, Lucas."

Lucas went to the closet and got his jacket. He looked at Noah and cracked his knuckles. "Okay. Let's go fold his ass up."

Nick grabbed Lucas' arm.

"No! No, Lucas, don't go look for him. Keith's acting crazy. Please."

He looked at her calmly, but there was anger behind his eyes.

"What's he gonna do, Nicole? Punch me in the mouth? Don't be afraid for me, be afraid for his ass. Let's go, Noah."

Nick turned on Noah. "You see? See what you've done? You just had to open your big mouth."

Noah blinked. If she hadn't been Lucas' woman, he would have grabbed her by the collar. "You listen to me. I did what I had to do. My loyalty is to Lucas, you hear me?"

Karma II

She was shrinking away from him, but Noah was tired of her ass, and he kept going. "You're sittin' here, hopin' this nigga is gonna go away, and his ass is plottin' and schemin'. I got news for you, I ain't gonna wait for him to pop my boy in the head when he ain't lookin', so fuck what you think, Nick! Fuck-"

Lucas stepped between them and looked Noah in the eye. "You made your point, Noah."

Noah stared back at him. He'd seen Lucas spraying blood like he was dying. She didn't understand at all. Noah fell back.

Lucas turned to Nick. "I'll be back soon. Don't wait up."

He kissed her forehead and followed Noah out the door. Noah got into his truck and slammed the door. He was surprised when Lucas started laughing.

"What's funny?"

Lucas' laughter faded to a smile. "I didn't know you cared."

Noah smiled, too. "Yeah, you did."

"What's the plan?"

"Unlike your lady, I didn't sit around wringin' my hands all day. I got the nigga's address."

Lucas settled back in his seat. "Well, shit, let's go."

They didn't say much as they drove out to Gravesend. Lucas sat up when they
turned off McDonald Avenue.

"This was a long way to go to kick a nigga's ass."

Noah smiled. "It's never too far. I'd drive all night to crack a man's forehead."

Lucas laughed. "Yeah, I bet you would."

"Can't help it, Luke. I had to fight all the time when I was a kid."

"Damn, No. The Grounds was like that?"

"Hell, yeah. I always had dudes tryin' me. Bein' Big John's kid kept 'em off my ass a little, but I always had somebody steppin' to me."

"Why? Trying to rob you?"

Noah looked at him like he was stupid. "Luke, I ain't never had nobody ask me for my wallet. By the time I was 17, I had screwed my way through half the neighborhood. Dudes wasn't feelin' me."

"Your ass is crazy, Noah."

Noah turned down 86th Street. "Maybe, but I ain't into tall tales."

He parked the car and they got out. "Sorry. I couldn't park too close. Fucker knows my car."

He looked at Lucas, who'd grown silent. He was frowning. "You alright?"

"I was just thinking."

Noah lit a Dunhill. "I'm just listenin'."

Lucas looked unhappy "I just want to know why this shit

190

Karma II

keeps happening to me."

"Where you goin' with this, bro?"

"I don't know, Noah. I guess I fucked over so many women, whenever I find it, I'll never be able to fall in love right. It's like a big slice of the best tasting cake in the world, but instead of whipped cream, it's got a giant helping of bullshit splashed down right on top of it."

"You paint a vivid picture, Luke, but it's not the same as with Justine. It is different. It's always different."

Lucas looked at him with amused skepticism. "How would you know? You only loved three women in your entire life. Your mother, Raine, and God help you, Nadine."

Noah smiled and tossed his smoke. "Yeah, and it was different each time."

He stopped walking and looked at the number on the small apartment building in front of them. "This is it. Get your screw face on, and we'll finish this conversation later."

They went up the steps and took the elevator to the second floor.

"It's 2D." Noah said.

They didn't have to search for it. It faced the elevator. Lucas slipped out of his jacket and handed it to Noah. Keith's ass was in a lot of trouble. Lucas rang the bell. They were both a bit shocked when a white girl answered the door. She had long brown hair, big brown eyes, and a lot of curves. Very nice. She looked them over and smiled brightly.

"May I help you?"

Lucas looked down at her. "Yes, you may. I'm looking for Keith Childs."

"May I ask who you are?"

"By all means. Tell him it's Lucas Cain."

"I'll tell him you're here, Mr. Cain." She walked away, and Noah watched her go with great appreciation. She had an ass like a black girl.

Keith's voice came back at them like a roar. "What?!"

Noah snickered. Lucas put one foot behind him and his fists up. Noah loved a good fight. Keith appeared in the doorway and Lucas hit him in the nose with everything he had. Before Keith could react, Lucas hit him again, square in the nose. Noah shook his head in disappointment. He'd hoped the fight would last a little longer. He was pretty sure Keith's nose had snapped. Keith rushed at Lucas, and Lucas grabbed his arm and tucked his body in. He tossed Keith neatly over his back, into the elevator door. Lucas' toss was elegant and efficient, but Keith hit the door like a hot mess. He sprawled on the floor, an untidy eyesore. Noah howled with laughter.

Lucas stood over him. "Get your ass up," he said.

Keith had enough piss and vinegar in him to get to his feet. He started to make a fist, but his right pinkie was leaning at a crazy angle. Lucas rolled up on him and grabbed him in the collar like a bitch.

"Why won't you fight me? Would you rather fight a woman? This is for Nicole."

He punched him in the mouth and Keith started sliding down the wall. Lucas punched him until he was too low to hit, then he kicked him in the chest. Lucas took his jacket from Noah and slipped it back on with a swagger.

"Look at you. You ain't shit. You're not even worth the gas we wasted to come kick your ass."

Lucas reached over him and rang for the elevator. The door to the elevator opened and Lucas stepped over Keith's crumpled body. Noah followed. He couldn't resist stepping on that disjointed pinkie.

"Oops. Sorry," he said with smothered laughter as Keith screamed.

The door started to close and Keith looked up at Lucas from his undignified position.

"You fucking snuck me."

Lucas grabbed the door and pulled it back.

"I didn't need to. There ain't shit to you. Stay away from me, and you really better stay away from Nicole."

He let the door go and it slid closed. When Lucas stepped back, his watch fell off and hit the floor. He picked it up and stared at it. He looked very pissed off.

"He broke my watch."

"Well, you broke his face."

"My grandfather gave me this watch."

Noah concealed the smile that wouldn't leave by sticking a Dunhill in his mouth. "It's probably sprung. You can probably get it fixed. Let's see it."

Lucas handed it to him and they started walking back to Noah's Escalade. Noah examined the watch, turning it over to read the back. It was just one word. Virtue. Noah looked over at Lucas. Lucas was looking at his right hand, curling and uncurling his fist.

"Thumb jammed again?"

"Think so."

That happened almost every time he had to hit something really hard. Noah looked down at the watch again. He'd be pissed, too. It was a Patek Phillipe.

Karma II

"Don't you think you should take care of that, Luke?" He asked, absently. The minute hand had stopped. Lucas wiggled his thumb around with his other hand.

"I can fix it myself."

Noah shrugged and put the watch to his ear. Nothing.

"You should have somebody look at it."

Noah shook the watch and something inside tinkled merrily. Lucas snatched it out of his hand.

"Gimme my watch. What the fuck is wrong with you, man, shakin' it like a little kid?"

Noah threw his hands up in mock dismay. "Whoa, man. Sor-ry. Thought I could fix it."

Lucas put the watch in his pocket. "You a jeweler, now? Don't quit your day job."

They stared at each other for a second, then started laughing.

"Fuck you, Luke."

"Yeah? Fuck you back."

They got into Noah's Escalade and drove back to his townhouse. They talked about a lot of things. Draco, women, Noah's kids, back to women. Then, the inevitable. Justine. Always back to her. It was a little different this time. He sounded more like he was reminiscing than deep in grief. That was a good thing.

"What made you ditch your earring?" He knew it had taken a lot for him to take it out.

"I took it off right before I slept with Nicole. I put her picture away, too. I didn't want her in the room with us."

Though he could appreciate the sentiment of the gesture, Noah couldn't stop what fell out of his mouth. "Why? You thought she'd be in the corner with a camcorder?"

Lucas laughed in spite of himself. "You're an asshole, Noah. You comin' in?"

Karma II

"Nah. I told the pregnant fighter I'd be home after I wrapped this shit up with you."

"Alright. Thanks for lookin' out, bro." They dapped each other with a smile.

"You know how we do, Luke. Anytime."

He drove home dreading dealing with Liz and her stink attitude, but he was willing to cajole her to keep her calm. He parked his truck and entered the house through the kitchen. Liz was sitting at the table with her hands folded in front of her. He knew he was in trouble from her posture. He stuck a white flag out anyway.

"Uh, hey, babe."

Liz got up and walked into the living room without looking at him. Oh, shit. Here we go. Noah thought. He was more than a little surprised to see her bags packed and waiting by the front door.

"You leavin' me, Liz?"

"It didn't take long for you to figure that out." She said.

"Why?" He asked.

She looked at him, then, and he hated the look on her face. "Because you fucked Nadine, Noah. That's why I'm leaving you."

Noah shook his head.

"Don't stand there shaking your head like you didn't, Noah. I knew you did when she showed up here, but I chose not to believe it. I was shopping today and I ran into her. You better believe she didn't hesitate to give me the facts when I asked her."

Tears were sliding down her pretty cheeks. Noah didn't know what to say, so he kept quiet.

"How could you do that to me? All I ever tried to do was love you. This baby is all about me loving you. God! I feel like you spit on me, Noah! You're a heartless bastard!"

Liz walked up to him and pushed him in the chest. "What's the matter with you, Noah? Don't you have anything to say to me? Did you ever love me at all?"

Noah wasn't the type of man to live in regret, but he was sorry he'd hurt her. "I'm sorry, Liz. I really am."

Karma II

"So, she was telling me the truth?"

Noah knew Liz well. He took his hands out of his pockets and watched her carefully. "Come on, Liz."

That dark look became fury. "You're a fucking pig, Noah!"

Noah blinked. That shit had stung. He'd been extremely unkind. All he'd been able to think about was Nadine, and he wasn't even sure that she was where he wanted to be.

"Where are you gonna go, Liz? Don't leave. Not like this."

"What am I supposed to do? Stay her with you and have a ringside seat to you fucking me over? Well, fuck you, Noah."

Her hand flew out and she slapped him across the face as hard as she could. Her hand came up again and Noah grabbed her wrist. Liz kicked him in the shin and he stepped back. She tried to claw his face with her other hand and Noah grabbed that wrist, too.

"Stop, Liz. Cut it out."

"Get off!" She yelled.

She stomped his instep and he let her go. A horn blew outside.

"At least you had the decency to ask me not to go. I wouldn't stay here with you another day. I hate you, Noah! I'm done!"

She picked up her lightest bag and put the strap over her shoulder. "I'll call you when your child is born."

Noah stared at her in shocked disbelief. Liz opened the door and picked up her suitcase. She was crying for real now, nearly sobbing. Noah started toward her, but she held up her hand.

"Get away from me. Don't come another step. I mean it."

Karma II

She maneuvered herself out the door with her baggage. She was struggling and Noah instinctively moved to help her.

"I said not another step. I hope you're happy."

"Liz, don't do this."

"You did this." She said, and slammed the door.

Noah wanted to stop her, but something in him wouldn't let him. Pride? Ego? He'd fucked up, royally. Noah sat on the edge of the sofa and put his face in his hands.

Chapter Eighteen

Taking the plunge

Leah watched Noah sleep.

Noah had rang her doorbell late last night. When she opened the door, he hadn't even said hello. He just started kissing her and taking her clothes off. Noah made love to her long and sweet. He'd made her respond in ways she'd never had before. He was perfection, but deeply flawed. Noah was an oxymoron. Two different things at once. Leah didn't care. She was in love with him, screw everything else. Leah put her fingers in his glorious curls and he opened his eyes. With all his other obvious beauty, his eyes were his best feature. Large, clear and shockingly gray.

Noah pulled her to him and started kissing her. Real soft at first, then more fervently as his passion grew. As delicious as he was, something that rich and delectable had to come with a price. What she was paying now was nil. All she felt was outrageous pleasure as his head drifted south and his tongue found her breasts. Leah put her fingers in Noah's hair and he let her guide him down to her most tender spot. Noah licked her with unrestrained indulgence until she was breathless and quivering, whimpering his name.

Noah pushed her hands out of his hair and came up suddenly, like a diver breaking through water. He grinned down at her in handsome, gleeful, wickedness, putting a hand on either side of her shoulders. His eyes sparkling, Noah plunged into her like he was impaling her.

"*Unnhh!*" He growled, loudly.

He slowly hammered her into submission and her reaction was raw and instantaneous. She screamed his name and dug her heels into the mattress as her hips slammed into his. An exquisite mixture of pleasure and warmth, like pin pricks, rushed through her. She spasmed around him, pulling him in deeper, like suction, then almost forcing him out. Leah let go and rode that crest of ecstasy until everything was suddenly wet. Noah's arms trembled and he dropped his head.

Karma II

"*Ahh! Ahh!*" The sound came out of his throat reflexively. He couldn't hold it in. Noah slowed way down and started moving in small, tight circles. He was still grinning and breathless himself.

"That was nice. Do it again." Leah said.

Noah raised up and pushed Leah's legs back toward her chest.

He worked on her with his thumb. It wasn't hard to get her to go back to the place she'd just left. It took her over like a seizure. Noah watched her climax and kept going, looking at her like she was bewitching him. He frowned hard and was helpless to stop himself.

"Oh, wow." His words came out in a hoarse whisper. He dipped in and out real slow, blowing his breath out through his teeth. He kept going until it went without saying that he'd reached the point of hypersensitivity men always fell into. He worked through it, shuddering, trembling, and cursing softly. He was hard again almost at once. Noah threw her leg over his shoulder and looked down at her quite seriously, still moving.

"Now I can't leave you alone." He said the words softly, and started kissing her.

Noah made love to her slow, as if they had all the time in the world. When it was finally, regrettably over, he lay with her, spooning like that first night. Noah ran his hand lazily over her hip and they didn't talk for a long time.

"Noah?"

"Hmm?"

"You asleep?"

"Nope. Can't. You gotta leave."

He was right. It was Monday morning, and she had to be at the Trinidad compound at eleven.

"You're right." She said.

Leah moved to get up, but Noah kept his hand firmly on her hip. He kissed her neck. It was a touching gesture, coming from him.

"You okay?"

"Nope. I got a lot on my mind, baby."

Leah tucked her lips in to keep from smiling at the endearment.

"I can imagine."

Noah sighed and sat up, running his hand through his hair. "No, you can't," he said and stood up. "I'm gonna get outta here. We got a ten o'clock meetin' with Griff, and you gotta go drive that asshole around."

"Okay. I'll get you some towels."

Noah smiled at her and disappeared into the bathroom. They got dressed with a minimum amount of talking. Noah looked at his watch.

"I gotta run."

"I know."

"You gonna be okay today?"

"I'll be fine."

They stared at each other for a moment, then Leah walked him to the door.

"I guess I'll see you tomorrow," he said and started out.

Leah suddenly found herself reaching for things to say. Things that never, ever would have fallen out of her mouth if this wasn't Noah Ramsey, and she didn't want him to leave so bad.

"What if I want to see you before then?" Noah sighed and looked at her patiently.

"Then you gotta take a number. I gotta see my kids tonight."

Leah tried her best not to let him see how much that bothered her. It wasn't him seeing his kids that rubbed her the wrong way. It was Noah being in close proximity to his ex-wife that didn't sit right.

"Okay, Noah. See ya."

Leah was horrified at the seeds of jealousy that had begun to sprout into small ugly flowers. Her mind conjured up a disturbing image of Noah doing something delightful to his ex-wife. She heard the door close. She didn't even turn around. Fuck his whorish ass, then.

"Fucking asshole." She mumbled.

She turned around to lock the door, and found Noah standing there with his hand on the knob. "I thought you left." She said quietly.

He had noticed she was upset. "So you call me names behind my back like everybody else, huh?"

"No. Not like everybody else."

He grunted softly in disagreement. "Come here, Leah."

"No. You come here."

"What's this? A battle of wills?"

Leah looked at him indifferently. "Guess so."

Noah let his breath out in mock resignation. "Alright. You win."

He closed the distance between them, and stood close,

not quite touching.

"You mad at me 'cause I gotta see my kids? I gotta see my kids, Leah."

"It's not your kids I'm worried about."

Noah raised an eyebrow. "You worried about my ex-wife?"

"Shouldn't I be?"

He stared at her. Leah watched his eyes change with some amusement. His eyes were like a mood ring.

"What's wrong, Noah? You gonna sleep with her, too?"

He smiled at her sarcastically. "I wasn't plannin' on it."

"Yeah, but you probably will."

"Maybe I won't."

He reached out and grabbed her, unexpectedly. The kiss he gave her was so soft and so sweet, Leah actually felt her knees go weak. He stopped kissing her with the same abruptness and patted her on the ass.

"See you tomorrow," he said in her ear, and walked out the door.

She'd thought she could handle getting involved with Noah, but she couldn't. She'd never been into men playing her too close, but Leah hadn't wanted Noah to leave. She'd played him close. Noah had made her feel like he honestly did care about her. She hoped with all her heart that she'd cracked his surface. She thought there was potential there if she played her cards right.

Leah looked at her watch and groaned loudly. She was about to become one of Troy Trinidad's flunkies, and she wasn't in the mood to deal with assholes. She drove the long-ass drive to the Upper East Side. Leah walked to the townhouse in the middle of the block. It wasn't a brownstone-type townhouse like Lucas' place. There was a small gated area with pretty potted plants at either side of the huge mahogany door. Leah looked up at the dainty, tasteful terraces with their beautifully intricate

Karma II

ironwork, and knew that even though the place looked small according to Manhattan standards, it was probably humongous on the inside.

Leah took a deep breath and rang the bell. It only took a second for a prissy female voice to answer in surround sound.

"May I help you?"

"Ayesha Singleton for Troy Trinidad." The door opened briskly, and the woman who answered smiled at her, but not with her eyes.

"Come in. Mr. Troy's been expecting you."

She turned on her heel and started down the hall. The drug trade had obviously made the Trinidad brothers filthy, stinking rich. This was only the entryway and already there was so much money in this room, she could practically smell it. Her eyes were trailing up to take in the elegant crown molding when the maid who answered the door stopped walking.

"This way." She said, impatience creeping into her voice.

"Alright. Sorry."

Damn, what was her problem?

"In the future, you use the service bell at the back of the house. Mr. Tate and Mr. Troy don't care for the help using the front door."

Leah shrugged. "My bad."

The maid stopped walking and turned to face her. She was a pretty girl. She looked to be in her late twenties. She had creamy amber skin and dark auburn hair, pulled tightly back from her face and twisted into a stylish bun. Her eyes were large, brown, and very clear. She surprised Leah by taking her by the arm and guiding her through the kitchen and into the pantry.

"Do you know what you're getting yourself into?"

Leah frowned. *Oh, shit. This girl was terrified.* "Are you okay?"

She looked at Leah urgently. "I know you're here to

drive Mr. Troy, but he doesn't even know you're here yet."

"Are you telling me to leave?"

"I'm saying they're not nice people."

Leah was a bit blown away by the look of terror in her eyes.

"What's your name?"

"Cherry."

"I can handle myself, Cherry. I really need this job. Don't worry. I know what kind of people they are."

"I took the risk of warning you. It's up to you to listen." She turned to leave and Leah grabbed her wrist.

"Wait a minute. Don't just-"

Cherry cut her off by removing her hand from her wrist. "I live here, Ayesha. I'll be around. Come with me."

Leah followed her up the back staircase to the second floor. "Mister Troy lives on this floor. There's an elevator off the library in the main part of the house, but it's not to be used without permission."

Karma II

"No problem. Is that what you call him?"

"Yes. That's what he requires. Mr. Tate, too. Especially Mr. Tate."

Especially Mr. Tate, huh? Leah was starting to get the creeps.

Chapter Nineteen

Meet and greet

Karma II

Lucas picked Noah up in a navy blue BMW sedan. Noah sat in his usual slouched position, his chin in his hand, staring out the window.

"Something on your mind?" Lucas asked.

Noah didn't even blink. "No."

Speaking in monosyllables was out of character.

"Worried about this-"

"I said no."

Alright. Enough of this bullshit. Lucas pulled the car off the road and looked at Noah. Now he was frowning. So what? So was Lucas. "Noah, what the fuck is wrong with you?"

"I don't know where my kid is."

Oh, shit! Lucas was instantly worried. "What?"

Noah took a deep breath and sighed loudly. He reached for his Dunhills and lit one. "Liz left me. I don't know where she is. I can't find her."

"Damn, No."

"Bitch." Noah said the word quietly, but it carried weight.

"Noah, just chill, bro. She'll come around."

"You really think so, Luke? Tell you what. Fuck her stupid ass, okay?" Noah was tripping hard.

"You don't mean that."

"I mean it right now."

Lucas stared at him. He recalled the time he'd asked Noah if he was on self-destruct. Hell, maybe he was.

"You gotta pull your shit together, No."

Noah looked at him and smiled brightly. "I'm on it, bro. Let's drive."

"You got it."

They were a block from the Trinidad place when Noah opened his mouth again. "Hey, Luke?"

"Yeah?"

"We cool?"

"Like ice." They dapped each other quickly.

They got out of the car and started toward the mansion. Lucas looked over at Noah as he buttoned his suit jacket and straightened his tie. Noah's blue suit was so dark, it almost looked black and his shirt was a strange blue, not quite cobalt, not quite royal. It looked like Prada.

"Nice suit." Lucas said, with a smile. Noah grinned back.

"Yours ain't bad either." Lucas' suit was a stylish, dark gray Dior. Noah squinted at him.

"Is that shirt purple?" He asked.

Lucas smiled. "It's mauve."

A pretty young maid answered the door. Noah appreciated the view of her backside as she guided him and Lucas to the office where Tate and Troy were waiting.

"Mr. McCoy and Mr. Black are here for you, Mr. Tate."

"Send them in."

Lucas and Noah walked into the room and were stopped

206

Karma II

short by two gentlemen at the door. One was taller than both of them, thin in a wiry sort of way, and darker than Lucas by about 10 shades. The second was about 5' 10" and 240 pounds. He looked like a fucking wall.

"Pat them down, please." This came from the obscured Tate Trinidad.

"Tate, that's my cousin. I don't think that's necessary." Tamiko said, walking into the room from another doorway.

"Hush. I believe it is." Tate said in a voice that invited no argument.

"Hands up, fellas," the solid one said.

Lucas and Noah complied. They were both carrying 9 mm pistols. Fat and skinny

removed their weapons and pronounced them clean. The solid one smiled.

"We'll hold onto these, if you don't mind."

"I do mind and I want it back." Noah said, darkly. Tate stood up from his seat behind his desk with an unlit Cuban in his hand.

Karma II

"You'll get it back, Craig. Sorry about that. One can never be too careful. Where are your men?" Noah smiled.

"I travel light. I got all I need right here." He gestured toward Lucas.

Tate sized him up and Lucas did the same. Tate wasn't very tall, maybe about 5'9", but he had a definite presence about him. He was wearing a champagne-colored Armani suit and a sable tie. His skin was unflawed and coppery. Tate wore his wavy hair short and neat. His moustache and goatee looked as if he'd just had them trimmed. Nice looking guy. Handsome, even. His eyes were his defining feature, large and slightly deep set, they glittered in his head like black diamonds - piercing, vibrant, shrewd, and a bit unkind.

"Ray Black?"

Lucas looked at him coolly. "Uh-huh."

Tate smiled. "We all have a mutual friend. Oscar Tirado speaks very highly of both of you. Forgive me for checking you out."

Bless Oscar's cold black heart. They must have promised him the moon for this.

"We understand." Lucas said.

They walked deeper into the room and Tamiko closed the space between them. She reached up and put her arms around Noah's neck and kissed his cheek. Noah gave her a warm, brotherly hug and held her at arm's length.

"Look at you. Good to see you."

"It's better to see you."

She turned to Lucas and surprised him by kissing his cheek, too. "Hey, Ray. It's been a long time."

Lucas played along. "Sure has."

Tate clipped the end of his cigar off with an expensive silver toy and lit it with a gold lighter.

Karma II

"Alright. Enough of that. Troy's waiting for us at the club."

"Where is it? We'll meet you there." Noah said.

"I'm afraid you won't. You and Ray will ride with us. If we part paths now, I'll just have to have you patted down again. Besides, I love entourages."

"However you want to do it. Let's go." Noah was smirking.

"Don't look so put out, gentlemen. I don't trust anybody. Come. We'll eat, drink and get to know each other, for tomorrow we may die."

Lucas raised an eyebrow. "That's not exactly the way it goes."

"Good observation, Ray, but it still applies."

They followed Tate out of the house, and everyone piled into two vehicles. It didn't take long to get there. They parked in front of the club and everyone got out of their cars. Tate turned to Noah and Lucas, holding his hands out, expansively.

"This is our newest venture, Façade. We just opened

last week."

They went in and found Nicole leaning against the bar. She looked excruciatingly beautiful in a short red dress, with her long hair curled and cascading down her back.

"Damn! Who's this?" Noah asked, checking Nick out.

Nicole smiled at him and crossed her gorgeous legs. If Noah had been someone else, Lucas would have been pissed at their little exchange, but he wasn't worried at all about Noah doing him greasy.

"This beautiful lady is Tiffany Allen. She's my personal assistant. New, but I think I'm fitting her in quite nicely."

Lucas could have broken his jaw, just for the way he said it, but he kept his face devoid of emotion. Noah was looking at him with his bemused little grin. Lucas could have knocked the shit out of him, too.

"Tiffany, say hello to Craig and Ray." He gestured to them respectively, and put a possessive hand on her arm.

Tate had a notable blackness to his personality that sizzled just below the surface of his smile. Like it made his dick hard to watch people's reactions to the fucked up things he did and said. Lucas hadn't known him an hour and he couldn't stand his ass. Nicole stood and picked up a black leather day planner from the bar.

"Hello," She threw her attention back to Tate. "Do you still need me?"

Tate stood close to her, his attraction to her unconcealed. His eyes drifted over her body like it belonged to him. "Not at the moment, but don't go far. I'll definitely need you later."

"I'll be around." She said and walked away.

Tate watched her go, then turned back to them. "Troy should be waiting for us in the VIP room. Let's join him."

They walked in to Troy standing behind the bar, loud and boisterous, with three other men, drinking liquor straight from the bottle. He took another swig out of the bottle, then slammed it down noisily.

"Tate! What's good, man?"

Tate picked up the bottle and put the top on it. He looked at Troy with a heavy dose of disapproval. "That remains to be seen, brother."

Troy watched Tate put the bottle back in its proper spot and put a tightly rolled joint in his mouth. Tate reached out and calmly removed it.

"Not now. I have some people I'd like you to meet. This is Craig McCoy and Ray Black. I'm thinking of letting them give us a connection."

Troy looked interested. "To replace Frankie?"

He smiled a parody of regret at Tamiko. "Sorry about your brother, Tammy."

She grimaced at his laughable apology and looked at him like she wanted to spit on him. "Go to hell, Troy."

"Meet you there, bitch."

Karma II

Noah leaned forward and delivered a nice rendition of indignation. "What did you say?"

Troy kept smiling, a flicker of something sinister was just behind his eyes. "You heard what I said. Whatcha gonna do about it, with your punk ass?"

Tate raised an eyebrow and looked at Noah. Lucas knew Troy had just authentically pissed Noah off. Noah stared back at him cold and hard.

"I don't play that shit," he said in a quiet voice.

Troy laughed and addressed his brother. "Pretty boy's showing some very large balls."

Noah leaned closer and put his hand flat on the table. That was a bad sign. It meant he didn't mind coming over it.

"I got colossal balls, and I ain't afraid of you."

Troy stood up, his laugh so black you could almost see it. Noah stood, too, and Lucas tensed up. Noah wasn't walking away and he'd gladly throw the first punch.

"Be real careful what you ask for."

Troy said in a voice just as low as Noah's. "Follow

your own advice."

His eyes sparkled darkly and he turned his back on Noah completely. He spoke to Tate.

"You were right about Kenny. He was living foul and lining his own pockets."

Troy reached into his back pocket and flipped a ziplocked mess onto the middle of the table. Tamiko recoiled with a yelp and hid her face in her hands. Lucas looked down at what seemed to be a wig covered in gore. He stood for a closer look, as Noah also leaned in for a better view. Lucas narrowed his eyes and stared at Troy. His hand itched for his gun. Noah took a step back and stared at Troy like he'd crawled out of a garbage can.

"I see we no longer have to worry about Kenny," Tate said, with a small cheery laugh. "Take this garbage off my table, Troy, and no more scalping. It's unconscionable."

Troy kept his eyes on Noah and removed the bag from the table. He casually tossed it to Tobias, who caught it as if it were no big deal.

"You scared yet?"

Karma II

Noah didn't break his cold stare, but he smiled. "It takes a lot more than your wild west, Texas chainsaw, bushwhackin' ass to scare me."

Tate looked at Lucas. "What about you? You haven't had much to say."

Lucas sat back down, as did Noah and Troy. He nodded at Troy. "Nice work."

"Thanks. I'm always willing to go that extra mile."

"Uh- huh. Nothing succeeds like excess."

Troy didn't know if that was a compliment or not. It wasn't.

Tate rubbed his hands together. "Let's have a drink and get down to business, shall we?" He signaled to Tobias, who politely took their drink orders. Tate held his hands out like a white flag.

"Gentlemen, I believe we've gotten off to a bad start," He turned his eyes on Noah. "Craig, I apologize for my brother's antics. He has a constant need to prove himself, though his reputation precedes him."

Noah smiled sarcastically. "Yeah, I'm sure he's really a nice guy."

Tate laughed. "No, he's really not, I'm afraid, but he's my brother and my business partner."

Noah frowned. "You let him talk to Tamiko like that?"

"I have no control over Troy. I can only try to rein him in."

Noah smirked. "A fuckin' leash might work."

Troy bristled and Tate shushed him with a hand on his shoulder. "That was very unkind, Craig. Not unwarranted, but unkind."

Noah stared at him and made no apology. Tobias returned with their drinks and disappeared. Noah leaned back in his chair and took a sip of his single malt. "Okay, I'm done with the freak show. You guys are weird. Let's make a deal."

Tate smiled. "I'm going to ignore that. I've got $250,000.00 if you can provide me with a superior product – 20 kilos - and procure a shipment to me by the seventeenth."

"That's in five days." Lucas said.

Tate put his elbows on the table and tented his fingers. "That's when I want it."

"That's when you'll have it." Lucas replied.

"Not so fast," Troy said. "We ain't givin' you that much money without knowing what you got."

"That's very true. We don't deal on blind faith." Tate added, eyeing Tamiko.

She sat very still, looking at her hands. She'd been that way since she'd uncovered her eyes. She'd probably known Kenny very well.

"Fine. Produce the product, Ray." Noah said.

Lucas reached into his breast pocket and produced two small plastic envelopes. One red, one blue. He handed them to Troy.

"The red one's coke, the blue one's heroin."

"I'm sure he can tell the difference." Tate said, snippily. He must have thought he was talking to one of his yes men. Lucas didn't appreciate it, but he conceded. Troy opened the red package, stuck his pinky in his mouth, then into the package and tasted it. He looked interested. He poured a small cone of it on the back of his hand and sniffed it up his nose. He closed his eyes for a moment, then looked at Tate.

"This is some exceptional shit."

He took another hit and reached for the heroin. Lucas and Noah glanced at each other as they watched Troy taste and snort that, too. A slow smile slid across his face and he took another hit. Tate stared at him patiently, waiting for his opinion. It appeared Troy was drifting a bit.

Lucas gave him a nudge. "Troy?"

Troy's eyes popped open and focused on him. "Damn, man! That's primo. Where'd you get this shit?"

He picked the heroin up again and Tate snatched it out of his hand. "That's enough, Troy."

Karma II

Lucas and Noah exchanged another glance. What was this? A chink in Draco's armor?

Tamiko looked disgusted. "Fucking dope addict." She muttered.

Tate gave her that chastising look he liked to throw around. "That's not nice, my love," he turned to Troy. "What do you think, brother?"

"I think we should invest the money. If they can be consistent with the quality and deliver on time, we got a goldmine."

Noah leaned forward and spoke to Troy. "The quality stays the same, and we can deliver. How much did you say we were talkin'?"

Tate smiled. "I thought we agreed on $250,000.00."

Lucas put his glass down and spoke to Troy, too. "How good is it?"

"Nigga, I ain't gotta tell you again! You know your shit is primo! Some of the best shit I ever had."

Lucas laughed. "No doubt, but if you want that much product in that amount of time, the price just went up."

Tate frowned. "That's a lot of money I'm offering you, Mr. Black."

Lucas smiled. "Uh-huh, and that's a lot of product you're asking us to move in a short amount of time. People are gonna be inconvenienced. They have to be compensated. Isn't that right, Craig?"

"Right as rain." Noah chimed in.

Tate looked at Tamiko. "You keep the books, my love. How much do you think is wise?"

"I think $350,000.00 is good. You'll make your profit in no time. Craig is my cousin, I've known him and Ray all my life. I trust them."

Tate raised an eyebrow. "Is that so? I don't have to remind you that Frankie was your brother, do I? He was stealing from me and using as much as his body could stand."

Karma II

Tamiko stared at him. "Frankie might have been using, but he wasn't the only one," She said, and gave Troy an insinuating look. "If you were going to clean your house, you could have started right here."

"Watch your mouth." Tate said with quiet vitriol.

Noah stepped in. "You know, Tate, I ain't got too much to say on the subject of poppin' Frankie. Cousin or not, I might have done the same thing in the same situation. Business does come first. We ain't on drugs, though, and we can back up a commitment. If you wanna deal, let's deal. If you don't, stop wastin' our time."

Tate looked at his brother.

"Troy?" Troy nodded.

"Let's make a deal."

"Okay, gentlemen. We have an agreement. I'll even give you until the twentieth."

"Price stays the same." Lucas reminded him.

"No problem," Troy said. He took the samples and put them in his pocket. "I'll hold onto these."

Lucas smiled. "Be my guest." Noah stood up and Lucas followed his lead.

"Fantastic," He offered his hand and Tate shook it. "Glad we could do business, but sorry, I think we're gonna duck out early."

Tamiko stood, too, a trace of panic in her eyes. "You're skipping lunch? Don't leave, Craig. You and Ray have to stay."

Noah looked apologetic. "Afraid we can't, sweetie pie. That scalp thing kinda took my appetite. Besides, we got a few phone calls to make to start puttin' this shit together."

Tate stood, too.

"We'll see you out."

"I really wish you'd stay," Tamiko said again.

Noah smiled at her. "No can do. Don't look so sad. We'll be back tomorrow and do some catchin' up, okay?"

She smiled back and kissed his cheek.

Karma II

"You better. It really is good to see you guys." She gave Lucas a hug.

"Likewise."

Troy was just hanging up his cell phone. "My driver's outside. She'll take you back to your ride."

Noah reached into his breast pocket and put his shades on.

"'Preciate that. See you tomorrow."

Chapter Twenty

The past or the future

Nick had been in love before, but she'd never felt quite this way. She'd never met a man like Lucas, and she was sure she wasn't the first woman to say that. The other men she'd loved had all pursued her. Lucas hadn't. He'd just been there when she needed him. The others had spit crazy game to get her. Lucas' mack was quiet, strong in its reserve. He was far from perfect, and Nick was sure he harbored deep hurts he'd never share with her.

It didn't take her long to get home. She went upstairs to the bedroom. Lucas had left some of his clothes strewn over the bed. He was usually fairly meticulous about his stuff. Nick scooped up his things and walked into his closet. She flipped the light on and was putting his things away when something caught her eye. It was an old hat box with pink and gray stripes, sitting on the topmost shelf. It stuck out like a sore thumb. She finished hanging his clothes and looked back up at the box, half hidden behind some sweaters. She put her hands on her hips and stared at it. Nick closed her eyes. Just walk away, Nick.

Her eyes popped back open and she pursed her lips. Who was she fooling? She'd cried into the world nosy as hell. Nick pushed the sweaters aside, making a mental note of where they'd been, and pulled the hatbox off the shelf. She went back into the bedroom and sat on the bed with it in her lap.

She took the lid off and put it beside her. There was a wooden jewelry box in the middle, some papers rolled into a tube and secured with a rubber band, and three bundles of letters. She opened the jewelry box. These were some really nice pieces. Cuff links, two wedding rings, a diamond brooch and some earrings. Nick picked up the earring he used to wear in his left ear. He'd replaced it with something smaller.

Karma II

Nick closed the jewelry box and removed the tube of papers. She smiled at his birth certificate. Lucas Matthew Cain. A marriage certificate for James and Delilah Cain. From the date on the certificate, these were his parents, James and Delilah. She saw his discharge papers from the Marines, and four funeral service obituaries. Two for James, one senior and one junior. One for Paula, his grandmother, and one for Justine. Nick rolled the papers back up and put them back in the box. She picked up a stack of letters. Most of them were still sealed, even though there had to be over a hundred letters here, tightly bound by rubber bands. They were all from one person. Delilah Cain.

Nick flipped through them quickly and did the math in her head. These letters had started when Lucas was eight or nine years old. What the hell was this? She slipped the first envelope out of the rubber bands. It was open and postmarked from Chicago. The letter was short and sweet, but it brought tears to Nick's eyes.

Nick put the letter back in the envelope and closed her

eyes. Lucas' mother had walked away from her family. God, what he must have gone through. Nick opened her eyes and looked at the picture in the cracked frame. How'd he break it? Had it fallen, or had he thrown it? Nick looked into the big brown eyes in the picture and wondered what was wrong with her. she could understand leaving her husband, but leaving her little boy? What kind of woman was she? She flipped through the letters again. The last one was postmarked from San Diego. The most recent letters were all unopened, but he hadn't thrown them away.

Her eyes returned to the box. There was something at the bottom. Nick moved everything and took it out. It was the picture of Justine. The last thing in the box was a card. Thinking of You. It was one of those blank cards that you put your own message in. Nick read it twice. It said he shouldn't blame himself, that Simone was destined to meet the end she met, and how sorry she was about everything that happened. She told him to always hold Justine near, but to go on with his life. It was signed, 'Always your friend, Holly'.

Karma II

Nick put everything back in place and returned the box to the shelf. She learned a lot about Lucas in that small space of time. She felt guilty about looking into his past without his permission. Nick took her clothes off and got into the shower. Lucas needed some happiness.

He deserved a happy ending after all the sadness he'd been forced to deal with, and she knew she loved him enough to do her damndest to make sure he was. She was going to ask him to marry her. The worse thing Lucas could do would be to turn her down. She got out of the shower and got dressed. She put on a flippy little red skirt and a white tank top that was about a size too small.

She lit a few candles and turned on some Marvin Gaye. Nick poured herself a glass of wine and put dinner in the oven. The front door opened and Lucas walked in, tall, dark and exceedingly handsome.

"Is this all for me?" He asked. Nick slipped her arms around his waist and his hands found their way into her hair. He kissed her forehead and she smiled back up at him.

"Well, we haven't spent a lot of time together since we started the sting. I figured you deserved a nice meal and some quality down time. I missed you, honeybunch."

"You did, huh?" Lucas took his hands out of her hair and tugged at the bottom of her tank top. "This is nice. Why don't you take it off?"

"It comes off after I feed you."

He kissed her neck. "Promise?"

Nick giggled. "I guarantee it."

Lucas spoke into her ear. "Alright. Let's get dinner out of the way."

"You're not supposed to rush through it. You're supposed to enjoy it."

Karma II

Lucas smiled at her, slow and sexy, and put his face close to hers. "I will, Nicole. I'll take my time. You'll enjoy it, too, especially when I lick my plate."

Nick smiled back at him, just as sexy. "Wow, Lucas. That was kind of lewd. Are you trying to get me into bed?"

He laughed and kissed her lips, teasingly, as he backed her up to the counter. "Always, but the bed's upstairs. This counter is just fine."

She laughed and playfully pushed him away. "Stop being bad and let me put dinner on the table."

Lucas looked at her devilishly and put his hand under her chin. He kissed her again, one of those sweet and soulful Lucas Cain kisses. He had no idea how powerful his kisses were. In a matter of seconds, they overwhelmed you with his presence and made you totally aware of him, how tall he was, the strength in his shoulders, and how damned good he smelled. Nick shivered and pushed him away, shakily. The way things were going, they'd be eating dinner for breakfast.

"Um, come on, baby, let's eat." She said, her voice a bit huskier than she wanted it to be.

Lucas looked at her with a smug little smile. "You alright?"

Nick looked back at him with mock annoyance, but she was a bit too breathless, and of course he noticed. Lucas laughed softly and walked away from her. Yeah, his mack was formidable and his swagger was sensational. All he'd done was kiss her, and he'd left her with her chest heaving. Nick was startled by the force of the emotion she felt for him. If he'd have her, Nick was marrying this man, and she wasn't afraid to ask. Lucas recorked the wine she'd been drinking and selected another one. He got two glasses, took everything to the table and picked up the remote. Marvin stopped singing about sure lovin' to ball, and the Isley's started wanting to groove with you. Lucas smiled and looked over at her.

"Stop staring at me."

Damn! She thought she was being discreet. Nick carried the food out and sat to his left.

"Sorry. I couldn't help myself." Nick tried not to stare as they began the meal. Lucas had great table manners.

"You're still staring."

Nick smiled. "I told you I couldn't help it. I've got an enormous crush on you."

Lucas smiled back and raised an eyebrow. "You're embarrassing me."

Nick laughed. "No, I'm not. I'm stroking your ego."

Lucas shrugged. "Okay, maybe that's closer to the truth. What happened today? You looked upset."

Nick took a sip of her wine. She'd walked in on Tate beating Tamiko with a belt like she was a child. It had taken tremendous willpower not to shoot his slimy ass. "I don't want to talk about that right now."

Lucas put his fork down and sat back in his chair. He was no longer joking and being fresh. His face was dead serious. "I don't have to tell you that was the absolute last thing you should have said to me about that. What happened, Nicole?"

"Tate's an asshole."

Lucas nodded at her. "Go on."

"He was beating Tamiko with a belt like she was a little kid. Did you know he kicks her ass, Lucas?"

"Yeah, I did. You better not come walking in here with fresh bruises."

Nick smirked. "I can handle Tate."

Lucas looked at her with more than a little concern. "If he ever puts you in a situation you can't handle-"

Nick held her hand up. "Lucas, baby, with all due respect, I was a detective way before I met you. I can handle myself."

"Nicole, don't patronize me and don't make me flex on you."

Nick couldn't believe it. He was dead serious. "I was just saying,"

"No. Tate decides he wants to put his hands on you, I'm takin' his ass out. Period. End of story. I'm done taking losses."

Nick nodded slowly. She decided to see if he felt like talking.

"Taking losses?"

Lucas looked at her a long time before he answered her. He pushed his plate away and ran his hand over his beard. "Let me tell you something about me, Nicole. I've got a pretty good image of myself as I may seem to other people, but I'm not all they may think. It is what it is. Nice looking guy, nice house, nice job, pushin' a five. Real nice woman. Good friends. But you know what? I can't seem to stay happy. Everyone I've ever loved has left me, with the exceptions of you and Noah. I'm not losing either of you. I don't give a shit about Draco. I'll put in all the work I have to, to keep that from happening. Are we clear, sweetheart?"

Nick nodded and felt a pang of guilt. "Crystal clear.

Um, Lucas, I know about your mom."

He smiled a bit sadly. "I know you do."

She frowned. "How'd you know I knew?"

He shrugged. "Nicole, you know I never leave my stuff like that. I let that box stick out just enough for you to see it. I knew you couldn't walk out of there without seeing what was inside."

"You set me up."

Lucas laughed a little. "Uh-huh. Yeah, I did."

"Why didn't you just tell me?"

"Because you didn't ask. You knew it was a sore subject, and you didn't want to drive me away by bringing it up. I put it out there because you had to know, Nicole. Everything in that box made me into the man I am right now."

Nick put her other hand on top of his and looked into his eyes. "I'm listening."

"Alright. I'll give you the abbreviated version. Jimmy Cain met Delilah Sadler the summer she turned 17. He was interning at the same hospital where my grandfather was Head of Cardiology, and Delilah was there to have her appendix removed. My father fell in love with her the moment he saw her. From what I heard, she felt the same way. Her parents told her she couldn't see him because he had 10 years on her. Jimmy and Delilah felt like they couldn't live without each other, so they devised a plan, and had Delilah come and volunteer at the hospital so they could carry on their affair."

Karma II

He paused, took his hands away and sat back in his chair. "My father was about two years into his marriage to a woman named Alyssa. Alyssa was the daughter of my grandmother's childhood friend. My grandmother thought the sun rose and set on my father's wife. My father told me with his own mouth that he never loved Alyssa, not like that. My grandfather was always so busy, he was fairly oblivious to what was going on, until the shit hit the fan."

Lucas took a sip of his wine and looked out the window. Nick wondered what was really on his mind just then. She called him back from wherever it was that he'd gone. "What happened, honeybunch?"

Lucas laughed ruefully. "I happened. Delilah got pregnant and there was a huge scandal."

Nick frowned. "Scandal? Lucas, shit like that happens every day."

Lucas turned his gaze back to her. "You know, Nicole, I grew up in the brownstone down the street. I live here because that house is full of bad memories. Take a look around you, sweetheart. That piano over there is a Steinway. The shit hangin' on these walls is real. The watch on my wrist cost a whole lot of money. My grandfather gave it to me. I didn't grow up in the Polo Grounds playing stick ball and pick up games like Noah. I took my black ass to private school and I didn't dare wild out until I was late in my teens. My family moved in that rare and elite circle of black people with money. Anything that muddied the waters and made you look like a nigger was severely frowned upon. It made you a pariah. Yeah, baby, it was a scandal."

"What did your father do?"

"What could he do? Against everyone's wishes, he divorced Alyssa and married my mother right after I was born. My grandmother never forgave him for it, and she made their lives miserable."

He said the last part like he had a bad taste in his mouth. "She was a horrible person."

Nick was a little shocked by that. "Lucas! Don't say that, baby."

"Fuck her. That bitch ran my mother away, and she wasn't a saint after she left. My grandmother had a huge Mastiff and she would lock me in the room with it when I was bad. Fucking dog was bigger than me. I was afraid to breathe hard. My father drank himself to death after my mother left. Her fault, too."

Karma II

Nick couldn't keep the sadness out of her voice. "I'm sorry, baby." Nick stood up. "I guess we're done here."

Lucas stood, too. "Let's go upstairs."

They went up and Lucas kicked his shoes off and sat on the bed with his back against the pillows. "I'm tired." He said, absently.

Nick climbed in beside him and watched him carefully. "Why won't you talk to her?" She asked, undoing the buttons on his shirt.

"Who?"

Nick smiled and kissed him softly on his mouth. "Delilah. Your mother. She wrote you just last week. You don't even open her letters anymore. Why?"

Lucas studied her hands as she undid the last button, looking down at them through his eyelashes. He stopped her hands with his own and looked up at her face. "I don't want to know about her. I don't want to know how her life is. I don't want to know if she's okay, and I really don't want to know about her son."

Nick was surprised. Damn! What else? "You have a brother?

What's his name?"

"His name is Myles. He's 10 years younger than me."

"Don't you want to know him?"

"No, and I'm done with Delilah, too, and before you ask me why again, I'll tell you. We can never go back. She made her decisions. There's too much hurt and animosity to make it right."

"I can see why you feel that way. I'm glad you told me. I feel closer to you."

"How close?"

Nick watched his face as she swung one leg across his body, so she was straddling him. She stripped off her tank top and pushed his shirt open. She sat down on him and did a slow bump and grind. Lucas grunted softly, a small sound of pleasure and surprise. His hands went instinctively to her hips. Nick smiled down at him and spread her body over his, her breasts pressing into his bare chest. She put her fingers in his hair and covered his face with soft kisses. She loved his face. He was so damned handsome. She nuzzled her face against his and enjoyed the softness of his light full beard. She felt him watching her with his incredible big brown eyes. Oh, yeah. She loved Lucas Cain. He was just as wonderful as he was delicious. Nick finally put her lips on his and kissed him slow, savoring the taste of him. Lucas hands left her hips and his arms went around her. He kissed her back just as intently. Nick pressed against him. Lucas couldn't possibly be closer to her than this, unless he was inside of her. She shivered in anticipation.

"This close." Nick whispered the words against his mouth and felt his lips smile against hers.

"That's pretty damn close."

She kissed him again, grinding against him like a teenager. Nick sat half-way up, bracing herself on her hands. She threw her head back and closed her eyes. She was almost there and she hadn't even gotten his pants off. Lucas wasn't just lying there. He was moving with her, his thumbs on her nipples. Nick moaned, as she glided along the length of him. His hands dropped to her thighs and forced her to stop moving.

Nick's eyes flew open in frustration. Lucas smiled and sat up with her now in his lap. He raised his hips and eased his pants off as Nick watched the muscles in his stomach ripple from the effort. Lucas slipped his delectable tongue in her mouth and eased into her. Nick melted at once. Lucas leaned back into the pillows with her and brought his knees up. When he put his hands on her ass, she realized she was trapped.

He was hitting her spot with every stroke. He was working her out with an even and practiced rhythm. He was building her steadily up to an explosion. The first flutters started and her body began to stiffen up, as Lucas' arms went around her body and held her tightly against him. Nick couldn't move, but she loved being held hostage this way. Lucas leaned forward and started slow grinding. He was all the way in and still kissing her, when that unmistakable throb began.

Nick's head went back and she threw her arms around his neck. Nope. The pleasure from that sweet, slippery friction was so intense, it brought tears to her eyes. Her body was quivering so hard, she couldn't stop, but Lucas wouldn't let her go. He shifted and went deeper. She leaned away so she wasn't so close. She wanted him to look at her and he did. His eyes traveled along her body and lingered where their bodies met. He pushed her legs back and used his thumb to guide her right into her next orgasm. Lucas turned her onto her back and put a hand under each knee.

He slid back into her long, deep, and at an angle. He had her g-spot covered and he was putting in extra work on it. Nick gasped and reflexively kicked her legs out of his grasp. She dug her heels into the mattress as her back arched, and she grabbed his ass, pulling him in as far as he could go. Lucas plunged into her with that sexy-ass growl. He dropped his head until his face was close to hers.

Karma II

"Open your eyes, Nicole." Her eyes fluttered open at his command. He was staring almost through her.

"Do you love me?"

"Yes, Lucas. Oh, yes baby. I do."

"Good, because I need you."

He dove into her again and came hard. He always did, like he was holding back until the very end, thrusting and grinding his hips against hers, until he was spent, breathless and empty. Nick was thoroughly content. She snuggled into him as he lay on his back beside her. Lucas pulled her close and kissed the top of her head.

"I love you, you know." He said softly.

Nick smiled. "Good, because I love you, too, honeybunch. I think I'd find it very hard to live without you."

"Don't talk like that. Don't even think like that. I'm not going anywhere."

"You better not." They lay there for a long while, snuggled against each other with their own thoughts. Nick knew she should probably leave it alone, but one thing kept resurfacing in her mind. Hell, all he could do was not answer her.

"Lucas, if your mother-"

He cut her off and sat up. "That's the story. I don't want to talk about it anymore."

"You can't just close the subject just like that, Lucas."

"Yes, I can." He said in a voice that let her know he'd had his fill of rehashing the past.

He stared at her briefly, then got up and went into the bathroom. A moment later, Nick heard the shower go on. She appreciated the insight into his past but, though she loved him dearly, Lucas irritated her to no end when he acted like he was the boss and shut her down.

Karma II

"Yes, I can." She mimicked him in a whisper and stuck her tongue out at the open door. Nick walked to the door and expected to see Lucas actually taking a shower, but he wasn't. He was standing under the spray with his hands over his face. She opened the shower door and stepped in. Nick stood behind him and put her arms around him, resting her cheek on his shoulder.

"Are you crying?" She asked quietly.

Lucas laughed a little and shook his head. "No, I'm not crying. All that stuff was just hard. It's always hard going back to Delilah."

"I know."

"No, you don't."

Nick raised her head and kissed his shoulder. "Don't get snippy with me, I love you."

"I know."

"No, you don't. " Nick countered, "I could be lying."

Lucas looked over his shoulder at her. The look on his

face was border-line arrogant. It turned her on like he'd struck a match. "Okay. Tell me you don't, then."

Nick looked at him standing there staring at her, his face so handsome and serious, and smiled as she felt heat rise in her belly. "I could never say that. You may very well be the love of my life."

Lucas smiled. "Is that so?"

Nick nodded. "I really think you might be. What do you plan on doing about it?"

Lucas put his lips to her forehead." I don't know. What do you want me to do, Nicole?"

Nick knew herself well enough to know she didn't know how to leave well enough alone. "I want you to be the last man that tells me he loves me. I want you to be the first thing I see in the morning and the last thing I see at night."

Lucas watched her carefully. "What are you saying?" He was looking at her so hard, it made her blush. She was suddenly unsure of putting her feelings out there like that. She turned away from him, but he put his hand on her wrist and turned her back.

Karma II

"Don't go. What are you saying?"

Nick was starting to get angry with him because she felt embarrassed and a bit more than just physically naked. She jerked her arm away harder than she should have, and slipped. Lucas caught her before she fell on her ass.

"You okay?" He asked quietly. He held his head up high and his lips tucked in. The dimple in his cheek stood out prominently. He was trying hard not to laugh at her.

"Asshole." She muttered and stepped out of the shower. Jesus, Leah was right. Nick snatched a towel off the heated rack, wrapped it around her body, and stomped her way back to the bedroom and flopped down on the bed. She wished she hadn't opened her big mouth.

Lucas didn't appear right away. He let her stew for a while and came back into the room, freshly washed and completely dry, then began to get dressed. Nick was surprised.

"You're leaving?"

"I have to. We've got to meet Tate at nine."

She was mad at him because he'd tried to make her put all the beautiful feelings she felt for him into precise and exact words, because he was a precise and exact man. Lucas really wasn't into flowery effusions. You had to lay it straight out for him. That was all well and good, because Nick wasn't a poet. She had never been one to mince words, and hell, she wasn't going to start now. She felt her backbone start to return as she watched him slip his tie around his neck and put on that irresistible cologne he wore.

Nick walked over and tied his tie. When she was done, she slipped her arms around his waist and looked up at him. He was back to watching her carefully with his beautiful chocolate eyes.

"What's on your mind, Nicole?"

"I'll never find another man that will even come close to making me feel the way you make me feel. Did you know that, Lucas?"

He smiled at her. "I can only hope."

"You don't have to. You got me, Lucas. I'm head over heels in love with you. I need you. I need your love. I want to marry you. Do you want to marry me?"

Lucas looked down at her, surprising her by not seeming surprised. Lucas had a great poker face. He didn't flinch. "Are you proposing to me?"

Her chest was tight, but she nodded. "Yeah, I am. I hope you don't think I'm moving too fast. Don't answer, because I know I probably am, but I had to ask you. I just need you to know how I feel about you, and I just blurted it out because I know you hate bullshit, so I thought that was the only way. If I'm rambling now, and not making sense anymore, maybe it's because I-"

She stopped herself abruptly and took a deep breath. "Look, Lucas, I know it was probably stupid of me to come at you like this, but honey, please, don't make me feel like a fool for doing it. You don't have to say yes right away, but, please, baby, don't say no."

When he looked away, her heart sank. She'd screwed up and assumed too much. Lucas ran his hand over his beard and sighed. Bad sign. He looked back at her and Nick held her breath.

"So, that's what you want, huh?"

"Yeah, Lucas, that's what I want. What do you want?"

He gave her a very sweet kiss and looked deep into her eyes.

"I'm gonna be honest with you. You ready for that?"

Nick wasn't sure if she was ready, but she nodded anyway.

"I'm gonna tell you what I want. I want to go on. I want to live my life and be happy, if I can. I'm tryin' real hard, Nicole. I love you. I'm letting you all the way in. I don't want you to rush me, Nicole. I'm almost where you need me to be. Okay?"

Karma II

She tried to keep her bottom lip in, but it slid out like it had a mind of its own. Her arms betrayed her, too, and folded themselves across her chest. Lucas hadn't exactly given her the answer she was looking for.

He watched her with some amusement, then kissed her forehead. "I'm not saying no, Nicole."

"Then what are you saying?"

"I'm saying, I still need some time."

She looked away. "Some time. Yeah, okay."

Lucas put his arms around her and spoke into her hair. "Yes, sweetheart, I need some time. Stop pouting. It's almost a done deal."

He let her go and put on his suit jacket. "I gotta go. I'm late."

Nick followed him down the stairs and walked him to the door. She felt clingy, but did her best to fight it off. Lucas picked up his car keys and smiled at her.

"Don't be mad at me, sweetheart. I'm doing the best I can with what I have left to work with."

Nick sighed. "I wish I'd met you… " She'd almost said, before her, but she cleaned it up quickly. "…a long time ago."

Lucas smiled again and tilted his head. "You met me when you met me, Nicole, and everything happens for a reason. Be patient. I'm not going anywhere." Nick returned his smile.

"You better not."

"Be back soon." Nick watched him leave, then went upstairs and got into bed. At least he hadn't shut her down.

Chapter Twenty-One

Can't trust nobody

Karma II

This was some bullshit. Noah couldn't believe he was up in Washington Heights chasing Liz. He couldn't believe she wouldn't take his calls, and he couldn't believe she'd stepped out of his life so abruptly without a forwarding address. Okay, yeah, he could. He may be a bit of a bastard regarding commitment issues, but Noah always took care of his kids, and he wasn't about to let Liz go traipsing off with one of them.

He was pissed because he wasn't in control of this situation. He was pissed at Liz for running off, he was pissed at Nadine for starting all this shit, he was even pissed at Leah for taking up increasing space in his head, his mind fell on Leah more often than was actually comfortable. He hadn't set out to give her a room in his thoughts, but she'd managed to take up residence. He was pissed at Lucas, too. He was pissed at him for being right. It was a lot easier to get over being pissed at Luke, though. After all, he was his best friend and he was also riding shotgun on this little excursion. Right on cue, Lucas opened his mouth.

"Where's your head at, Noah?"

Shit, he'd been on low simmer since Liz did her disappearing act, but he smiled and stuck a Dunhill in his mouth. "I'm good. Just gonna ask a few questions. That's all."

Noah stared straight ahead as he patted his pockets for his lighter. He didn't look at him because he didn't want Lucas to know how upset he was. He'd gone way past just being mad, days ago. He was so enraged, he felt like it was welling up in him like lava. Noah felt like he wanted to scream until his throat was raw, like he wanted to hit something until his hands hurt. Liz couldn't be found, so he was completely at the mercy of her mother. He'd never been her favorite person, and here he was, hoping she'd throw him a fucking bone, for God's sake. Noah frowned and lit his smoke.

"You alright, No?"

He turned his head and looked at Lucas. "Yeah, Luke. Peachy."

Lucas shook his head, slowly. "Aw, shit, Noah. Come on, man. Bring your shit down a thousand."

Noah got out of the truck. Fuck it, now. If anybody said anything to him, he was letting them have it. He took another drag off his Dunhill and threw it on the ground. Noah heard Lucas' door open and close as he started up Ava Maldonado's front walk. Noah's hand went up to ring the doorbell and Lucas brought it back down.

"Say what you gotta say, Luke, then I'm ringin' the fuckin' doorbell."

Lucas took his hand off Noah's wrist slow, like he was taking the muzzle off a mad dog. "You can't go in there like that, Noah. You're two seconds from apeshit. Calm down, man."

Noah took a deep breath and looked at his shoes. He

took a moment to let his ire dissipate from boiling and raging back to a simmer.

"You alright?" Lucas asked again.

Noah rang the bell. "Right as rain."

Lucas positioned himself behind him just as the front door was flung open. It wasn't Ava, it was Liz's youngest brother, Bobby. His young, handsome face was twisted into a grave look of disdain.

"What you want, Noah?" Bobby was 20. He was a kid, and Noah wanted to speak to an adult.

"I'll give you three guesses. Where's your mom, Bobby?" Bobby stepped out of the door and blocked it with his body. He looked at Noah with extreme insolence.

"She don't wanna see you either."

Noah cocked his head and nodded. The anger was coming back quick. He didn't appreciate this kid talking to him like that. He was a grown-ass man. Noah fought hard against his natural urge to snatch him up in his collar. His hands actually reached out to grab him, but he pulled them back. He felt Lucas take a precautionary step forward. Noah knew if he moved on Bobby, Lucas was going to stop him. That was the real reason Lucas was with him. Sure, he had Noah's back if some shit jumped off, but he was there to make sure Noah didn't start any himself. Noah dropped his hands and moved in close. Bobby's chin went up defiantly and he took up a fighting stance, one foot behind him and his hands up.

"You wanna grab me? Go ahead!"

Noah's head went back in amazement. Before he thought about it hard, Noah had Bobby's collar in his right hand. He jerked him forward so hard his shirt ripped. Bobby's snarl melted into a childlike look of surprise, as he flailed his arms so he wouldn't lose his balance.

"Listen, boy, go in the house and get your mother before I drop your ass on your own doorstep." Noah pushed Bobby away from him and Bobby fell clumsily back against the door.

Lucas, who'd been near his elbow, took a step back, convinced he wouldn't have to peel Noah off Bobby's ass anytime soon. Bobby stared at Noah hard, and started to open his mouth, but Noah advanced on him so that the only place left for him to go, was back through the front door.

"Go right now, Bobby. Stop thinkin' so hard."

Bobby dropped his head and went back inside, leaving the door open behind him. Noah made no attempt to enter the house. He looked over his shoulder at Lucas.

"I'm alright."

Lucas nodded, doubtfully. "Uh-huh. Right as rain."

Noah heard footsteps approaching, and turned just as Ava Maldonado appeared in the doorway. Ava was not the conventional conception of someone's mother. She looked more like Liz's older sister. The same face, same hair, dressed in a pair of jeans and a semitight shirt, she was Liz, in a few years. She put her hands on her hips, threw her head back and let Noah have it.

"What you doin' here? Lissette don't want you no more."

Noah smiled at her, pleasantly. "Hey, Ava, how you doin'? Where's your daughter at?"

"She's not here, and she's not lookin' for your no good ass. You got no right to be here."

Noah kept smiling. "I got every right in the world to be here. You don't have to like it, but you need to tell me how to get in touch with her."

"For what? There's nothing to say. Nada."

Noah's smile vaporized. He took a step back and drew a deep breath. He was a lot angrier than he thought. Ava assumed his step back was retreat. She squared her feet and laid into him, pointing her finger in his face.

"I told Lissette not to get involved with you! Look at you! You can't even look me in the eye! You know what you did to my daughter! You bastard! Pendejo! Why? All she did was love you and you shit on her! Don't you come here looking for Lissette. She don't need you!"

Noah stared at her finger resentfully. Stared at it so hard, Ava took it down. His Spanish wasn't strong, but he knew she'd just called him an idiot like it was his name. His control started to unravel. The only reason he didn't totally flip on her was because he felt his boy standing quietly behind him.

"Okay, Ava. I understand you're upset, and I know you think I'm a shit, but you standin' here callin' me names ain't makin' the situation better. Now I'm gonna ask you again, real nice, okay? Ava, would you please tell me where Lissette is? Please?"

Ava's hand's returned to her hips and she looked at him with contempt. "Please? What you gonna do, Noah? Are you gonna lie and tell her how much you love her? Are you gonna pull a ring out of your pocket and ask Lissette to marry you? Are you?"

Noah stared at her. He was taking a lot of shit off this lady – even if she was right. Ava stepped up into his face.

"No, you listen, Noah. Leave her alone! You don't want her. If she wasn't pregnant, you wouldn't be here. You wouldn't give a shit. You don't care about how you broke her heart and how much you hurt her. You're probably only worried about the baby because you want to work something out so you don't have to take care of it."

Noah's mouth dropped open. "What? Look, lady, that baby is the only reason I'm here. I take care of my kids. Don't you accuse me of not steppin' up."

His tone was low and quiet. He'd just about had it. Ava looked at him pointedly.

"What about Lissette?"

Noah had a mean streak he wasn't particularly proud of, and it was rearing its ugly head. "What about her?"

"You're just gonna leave her pregnant and alone. I knew it! How could you do that?"

"Do what? I asked her not to go. She left me. This is what she wanted. As for bein' alone, she's not. She's got you guys. Think you can tell her to get in touch?"

Ava narrowed her eyes at him. "You're a bastard. Get off my stoop. Go away and don't come back!"

Noah smiled at her. "I been called a lot worse than that, Ava. You better tell your daughter to get in touch with me, or I will be back."

"Yeah? I'll call the cops!"

"I am the fuckin' cops. Just make sure she calls." Ava surprised him by reaching out with both hands and shoving him in the chest as hard as she could. She shoved him so hard, and he was so unprepared for it, she might have knocked him down if Lucas hadn't been standing behind him. Noah snapped. He grabbed her wrists. Lucas immediately tried to wedge himself between them, but Noah had Ava's wrists in a vise grip and he wasn't letting go. The lava spewed from the volcano.

"You put your hands on me?" He said, somewhere between an outraged question and a statement. Noah clamped his hands down and Ava cried out. "Don't you ever put your hands on me!"

Karma II

Lucas grabbed Noah's forearms and put his weight against him. "Noah, let her go."

He didn't want to get into a shoving match with Lucas, but he was in his way. He pushed him and Lucas pushed back. "I'm done takin' shit, Luke. Move!"

Lucas looked him in the eye. "I won't. Let her go, Noah." Lucas wasn't budging, so Noah leaned his head over and pulled Ava as close as Lucas being between them would allow.

"You listen to me. I didn't come here for this shit. You make sure you tell your crazy-ass daughter if I have to come back here and look for her, ain't nobody gonna be happy. You think I'm not here for my kid? Well, fuck you! That's the only fuckin' reason! Liz's ass is history. You just sealed that deal yourself, you bitch!"

He pushed her away from him, and her back hit the door jamb with great exaggeration.

Lucas turned him around and began to forcibly walk him away, while Ava cursed in Spanish.

"Bad scene, Noah. Walk away." Lucas walked so close to him, he couldn't turn around without pushing him out of the way.

When Noah reached his truck, Ava was still yelling and screaming on the stoop. "If you come back here, I'm callin' the cops!" She repeated. "I'll get a restraining order on you! You don't come to my house and push me around!"

Noah gave Lucas his keys and opened the door on the passenger side. He lit a cigarette and turned back to her. "You started that pushin' shit. Get your fuckin' restrainin' order. If you don't do what I told you to do, you'll fuckin' need it!"

Ava twisted her pretty face up and spit on the ground. "Asshole!"

Noah was a little shocked at her vehemence. He'd hardly ever been spit at before, but he never found it any less repugnant. He got back in his truck without replying and slouched in his seat.

"You okay?" Lucas asked, pulling into traffic.

"She spit at me."

"She spit on the ground, Noah."

"Same difference."

"I guess you're right. I think you should step away now, No. You said what you had to say."

Noah blew smoke out the side of his mouth and looked at Lucas. He wasn't trying to hear the voice of reason right now. He was furious. "I ain't said half of what I got to say. I made this visit 'cause I care about my kid. Ava treated me like some chump with no right to be there, pushin' on me and spittin' at me, like she lost her fuckin' mind. Man, I put bullets in niggas for less shit than that."

There was a hint of a smile on Lucas' face. "Yeah, you have. Leave it alone, No."

Noah finished his smoke and replayed his meeting with

Ava in his head. He looked over at Lucas. Lucas glanced at him. "Yeah, I know. I'm right."

Noah smirked. "Fuck you, Luke."

"Fuck you back."

"Thanks for comin' with me. If you weren't there, I'd still be shakin' the shit outta Ava."

Lucas laughed. "It's all good. Besides, your drama is a distraction from my drama."

Noah snickered. "Keith actin' up again?"

"Nah. Keith I can handle."

Noah was slightly disappointed. He wouldn't mind seeing Lucas kick Keith's ass again. Lucas was an excellent ass kicker. "So what is it? Nick?"

"Yeah. She asked me to marry her."

Noah raised an eyebrow and whistled low. "Wow. What brought that on?"

"I told her about Delilah. You know how women are. She was probably feeling extremely close to me."

Noah frowned. "You told her about Delilah? Damn, Luke, what made you do that?"

He smiled a genuine smile. Teeth and all. "I was feeling extremely close to her."

Noah smiled, too. "You feelin' her like that, Luke?"

"Uh-huh. Yeah, I think I am, maybe. Absolutely. Almost definitely."

Noah studied his friend with his usual skepticism. "Man, you talkin' out of both sides of your mouth. You scared?"

Lucas stopped smiling. "For obvious reasons, Noah."

Noah nodded. "Loud and clear."

They rode in silence for a spell. Noah might not have hand-picked Nick for Lucas, she was fine as hell, but she irritated Noah to no end. She was bossy, nosy and opinionated. She also ran her words together, like one long run-on sentence. She never took a breath. He personally, could take her in doses, but he also knew, in all fairness, that Nick treated him the way she did because she didn't want him hurting Leah. Leah appeared in his mind so

240

Karma II

vividly, he had to close his eyes. It was making his head hurt. Noah returned to the matter at hand.

"You gonna say yes?"

Lucas rubbed his hand over his beard and sighed. "I don't know. I want to. I feel like it's right."

"But?" Noah prodded him along.

"But there's too much shit going on, No. Unresolved shit."

"Yeah? Like what?"

"Like this case. Like Keith Childs."

"Later for Keith, Luke. He ain't important."

"I learned a long time ago not to sleep on people."

"You think he's layin' in the cut for you?"

Lucas glanced at him. "Come on, Noah. His ego won't let him just lay down and be quiet. He's gonna try to hurt me, I know it, and it's probably not even about Nicole anymore."

Noah's initial take on Keith was that he was a cowardly asshole who deserved the beat down he got. End of story. But if Lucas was feeling something a little more sinister coming from him, Noah would be the last person in the world to wave it off.

"If you need me to help you shut his ass down, let me know."

Lucas nodded, but his cell phone rang before he could comment. Visions of Simone bashing Justine's brains out danced through Noah's thoughts. He didn't want to think every woman Lucas fell for came with her own private lunatic. Brother deserved some peace. Lucas caught his attention. He was obviously talking to Griff.

"Not a problem. Don't bother, he's with me. We'll be right there." He hung up and looked over at Noah. "Griff wants to see us."

Noah made a small grunt of displeasure. He'd wanted to see his kids, but that seemed to be down the toilet now.

"He give you a reason?"

"Nope."

"Usual place?"

"No. different place. BBQ's downtown Brooklyn."

They slipped back into their usual companionable silence, eager to see what was in store for the Trinidad brothers.

They found Griff sitting at a table in the corner, talking into his Bluetooth and nursing a Heineken. He picked up the frosty bottle and took a swig, gesturing for them to sit with the same hand. They sat and waited five minutes for him to end his conversation.

"Sorry about that. Have a drink with me. I have news."

Griff beckoned for the waitress and took his Bluetooth off and deposited it in his pocket. Lucas sat back in his chair. "I take it that it's good news, since we're having a drink."

Griff smiled. "That's open to interpretation. It's progress, anyway. Amazing progress."

The waitress swung by and dropped off two more Heinekens. Noah looked at his in resignation. He picked it up, tasted it and grimaced. "So, what's the deal, Griff? You got us sittin' here drinkin' piss water on date night at the barbeque joint."

Griff laughed. "I must have spoiled your evening. Sorry. Anyway, we're not staying here," He looked at his watch. "We've got to be at the Promenade in 15 minutes. I've got someone I want you to talk to."

Lucas looked at his watch. "That ain't gonna happen unless we leave right now."

Griff stood and put a twenty on the table. "Let's go."

They left the restaurant and drove to the Promenade in virtual silence. They got out of the car and followed Griff to the balustrade. Dusk had come and gone. The bright sunny day had become a balmy June night.

"Here's our guy." Griff said, motioning behind Noah.

Noah turned his head. There was a guy walking toward them in black sweats and a white tee shirt. He was wearing a black Yankees cap and had an iPod plugged in his ears. He took the ear buds out as he approached them.

"Oh, shit." Lucas mumbled in quiet disbelief.

The sight of him shocked Noah. It was him, in the flesh. "Well, I'll be damned if it ain't Old Scratch." He mumbled back with the same amount of disbelief. Fucking Oscar Tirado!

Oscar's face broke into a wide grin. "You'll be damned? If it ain't Noah and Lucas! The fuckin' Bible Brothers! How's tricks? Locked up any cops lately?"

Lucas and Noah hadn't locked Oscar up themselves, but they'd had key roles in bringing about his downfall. When he went down, Oscar had fired off a shot that came so close to Noah's ear, he couldn't hear shit out of it for a week. It was the sting they were working on when Lucas met Justine. Noah narrowed his eyes at him.

Karma II

"Shot any?"

Oscar looked amused. "Nah. Not lately. How's your ear? Hearin' okay?"

Noah smiled and took a step toward him. "You could get your ass kicked for that shit, Oscar."

"Let's see you try." He stepped into his face so hard, they almost collided.

Griff stuck his arms between them, moving them away from each other. He looked at Lucas for help. All of a sudden, Lucas seemed to find the view of the water real interesting. He wasn't pulling Noah off Oscar. Oscar needed his ass kicked. Noah fell back, in deference to Griff, remembering what he'd said about loose cannon behavior. He knew his reputation preceded him. He knew people thought he had a smart mouth and a problem controlling his temper. He knew they said he shot first and asked questions later.

Noah smiled. All that shit was true, but Griff was leading this investigation and he wasn't trying to disrespect him, no matter how much he wanted to punch Oscar in the face.

"You guys have to control yourselves. I can't have you going at each other," He looked at Oscar. "Remember, you made a deal. You're out conditionally. If you choose to be disruptive and not follow through, you can go right back."

Oscar didn't look happy about it, but he retreated.

"What are the conditions?" Lucas asked.

"The exact conditions of Mr. Tirado's release are not relevant to this meeting, Lucas." Griff replied, evasively "He's here to give us some information to help us decide the best way to proceed with the takedown. That's all."

"Is that a direct quote from the Fed manual? We don't need him for that." Lucas came back at him.

Karma II

Noah was surprised. Snide was his department. Griff chose to ignore Lucas' attitude. "Tirado knows where the drugs are. We'll use the information he gives up for seizure. He also has insider knowledge about how, where, and when they process and move. He's a gold mine. Mr. Tirado will help us close this investigation in half the time and knock out at least two other crews at the same time."

Noah stuck a cigarette in the corner of his mouth, he lit it and squinted through the smoke at Oscar. "Okay, good. Start singin'."

Oscar laughed. "What, I don't get a drink before I let you fuck me?"

"I'm sure the DEA slipped you a little tongue first. That's all the foreplay you need." Lucas said, dryly.

They stayed at the Promenade with Oscar Tirado for over an hour. When they left, they had a king's ransom of information about millions of dollars worth of heroin, cocaine, marijuana and ecstasy. There were crews they'd kept an eye on for years that were nothing but extensions of Draco. Their empire was huge and far reaching. The

Trinidad brothers evil, inky, tentacles of drugs, murder and degeneration were spreading quickly into three other states. With the info Oscar gave them, Draco and its festering little offshoots were about to get a stake right through the heart... if Oscar was telling the truth.

Karma II

Chapter Twenty-Two

They popped Cherry

This was taking forever, Leah thought to herself. The longer this sting took, the scarier it got. She wasn't running and screaming scared, it was a low and building terror. These guys were violently out of their minds. Leah had seen some crazy stuff since she'd started hanging with the Trinidad brothers. Skin crawling, nightmare inducing, murderous stuff. Leah shuddered and went into the powder room down the hall from the kitchen. She closed the door and washed her hands like she was about to perform brain surgery.

The afternoon had been grueling. Tate and Troy told Noah and Lucas they had some people they wanted them to meet. They'd taken a ride out to Newark, and Troy had become a homicidal maniac. Leah felt the bile rise in her throat as the image of Troy taking the guy's scalp off flashed through her mind.

These motherfuckers were crazy. She traced her fingers lightly over the wire she was wearing. If they found it, she was dead. There was a soft double knock on the door and it swung open before she could get scared. Noah stepped soundlessly inside, with his finger to his lips. He got real close to her, in all his fine-ass splendor. Noah's hand slipped beneath her blouse and he put his thumb over the microphone of the wire. He leaned down and put his mouth close to her ear.

"You okay?" He asked, his voice so low, she could barely hear him. He smelled like cinnamon, tobacco and the light cologne he wore.

Leah's heart was hammering in her chest, but not from the atrocious thing Troy had done. It was Noah. She nodded, weak in the knees. Noah looked at her like he didn't believe her.

"You sure?" He asked, whispering in her ear again.

She shivered, though his breath was incredibly warm. "Noah, what are you doing in here? What if they come looking for you?"

Noah seemed unfazed. "Luke's got my back. You didn't look too good when Troy did his thing, you know."

Leah smiled. "You were worried about me?"

Noah's face changed. He frowned like he was furious with her, then he did the oddest thing. He ran his fingers through her short hair and let his hand settle on the nape of her neck. "Leah, why are you doin' this shit to me?"

Leah's head went back like he'd slapped her. No, he didn't! Rolling up on her and grabbing the back of her neck? Oh, hell to the no!

"Noah, what the hell-"

His mouth was on hers, stopping her mid-sentence. He kissed her soft and slow, like he missed her. His hand moved from her neck to her face. His tongue moved over hers like a slow dance. Noah had never kissed her like that before. Her breath hitched and a tear slid down her cheek. Leah put her arms around his neck and kissed him back with just as much quiet passion.

"Been away too long. I gotta get back." He said, breaking contact, briefly.

Leah opened her mouth to speak, and he kissed her again. Shorter this time, but with that same sweetness. Noah took her hand, replaced his thumb with hers on the open mike, and moved to the door. Before he opened it, he turned back to her.

"It's gonna get ugly in a minute. Today was nothin'."

She smiled a little. "Noah,"

He put his hand up and stopped her. "Don't do that. I don't want talk about it right now. Soon, maybe."

"Alright, Noah."

Noah put his hand down and finally offered a small smile of his own. "Okay. If you need me, I'm right here, Leah."

She nodded as another tear fell. "I'll remember that."

He gave her that rakish grin she'd been waiting for. "You better."

Karma II

He said and slipped out the door. She couldn't stop smiling, despite the horrors of the day. She now knew she had a much better shot with Noah than she'd thought. Leah waited a few minutes to make sure Noah was gone, then she went down the hall to the library where everyone was having a cocktail and smoking cigars. She entered on the ass end of what Troy was saying.

"You nip it in the bud, man. Fuckin' traitor's gotta pay."

Noah put his drink down and leaned toward him. "Fine. Then you put a bullet in his forehead and call it a day. Ain't no need to take the top of a man's head off."

"I think it's an effective deterrent. I really don't think he'll be cutting up again." Lucas said, pointing his cigar at Noah.

Noah looked back at him darkly. "You would say that."

Lucas gave him a bright smile. "Yeah, I would."

Tate narrowed his eyes and looked at him cautiously. "My brother's known for being a bit of a sadist. Are you one as well, Ray?"

Lucas never even blinked. "Not really. Torture's a last resort, but it gets the point across."

Noah smiled. "So does one between the eyes. Pop 'em quick and wash your hands."

Tate puffed his cigar luxuriously. "We don't bother. Our hands will never be clean."

Nick walked into the room and went straight to Tate. "You need to be at Façade in an hour. The contractor wants your final approval and his check."

Tate put a hand on the small of her back and smiled. "Not even a hello? Tiffany, you treat me badly."

Nick shrugged and removed his hand. "That's your last appointment of the day. Do you still need me?"

"No. You're free to go. I'll see you in the morning."

Karma II

Nick nodded and turned on her heel. She looked Leah in the eye long enough for Leah to know something was up, but not long enough to catch anyone's attention. Tate knocked the ash off his cigar and crossed his legs.

"Tiffany's always running off. I try to get to know her better, but she won't have it."

"Probably got a man at home, Tate," Troy said, taking a swig of his drink. He looked at Lucas. "I wouldn't mind hittin' that, though, know what I'm sayin', Ray?"

Lucas laughed and gave him dap, the smile not quite touching his eyes. "I heard. Lucky bastard."

Leah smiled to herself and left the room. Troy didn't know the half. She went into the kitchen and found Nick waiting for her. She silently beckoned for Leah to follow her through the back hallway, into the maid's quarters. Nick stopped outside Cherry's door.

"Brace yourself," she said, quietly, and opened the door. The first thing that hit Leah was the heavy, coppery, scent of blood. She stepped into the room behind Nick as she switched on the lights.

Leah blinked as her eyes adjusted and her heart sank. "Oh, Cherry." She whispered, as she took in the scene before her. "Oh, God."

Nick nodded grimly. "Yeah. Those guys are fucking monsters. I wonder which one did it?"

Leah frowned. "No telling. She's still wearing her scalp, maybe it was Tate."

Nick slipped on a pair of Playtex gloves she boosted from the kitchen. "I was leaning that way myself. Come look."

Nick walked over to the bed where Cherry was sprawled on her back. Her head was hanging over the edge, so her face was obscured, but you could see that her body was covered with stab wounds. At least eight that Leah counted. The obvious murder weapon was sticking out of her chest with the handle snapped off. The simple cotton nightgown she wore was pushed rudely up past her breasts, so that her entire body was exposed, her legs spread wide. There was little doubt that there'd been some sexual activity. Nick put her hand under Cherry's head and lifted one of her eyelids with the other.

"She's frozen. Full rigor. Eyes are cloudy."

She paused and lifted Cherry's shoulder up off the bed. Leah moved closer to get a better look at the dark mottled stain that covered her back. When someone dies, the blood pools to the lowest point, and Cherry was on her back.

"Lividity." Leah said, quietly.

"Yeah. Looks like she's been dead since last night. Fucker killed her, then went on about his business, like she didn't matter."

Nick took the gloves off and folded them into each other. Leah looked down at Cherry. Poor Cherry. Cherry had tried to warn her out of being here. Shit, with good reason. Leah looked at Nick.

"What do you want to do?"

Nick whipped out her cell phone and started taking

pictures. "If you're miked, they've got everything. These pictures will help. Nothing else we can really do right now."

She was right. Any other action could ruin the sting. Leah looked at Cherry's blood splashed on the walls like some gruesome tapestry. She shook her head, noting the cruelty of the broken knife sticking out of her chest. There were dried tears on her face. Leah could almost see Troy smiling maniacally with every blow of the knife.

Sudden movement outside the door snapped her back to reality. Leah had her gun off her ankle and in her hand before she could think about it. The door opened slowly, and Tamiko stepped inside, looking small, dazed and brutalized. Her left eye was swollen almost shut, and the cheek was bruised and scraped. She was crying.

"He killed my friend."

"Who killed her?" Leah asked, as she and Nick both tucked their guns back where they had gotten them.

"Tate. Tate did it. Tate killed Cherry." She was slurring her words badly.

"Are you on something?" Nick asked. Leah raised Tamiko's eyebrow with her thumb. Her pupil was dilated.

"What did you take?" Leah asked, shaking her a little.

"Some stuff. Some pills for the pain. Tate killed Cherry."

"Okay, honey. We got that," Nick said. She looked over her head at Leah. "Let's get her out of here." They ran into Tobias and Smitty in the hallway, obviously here to get rid of the body. They saw them and drew together, making the hallway impassable.

"What are you doing back here? What's wrong with Tamiko?" Tobias demanded. Tamiko flinched away from him.

"Don't you touch me! I fell. I fell down the stairs!"

"What?" He attempted to pull her away from Leah

and Nick, but Tamiko surprised everyone by shrugging them off and running down the hallway, screaming at the top of her lungs. Leah exchanged a glance with Nick, as Smitty and Tobias went after her. They all followed her out of the servants' quarters, Tamiko still screaming like she was crazy.

She made it to the kitchen where Smitty grabbed her, but she kicked and flailed so hysterically he let her go. She spun around and ran out into the main part of the house screaming like a lunatic. Her screams were so loud they bounced off the walls and reverberated through the house. She was shrieking so loud, Leah was late realizing Nick was yelling, too.

"Stop screaming! Stop running, Tamiko! Stop!"

The door to the library flew open and Tate stepped out like he was the leader of the

free world. Tamiko braked hard, dropped, and skidded on her ass right in front of him. She cowered and cringed, but she pointed her finger.

Karma II

"You killed her! You bastard!" She turned and realized Lucas, Noah, and Troy were standing behind him.

"He did it! Tate did it! He killed my friend! He raped her, then he killed her, and he did it because she was my friend!"

Tate stared down at her. He reached for her and she pushed away from him with her heels. "No! No! Get away! I hate you, Tate, I swear to God I do!"

Tate chuckled and grabbed her up by the scruff of her neck like she was a kitten. "Nonsense." He said, barely above a whisper. Everyone was shocked again when Tamiko brought her hand across his face like a claw.

Troy laughed out loud. "Uh-oh! The bitch finally snapped!" He jeered.

Tate drew back his hand to hit her, Lucas grabbed it and Noah pushed Tamiko behind his body. "Whoa, man. Chill, baby." Noah said, frowning at him.

Tamiko had left four scratches on Tate's cheek. He

wiped at it with his hand and looked at the blood on his fingers. Tate smiled and turned to Lucas. "Take your hand off me, please."

Lucas tossed his hand away like it was something nasty, a mixture of anger and disgust on his face. Tate laughed and gestured to Tobias and Smitty.

"Take her upstairs. Get her out of my sight."

Noah stepped in front of him. "Not today." He said, emphatically. A hint of a smile shimmered across his lips, but not in amusement, it was more like a challenge. Leah felt a knot in her stomach.

Tate picked up the gauntlet. "You're not going to prove to be a problem, are you Craig? Let's not forget, we've got a very big deal about to go through in a few days. Let's not sever ties over something as simple as this."

Noah laughed softly. "Simple as this, huh? I don't see what's so simple about this. Maybe you can tell me, Tate, 'cause all I'm seein' right now is a small woman with two different eyes and a fat lip."

Lucas, meanwhile, had reclaimed his cool. "What's simple about it, Craig, is the fact that none of this shit concerns us."

Lucas looked at him evenly, with ice in his eyes. He talked to Noah straight without going far enough to blow their cover. "You and I both know exactly why we're here. Let these people settle their own domestic disputes. We're not here to referee, Craig. I can feel you about family ties, man, but this is too much money. I ain't takin' shorts for this. Let it go."

Noah did not look pleased. "This is some bullshit, Ray."

Lucas nodded in concession. "Maybe, but don't shoot yourself in the foot and hurt your pockets over something that has nothing to do with you."

Leah breathed a sigh of relief as she watched the distaste of backing down wash over Noah's face. He stepped away from Tamiko without a word and walked away.

"Where you goin', Craig? Stay and fight!" Troy called after him, chuckling.

Noah walked right out the front door. Tate turned to Lucas, smiling his darkly sparkling smile. "Well done, Ray."

Lucas looked at Tamiko, who was standing with her head down, hugging herself. Though she was silent, her tears were falling so hard they were splashing on the floor. Lucas fixed his gaze on Tate and spoke very low.

"I don't condone the shit you do, but like they say, cash rules everything around me. I'll talk to Craig. Your shipment will be there but," he paused and looked back at Tamiko, then he returned to Tate, "I don't want to see this again, Tate. This is some sloppy, disrespectful shit. I'll be in touch."

Lucas turned to go and Tamiko touched his arm. She looked up at him with beseeching eyes. Pleading with him silently. "Ray…"

It came out as a sob and Lucas let the ice drop out of his eyes. "Don't worry, honey. You'll survive."

He walked out the door in search of Noah. Troy whooped his crazy man laugh.

"See! That's what I'm talkin' 'bout! I love that nigga. He straight gangster with his shit." Tate failed to share Troy's opinion or his amusement.

"Shut up, Troy. Take Tobias and Smitty and bring the Mercedes around."

Troy screwed his face up and gestured toward Leah. "Why ain't she drivin'?"

"She and Tiffany are going to stay here and babysit Tamiko while we're gone," He turned to address them. "I don't want her out of your sight. She'll calm down soon enough, but until then, you make sure she doesn't leave this house."

"Understood." Leah replied. Nick nodded her head to show that she also understood. Tate looked at them carefully, then turned to go, followed by Troy Tobias and Smitty. Leah heard Tobias speak as they exited the house.

"What about Cherry? Don't you want her out of here?"

Leah could hear the smile in Tate's voice. "She'll keep." He said, and closed the door behind him.

Leah looked at Nick. "You thinking what I'm thinking?"

"Damn straight. Let's get her out of here." Leah put an arm around Tamiko and followed Nick upstairs.

"Where's Christian, sweetie?"

"He's with my mom. Are you really gonna get me out of here?"

"Yeah. Now get what you need, we've got to hurry." That seemed to light a fire under her. Leah let go of her and they trailed her into the master suite, and watched her as she gathered her essentials and packed them in a large Prada bag. Nick looked around.

"Where's the dog?" Tamiko put on her Fendi shades and threw the bag over her shoulder.

"Fuck the dog. Let's go."

They went back downstairs and were about to leave. "I almost forgot," Tamiko said.

She threw open the doors to the library and went straight to Tate's desk. She opened the drawer and took out three disc files. Tamiko handed Nick the discs.

"Offshore and Swiss accounts. Make it hurt."

Nick put the discs in her pocket and nodded. "Don't worry, we will."

They left the house quickly and got into Leah's car. "Okay. Where to?" Leah asked Nick.

"I didn't think that far ahead. Let me call Griff."

Leah didn't want to sit and wait for instructions. She started driving, while Nick called Griff. When Leah stopped for a light at the corner, Tony got out of a Park's Department truck and walked over to her. Leah rolled her window down and he handed her a piece of paper.

"That's a safe house. Griff says take her there now. We'll see you there."

He walked away from the car and got back in the truck. Leah started driving.

Karma II

Chapter Twenty-Three

Dirty deeds

Keith sat in a back booth of a titty bar in the East Village and waited for his company. He'd been nursing a gin and tonic for the past 20 minutes. Dude was running late and the waitress was starting to look at him salty.

It had been a long time since he'd seen Oscar Tirado. Last time he'd seen him, he'd been on his way to a forever bid. Now, here he was, back in the world, like a fucking miracle. When Oscar got sent up, Keith was almost certain he'd find a way out of it. Lo and behold, he had.

Keith was watching the current dancer do her thing. She had a mean pole dance. The waitress appeared at his elbow. "You waitin' for somethin' to grow up outta that glass, or are you gonna order another one?"

Keith looked down. He hadn't realized he'd finished his drink, but he didn't appreciate her smart remark. He took his time looking her up and down before he answered.

"I'm minding my business, honey. Move along."

Keith took a closer look and licked his lips. Honey was fine. She noticed the look and dropped the frost out of her voice, even smiled.

"So, you want another one, playa? Maybe something else?"

Keith smiled back. "Maybe later, boo. Hold off on the drink. I'm waiting for someone." She winked at him. "Holla when you're ready."

She walked away shaking her ass. He was looking at the door when Oscar walked in dressed in mint green linen and matching gator shoes. He wore a very subtle, but effective, diamond watch and a fresh cut. He wasn't alone. He had two very big dudes with him. Oscar smiled when he saw Keith and motioned for his boys to stay at the bar. Oscar grinned and walked over with an exaggerated gangster swagger. Keith laughed and stood up. He applauded and greeted him with a bear hug.

Karma II

"Damn, man, look at you! It's like you're back from the dead and you never missed a beat." Oscar laughed.

"Funny you said that, 'cause that's what it feels like, and believe me, I never did."

They sat and ordered drinks, then talked for a while.

"It wasn't all that bad. Just about everybody up there was terrified to fuck with me."

"No doubt." Keith replied, knowing Oscar was telling the truth. Respect he didn't have on his own, he had through his other connections. He had always been the dirtiest cop Keith knew.

"So, what happened? How'd you manage to get out?"

"It just so happens, the Feds got a hard-on for the Trinidad brothers. They're tryin' to take 'em down as we speak."

Keith knew Tate and Troy very well. He was privy to the outcome of previous attempts at shutting them down, and was surprised they would even bother to try again.

"Ah... I see. That's major news."

"I thought so, too. Anyway, they want me to give 'em up, turn state's evidence, and provide them with financial information and trafficking connections, you know, major suppliers, low level dealers, turf domain, stuff like that." He said it all so nonchalantly.

Keith narrowed his eyes and looked at him. "Don't tell me you're gonna comply?"

Oscar waved his hand lazily in a dismissive gesture. "Relax. You know me better than that. Let's just say I threw them a bone to get my get out of jail free card."

Keith started to shake his head slowly and Oscar threw his hands up and smiled. "What's the look for, Keith? I didn't do nothin' to nobody that wouldn't have happened eventually."

Keith looked at him hard. "So you gave up Draco?"

Oscar laughed. "I wouldn't exactly say that. I gave up what Tate and Troy would have gotten rid of themselves. A few runners, a couple of factories, some places where they do their laundering. You gotta be real about this shit, Keith. They were gonna burn themselves out sooner or later."

Karma II

Keith's look turned shrewd. "You don't have to justify shit to me, Oscar."

"Gettin' in with the Trinidads was necessary. We made a lot of cash together, but I never intended to hold ties with them forever. I'm not indebted, and I'm not necessarily loyal, but I feel like I need to give them a heads up."

Keith finished his drink. He remembered his first deals with Oscar, being on the pad, and shaking people down. Oscar had become a big player while never quitting his day job. Keith had never become quite as large, because he had absolutely no desire to go to jail, but Oscar always looked out and made sure Keith got his gravy. Oscar had always ridden both sides of the fence. One foot in as a decorated NYPD detective, the other firmly in the street as one of the dirtiest cops in his lifetime.

"Why are you giving them a heads up?"

Oscar smiled at him with an evil glint in his eye. "It's revenge I'm lookin' for."

"Revenge? Against who?"

Oscar finished his drink and looked into his empty glass. "I met with the DEA on the Promenade in Brooklyn, Griffin is his name. Guess who he had with him?"

"I'm not really in the mood for guessing, Oscar."

"A couple of first-grade detectives, whose actions and sworn testimony, helped to bring about the downfall of yours truly."

Keith smiled. "Cain and Ramsey got Draco?"

"Yep. Lucky me, huh?"

Keith laughed. "Lucky us. I got a get-back for those motherfuckers myself."

"Yeah? How come?"

The smile left Keith's face. "I got my reasons."

Oscar studied him as he sipped his drink. "So what's up with you, Keith? How's Nicky?"

Keith shrugged. "I don't know. These days I guess

Karma II you'd have to ask Lucas Fucking Cain."

Oscar's mouth dropped open. "What? You're shittin' me, right? Are you sayin' you let Cain take your woman?"

Keith was instantly annoyed. "Fuck him. All he's got are my leftovers. Sloppy seconds."

Oscar snickered. "Sloppy seconds? Every man should be that lucky. I guess she finally got tired of you bullshit. But how'd she end up with Cain?"

"I don't know. I guess she's on the Draco case. I don't think she knew him before."

Oscar gave him a magnanimous shrug. "Well, look at it this way, my friend, those boys have always been high on a lot of women's wish lists. If your woman left you, at least she left you for Lucas Cain."

Oscar looked him in the eye and laughed with great delight, "I can't believe you let Cain walk off with your woman! Did you at least kick his ass?"

Oscar's hilarity was pissing Keith off. Nicky was a sore enough spot for him without adding the humiliation he'd suffered at the hands of Cain. He'd scrapped with him twice and each time he'd dusted Keith's ass like dirt off his collar. He was undecided about what he hated him more for, kicking his ass or fucking his woman. He looked at Oscar and tried to keep the resentment for his remarks out of his face.

"We ended the relationship before she met him."

"Who ended it? My money's on Nicky."

"It doesn't matter."

"You're right," Oscar said," It doesn't matter. The only thing that matters is for Cain and Ramsey to reap what they sowed when they got my ass sent up, and Cain gets an extra scoop of disaster for stealin' your woman."

"He didn't steal her."

Oscar smiled. "Whatever you say, old friend. When this jumps off, I'm taking my ass down to Costa Rica. That's where I got my set up. If this shit gets too hot, you come, too. You may have no choice."

Karma II

Keith smiled. An escape hatch was always necessary. "Sounds like a plan."

"Great, then break out your cell and hit Tate." Keith raised an eyebrow.

"You want to do it now?"

"No time like the present. The sooner we move, the more time Tate has to lay in the cut for Cain and Ramsey."

"You got a point."

Keith hit Tate's number. It was ringing when Oscar looked at Keith and laughed. "About Nicky, it could always be worse. If it had been Ramsey, not only would he have taken your woman, he would have talked cold cash shit to you about it."

Chapter Twenty-Four

The last supper

Nadine had never been this nervous around Noah in her life. She'd asked him to meet her for an early dinner and here he was. To her dismay, his mind was somewhere else. Noah was so preoccupied, he wasn't even eating. Nadine took a sip of her drink and tried to find out what was eating at him.

"What's wrong, Lover? Something on your mind?"

Nadine was so shocked at the annoyance in the look he gave her, her neck snapped back. "Did I do something wrong?" She asked.

Noah turned his eyes to his plate and fiddled with his fork. "I got a lot of things goin' on right now, Nadine." He looked back up at her with his beautiful gray eyes. "What, exactly, was it that you needed to see me for? Alone?"

Nadine noted the subtle hostility in his voice. He was looking at her with that snarky little smirk he wore when he thought he wasn't going to like what he was about to hear.

"You seem a little tight. What, exactly, is going on with you?"

Noah leaned forward with his elbows on the table and stared at her for a long time.

"Noah? What is it?"

Noah sat back in his chair, staring at her coldly. A small smile touched his lips. "Go ahead, Nadine. Play your ace in the hole."

"What are you talking about, Noah?"

He smiled, but it wasn't one of his nice smiles. It was a pissed smile. Oh God, he knew!

"Don't look scared now, Nadine. You had nerves of steel until now."

Nadine stared at her plate and wrung her hands in her lap. "Noah-"

Noah chuckled again, a dry little non-amused sound. "C'mon, Nadine. Don't cave in and start actin' like a girl. Show me your balls."

"Noah, I think-"

Noah cut her off sharply.

"You think what, Nadine? You think you can walk into this restaurant, lookin' the way you do, and I wouldn't know? You look like you swallowed the goddamned sun! You think I don't know when you're pregnant?"

"I didn't… No, I didn't think you'd notice."

As soon as the words were out of her mouth she regretted them. Noah leaned forward, his eyes were storm clouds.

"You didn't think I'd notice? I get paid to notice shit, Nadine! That was your plan all along, right? To force me to choose, right?"

"No. It wasn't like that at all."

"No? Then what was it like, Nadine?" His voice was escalating.

"You think I can't see the fucking trap you set for me?

Huh?"

Nadine glanced around, nervously. People were staring right at them. She almost jumped out of her seat when Noah slammed his fist on the table so hard his water glass fell off and exploded on the floor.

"Look at me when I'm talkin' to you, Nadine! Goddamn it! How could you put me in a position like this?"

Noah hit the table in frustration. Silverware skittered and teetered over the edge of the table. "Goddamn it! Goddamn it, Nadine! You of all people! I never thought in a million years you'd fuck me like this! Goddamn it! Goddamn you!"

He stood up and ran his hands through his hair. He was so angry she could see the pulse pounding in his neck.

"Noah," She said, in a soothing voice, "Please, honey, sit down and lower your voice."

Noah laughed bitterly. "Man, fuck these people, Nadine!" He took his wallet out and threw money on the table.

She never thought Noah would flip out like this. He was supposed to be happy and come home. She stepped around the table and touched his arm.

"Noah, this isn't the way you think it is. You have to listen to me. Please, Noah."

Noah removed her hand from his arm and shook his head. "Uhuh. I ain't gotta do shit. You set me up, Nadine. You set me up."

Noah walked out of the restaurant, leaving Nadine standing there with her mouth hanging open. Panic got her moving. She caught up with him at his truck.

"Noah! Please, baby, don't go like this. Let's talk."

"Talk? What the fuck are we gonna talk about, Nadine? You gonna try and convince me you didn't plan this shit?"

"Noah, I didn't!" She sobbed.

Noah was unaffected by her tears. He stuck his finger in her face. "You did! What is this shit about, anyway? Do

Karma II

you want me back that bad, or is it revenge? What the fuck is it, Nadine?"

Revenge? Revenge had never even crossed her mind. She just didn't want to lose him forever. She didn't want to lose him to some chick he was bound to by a child. Noah was bound to her! Noah was supposed to be hers forever, and she would fight to keep it that way.

"You don't understand. I wasn't trying to trap you. Baby, I love you. I just wanted you back. I want you to come home."

"I do understand!" Noah yelled at her, pointing his accusing finger. "I understand that I asked you if you were still on the pill, and you said yes. I understand that you fuckin' lied to me, Nadine! You flat out lied to me, with your plottin', schemin' ass! I can't fuckin' believe you!"

Oh, no he didn't. "You never flat out lied to me, Noah? You never plotted and schemed? I recall you doing just that, so be careful of how you throw the word liar around, while you stand there in your righteous indignation."

Noah stared at her for a second then looked away. Nadine knew she hadn't thrust the dagger in the dragon's eye, but she'd damn sure broke the skin.

"Okay." He said, quietly.

"I'm not trying to hurt you, Noah. I just want you back."

Noah raised an eyebrow. "So you did do it on purpose."

Okay. This was it. Lying wasn't her forte. "Yes, I did. Don't hate me because I love you. Don't bend this into what you need it to be so you can deal with it. I've always loved you, Noah. The divorce was your punishment for your infidelity. I have never put you out of my heart, Noah. I was hoping extreme measures would change you, but I was wrong. I can't change you, Noah. You have to change yourself. It's not my place to pick you apart and try to figure out why you tick the way you do. All I can do is love you anyway. When you told me that woman was pregnant, not only did it hurt me, it scared me. It made me panic, because finally, here was some real competition. I don't know what you feel for her, and to be honest, I'm not very concerned about that."

Nadine paused and stepped into his line of vision. "I will not let Lissette take you away from me, Noah, I will not do it. We were meant to end up together, Noah."

That accusing finger was at it again, and Noah was frowning at her. "Wait a minute. You're tellin' me you divorced me to punish me? You put me on punishment?"

Nadine was surprised by the question. "Yes. Yes, I did, Noah. You deserved it."

He shook his head. "That's fucked up, Nadine."

"I love you, Noah, and I know you love me. Come home to your family."

Noah ran his hand through his hair and looked at her. "How far along are you?"

Ah, a breakthrough. "About six weeks."

Noah sighed and Nadine wasn't thrilled by the look on his face. He looked unhappy. "You're fuckin' me, Nadine."

"I'm not."

He looked her dead in the eye. "You are." Noah looked at his watch. "I got a meetin' in an hour."

"I understand."

Noah smirked. "No, you don't. All you can think about, right now, is yourself."

"Noah, that's not true, baby. I'm thinking about us."

Noah laughed a fed up little chuckle. "Us? Yeah, right. Thanks, Nadine."

He turned to get in his truck and Nadine stepped between him and the door. Noah cocked his head. "What's the matter? You want me to put you back on the seat?"

Nadine looked at him coldly. "Don't you talk to me like I'm one of your whores, Noah, how dare you?"

Noah looked at her sharply and stepped in real close. "Who you talkin' to?"

Nadine bravely closed the distance between them. He might talk big, but she knew Noah would never violently put his hands on her.

"I'm talking to you. That was more than disrespectful and I won't tolerate you speaking to me like that, you hear? You better respect me, Noah Ramsey."

Noah let his breath out like he'd been holding it in. He reached past her for the handle on his truck and Nadine moved into him, putting her arms around his waist and pressing her body against his. Noah sighed as his body responded to hers. Nadine smiled to herself and reveled in that small power she had over him.

"We'll work this out, Daddy. Don't worry."

Noah laughed, gently pushed her away from him, and opened the door to his Escalade. "You know what, Nadine? Maybe God will work this shit out. I got somethin' real heavy goin' down tomorrow, if I'm lucky, maybe I'll catch a bullet in the forehead and He'll put me outta my misery."

Nadine was shocked. "Noah, don't say stuff like that out loud! Don't even put it in the universe."

He got into his truck and closed the door. "Don't stress yourself. Your name's still on all my shit.

Somethin' happens to me, you're sittin' pretty. You and my gang of kids."

Nadine pursed her lips to keep from blurting out something she'd regret later.

"See ya later, Sweetie. I gotta punch my time card."

Nadine stepped back and looked at him. Even after the divorce, she'd still cringe and hold her breath whenever the news said a cop was injured or dead. Nadine would pray it wasn't Noah and she was never okay until she heard his voice.

"You be careful." She said, seriously.

Noah lit his smoke and turned the ignition. "You bet. I gotta keep my balls attached so you and Liz can rip 'em off later."

"Just be careful, Noah. I love you."

"I'll try. See ya, Nadine."

Karma II

Chapter Twenty-Five

Where there's smoke, there's fire

Lucas sat behind the wheel of the fancy, unmarked BMW with Noah riding shotgun. The sudden and unplanned removal of Tamiko from the Trinidad mansion had changed the game completely. Lucas glanced into the rearview at the black Lexus that trailed him. Mack and Foster, two DEA agents, were riding with the drugs. Griff wasn't fucking around with Tate and Troy. The current shipment was not intended to change hands. They were to take them down immediately after they made the deal.

They were on their way to Façade now. Lucas had never been a nervous man, and it had taken him a while to figure out exactly what it was that he was feeling. At first he thought it was adrenaline, but then his stomach had flipped over and gone flat. Then it hit him like someone had just turned the lights on. It was dread. He hadn't felt any feeling this strong since the countdown to Justine's death. Lucas felt like something really bad was about to happen.

He looked over at Noah. Noah was low in his seat, face pointed toward his hands. He appeared to be sleeping, but Lucas could see that his eyes were open behind his dark sunglasses.

"Noah?"

He turned his head Lucas' way. "Yeah?"

"You okay?"

"Nadine's pregnant."

Lucas' shoulders slumped. He looked over at Noah and quickly tamed the urge to hit him. Noah looked back at him, then turned his head toward the window.

"I know, Luke. Don't say it."

Lucas was severely pissed at Noah. He'd told him. Fuck it. Noah would tell you himself he didn't change. All Lucas could do was be his friend.

"You need to talk this shit out?"

"Not right now. Ain't really shit to say."

Lucas was quick to agree. "Nope."

"I fucked up, Luke."

"We all fuck up, No."

"Yeah, but-"

"But nothin', bro. We all do. Get your mind off it. You don't need it in the way. Right now, you need to be on your game. No distractions."

"I know it," He said. "It ain't just that, Luke. I don't feel right. I feel off."

Lucas frowned and glanced at him. "You feel off, or does this deal feel off?"

Noah frowned, too. "It's the deal. Definitely the deal. Bad vibes, Luke."

"Uh-huh. Bad vibes."

Noah faced forward and ran his hand over his mouth. They were a block away from Façade.

"Hey, Luke?" Lucas stopped at the red light and they looked at each other.

"Yeah?"

"Nothin'. Never mind. Light's green."

They looked at each other a second longer, then Lucas drove the last block to the club. There was an almost tangible feeling of unease in the car.

Noah read his mind. "It's mutual. Probably Griff and Myers fault, with all that be careful death talk shit they spoon fed us."

"Probably. You good?"

"Not really, but my knees ain't knockin'."

"Mine either, but I still feel a little weird. Safety's off?"

"Damn straight." They both checked their weapons and took off the safety's in unison.

"I got your back, Noah."

"And you know I've got yours. Let's do this."

They dapped each other and got out of the car. Mack and Foster emerged from the Lexus and joined them, carrying two extra large duffel bags. Lucas looked across the street at the Federal Express truck that held Griff, Nicole and Leah. Tony, Vic and Nate were in there, too. Further up the block was an Academy bus with the windows tinted black, that was full of Feds, joined by officers and detectives from the NYPD Narcotics Enforcement Unit. He turned back to the business at hand.

Karma II

"Everybody ready?" Lucas asked, looking at everybody at once. No response.

"Let's go, then." Noah said.

He turned on his heel and walked toward the entrance to Façade. Tate had a giant posted at the door. Brother had to be at least 350 pounds, and he was easily four inches taller than Lucas. Noah tilted his head and raised an eyebrow. "Look at this fat motherfucker." He said, under his breath.

He rapped on the glass with his knuckles and big boy lumbered over to the door with the screw face on and cracked it open. "Who the hell are you?" He asked with an excessive amount of bass in his voice.

Noah looked at him like he had a horn in the middle of his giant head. "Who the hell am I? my name's Craig McCoy," He gestured to Lucas, "This is my business associate, Ray Black. We're here to see Tate and Troy. Now open up the fuckin' door, Sluggo, and step aside."

His eyes widened, then narrowed at the insult, but he moved a lot faster than Noah or Lucas thought possible. He was also very apologetic. "I'm sorry, Mr. McCoy. I didn't realize,"

Noah held his hand up and silenced him with a look. "Tell your story walkin'. Where's Tate?"

"Give me a minute, Mr. McCoy, and I'll have Smitty escort you back."

Noah looked at his watch. "Time is money, Sluggo."

"Yes, sir." He got on the phone and made a quick call. Smitty appeared, wearing his own 9 mm.

"Afternoon, gentlemen. Mr. Tate and Mr. Troy are waiting in the office. Follow me." They followed Smitty to Tate's inner sanctum.

Smitty opened the door and Lucas wasn't surprised to find Tate wasn't alone. Troy was there, too, of course, and the loyal Tobias, but the room also held six members of their personal goon squad. Enforcers. Tate stood from behind his antique mahogany desk and spread his arms with a smile. "Craig, Ray, it's truly a pleasure to see you this afternoon."

"Likewise." Noah said. Lucas nodded and looked at Troy, who was perched on the edge of Tate's desk like a fucking gargoyle. Troy looked back at him. His eyes seemed void of everything.

"Tobias, get the champagne," Tate said, opening his humidor. "You gentlemen care for a Cuban?"

Noah begged off. "No, thanks. We're good."

"No? Then you must have a celebratory glass of champagne with us. This should be toasted, am I not right?"

"As rain," Noah replied with a smile. "Sure, Tate, we'll drink with you."

Tobias poured the flutes of champagne as Smitty handed them out. Tate made small talk. "Have you heard from Tamiko at all, Craig?"

"No. Why?"

"I can't seem to find her anywhere."

"Is that so? Well, maybe she's still mad at you about the... little spat you had. She'll turn up."

Tate smiled slyly. "I'm sure she will."

Tate waited until everyone had a drink, then he raised his. "To what's to come." He said. His eyes passed from Noah to Lucas, as everyone echoed his sentiment. Lucas stayed silent, but he put the flute to his lips and pretended to drink. He was concentrating hard on Tate and Troy. Something was up with them. He didn't want to check for Noah too hard, but he did glance at him. He wore a very faint frown on his face. He felt it, too. Tate was smiling at him.

"Something wrong, Ray?"

Lucas positioned himself a bit further away from Noah so he'd have room to move.

"That was an odd toast, Tate." Lucas said.

"Ah, but very poignant. Would you rather I'd said L'Chaim. That means to life."

Noah put his down. "We know what it means, Tate. To you, too."

Tate looked slightly offended. "You seem to be in a rush, Craig. Relax."

"I could relax a lot better if we got the deal out of the way. Once I get my cash, I won't mind givin' dap and talkin' shit."

Troy eased himself off the desk and motioned to Mack. "Put the bag on the floor, man."

Noah held his hand up. "Not so fast, Slick. Where's the cash?"

Tate laughed softly. "Don't worry. You're about to get

what's coming to you."

Lucas didn't care for the innuendo in that. "Stop with the bullshit, Tate, before I stop trustin' you." Noah said flatly.

Tate smiled and waved his hand. "Smitty, give him the money."

Smitty picked up two cases and put them down in front of Noah. Noah took a step back and cracked his knuckles.

"Mack, get the money."

That knuckle cracking was a bad sign. Noah was about to grab his gun and he wanted Lucas to know it. It seemed the Trinidad brothers were about to pull some sheisty shit. He wasn't prepared for what Tate said next.

"I gave you no reason to stop trusting me, but you two, unfortunately, have given cause to stop trusting you."

Noah frowned and let his arms hang loosely at his sides. He didn't look at Lucas because he didn't need to. They both knew their cover was blown.

"What?" Noah asked.

Tate shook his head sadly. "You people never learn, do you Noah?"

Troy stepped quickly to the right, pulling his gun out and popped Taylor between the eyes. Lucas and Noah instinctively dropped into crouches. Noah shot straight up and got Smitty under the chin.

That's all Lucas had time to see. He ducked and rolled as Troy pointed his gun at him and came up shooting. Lucas dropped one of the goon squad. Everyone was shooting at once. Noah cursed loudly and ducked behind Tate's desk. Lucas felt hot and searing pain in his neck. His hand flew there and came away red. Noah's left hand was dripping blood. Tate's boys were no marksmen. They were shooting like they do in the movies. Lucas popped his head up over the desk in time to see Mack get riddled and fall. Lucas aimed his own gun at Tobias. He caught him in the left side of his head and he fell with a tremendous thud.

Noah scrambled past him. He looked over the desk and ducked his head back down as bullets hit the top of it and sent sharp wooden shrapnel flying into the air. A few sharp pieces hit Noah in the face. He swore and stuck his head back up. He fired his gun twice and that particular shooting stopped. The air in the room was smoky and acrid from the gunfire. Someone was still firing. Lucas leaned around and shot that one in the chest. Blood spurted from the hole in his heart and he fell on his face.

Noah was suddenly on his feet, stepping over bodies. They were the only ones left standing. Noah grinned at Lucas.

"That was damn fine shootin', bro!" He said, in an exaggerated southern drawl.

Lucas smiled. "I try." They reloaded.

"Where's Tate and Troy?" Noah asked, locking in his clip. A door stood open at the rear of the room.

"There." He and Noah were halfway across the room when the door to the office flew open and Griff burst in with Nicole, Leah and Tony. They all had their weapons drawn and Griff was yelling into his radio. He stopped dead in his tracks when he took in the scene.

"Damn!" Griff said in astonishment.

Lucas went to the door Tate and Troy escaped through and looked in. It opened onto a stairway that led down to the basement.

"It's dark as hell down there, Luke." Noah said over his shoulder.

Lucas looked at him sideways. "I ain't blind, Noah."

"Wait!" Griff yelled.

Lucas turned around. He saw that Nicole and Leah had joined them at the door. Nicole was looking at Lucas' neck, trying hard not to seem worried. Griff walked over and reached into his windbreaker. He produced a radio and handed it to Nicole.

"There's four floors to this club. I'm deploying most of the unit to those floors, but I'm holding some over.

If you need back up, give me a holler, and they're there yesterday."

Griff also gave her his standard issue flashlight. Noah plucked it out of her hand immediately and handed it to Lucas.

"Luke's in front. He'll need it before we do."

Tony moved toward the door.

"Where are you going?" Griff asked

"I'm going with them."

Lucas turned on the flashlight and started down the stairs. There was light, low and murky, but it was there.

He killed the flashlight and tucked it into his belt. Twenty feet in, the narrow hallway opened onto a large chamber. The light was better here, provided by a single bulb hanging from the middle of the ceiling. There was a door to the left and a door to the right. Straight ahead was an arch that led to another hallway. Lucas stopped in front of the door on the left. Everyone spread out and took up defensive positions. Tony went in low and put his hand on the knob.

"On three." He said.

Tony counted off and threw the door open. Lucas turned the flashlight on and ran it over the room. It was empty. They turned to the other door. Lucas nodded at Noah and Noah crouched and threw it open. Oscar Tirado sat, tied to a straight chair in the middle of the room, his hands holding his own head in his lap.

"Well, if it ain't the guy who blew our cover." Noah said, in a low voice.

"Good riddance." Tony added.

Oscar Tirado had finally gotten his just desserts. Lucas wasn't tap dancing, but he wouldn't be buying flowers either.

"Shit. He shoulda stayed in jail." Noah said.

Lucas couldn't see it, but he could hear the smirk he wore.

"Let's move on." Lucas said.

Major shit had happened, but the dread was still there. He held his weapon up and ready to fire as he walked through the arch. Nicole was right behind him, Tony was between her and Leah, and Noah brought up the rear. Lucas kept going. Deep in the darkness he thought he heard something. He cocked his head and stopped in his tracks. The way everyone bumped into one other would have been comical under different circumstances, but this shit was too creepy to laugh.

"Why'd you stop?" Noah asked. He sounded further away from him that Lucas would ever admit he was comfortable with.

"Lucas, what's wrong?" Nicole whispered.

"Be quiet. Listen." Someone was singing. No, Troy was singing. He sounded like he was above them, but not that far away. He was singing "I Shot the Sherriff."

They started moving again, following Troy's lunatic serenade. They reached the end of the hallway and there was nothing else but a stairway going up. Lucas frowned. What the hell kind of funhouse shit was this? They went up and found themselves in a room at what was most likely the back of the club. Tate appeared in the door of the only other way out, holding a TEC-9. Lucas raised and aimed automatically.

Karma II

"Stop where you are. I'm not alone and this is not the only gun like this in this building. Put your weapons on the floor in front of you and get your hands where I can see them, please."

"You gotta be kidding me." Lucas said.

Tate smiled. "On the contrary. I kid you not."

With a puff of smoke, Tate let off a short round into the floor near Lucas' feet, sending sharp chips of concrete flying. Nicole let out a small gasp of pain. Lucas wanted to turn his head and check for her, but no way was he turning his back on Tate. Tate laughed.

"Are you alright, Nicole? I'd hate to ruin your beautiful face. That seems like an awful lot of blood."

Lucas risked a look over his shoulder. Blood was dripping down her face from a slash in her eyebrow. Okay. That pissed him off.

"Put the fuckin' gun down, Tate."

Tate was full of hilarity. "I beg your pardon? You put your fucking gun down! You are not in control here, Lucas!"

Tate's gun burst again, ripping the floor on Lucas' other side. "I have no qualms about shooting you, any of you. Now for the last time, put your guns down and come with me."

Lucas hesitated, but he put his gun down. He had a failsafe weapon on his ankle. He new for a fact Noah also carried an alternate. Tate kept the TEC-9 leveled at them, and when he was satisfied, he stepped back into the archway to allow them room to pass. They filed by him to a stairway leading up.

Tate smiled serenely. "Go on. Up the stairs, please."

Lucas looked at him hard. "Give up now, Tate. If you don't, you'll be leaving here in a body bag. I guarantee it."

"Perhaps. Who's to say, Lucas? Now shut up and get up the stairs before I kill you."

Lucas looked at Noah. Their eyes met and Lucas was assured. Noah's mind was in overdrive, like his own. Lucas started up the stairs.

"That's it. Follow the leader. You, too, Mr. Ramsey."

"If you poke me with that thing again, you're gonna have to kill me." Noah said, bristling, "Why are you here anyway? Why don't you have one of your bootlickers doin' your dirty work?"

Tate chuckled. "You're a brave man, Noah. I prefer to do my dirty work myself. I do have my bootlickers waiting, though, I promise."

They reached the top of the stairs, and true to his word, a group of men were waiting with their own weapons pointed at the group of cops.

Tate smiled smugly. "Your escorts, as promised. Gentlemen, lead these police officers to their holding cell."

"Holding cell? You can't believe you're gonna-" Tony started.

Tate interrupted him with a nudge of his gun. "I do believe it, and I will. Now shut up, pig."

There was a large room with double doors to Lucas' left. The only things in it was a door to the far left corner and four chairs. Tate turned to one of his men. "One more chair, please," he said, looking at Tony.

They ushered them in and pointed their guns at them until they sat down. Lucas looked past everyone else and glanced at Noah, who was already looking at him. Tate wagged his finger at them.

"You boys stop looking at each other. We don't want the dynamic duo plotting any heroic schemes."

Lucas stared at him. "You gonna kill us, Tate? Go ahead."

He wasn't quite yelling and Noah followed his lead in the same loud voice as Tate's men started to bind them to their chairs with duct tape.

"Yeah, Tate. What you waitin' for? They ain't gonna make deals with you. Do it now and get it over with."

Tate strolled over to where Noah sat. "Make sure his bonds are tight." He said to his man.

Noah smirked. "Don't trust me?"

"Shut up."

Noah smiled. "Make me, bitch."

Tate brought his gun up and swiftly brought it down hard on Noah's head. He was aiming for his temple, but Noah turned his head and Tate got his ear instead.

"Son of a bitch!" Noah yelled, in pain. That one action created instant chaos. Lucas had one guy behind him, starting to tape his hands, but he'd only gone around once with the tape. Lucas pushed back with his feet and tilted himself backwards and fell into him, knocking him off his feet. He pulled his hands free and got to his feet, pulling his other weapon off his ankle.

Tate turned toward him with surprised eyes and raised his gun.

Lucas shot him in the shoulder and Tate fell on his back, firing reflexively at the ceiling. Leah, who'd stayed quiet until now, reached behind her and pulled a pistol out of her waistband. She pulled the trigger and shot the guy securing her feet right in the adam's apple. She pulled a knife out of his back pocket and cut Noah loose. Tate raised his gun and Tony leapt for him.

Nicole already had her backup gun in her hands and pumped two bullets into the man who'd turned his gun toward Leah and Noah. Lucas dropped his gun and picked up one of the TEC-9 pieces from the floor and smiled grimly as he squeezed the trigger and took out two others. He kicked one of the weapons to Nicole, who snatched it up and immediately fired on one of the three remaining men. He screamed, choked on his own blood, and went down. Lucas picked up the other weapon and made his way to Noah. The room had gone smoky, and when he reached Noah, Lucas noticed he had a TEC-9 of his own. Noah took the weapon from Lucas and handed it to Leah, whom he had protectively tucked behind him.

"Thanks, bro." Noah turned and shot the remaining two like an afterthought.

Tony was struggling with Tate for his gun, trying to keep being shot. Nicole stood over them looking for a clean shot. Lucas ran to her.

"Don't shoot! Don't shoot! We got him."

Noah was right behind him. They leveled their guns at him and Tony put both hands on his gun. With the four of them aiming at his forehead, Tate had no choice but to let go. Tony snatched the gun from him and got to his feet.

Tate sighed in surrender and sat up. "You seem to have turned the tables. I'm impressed."

Noah's hand had started bleeding again, but he grabbed

Tate's collar with it anyway. "Fuck you. Get your dumb ass up."

He hauled Tate to his feet. "Where's Troy?" Lucas asked.

Tate stared at him until Noah lost patience. He hit him in the face with his gun, grunting with satisfaction when Tate spit one of his teeth out.

"Answer the man, asshole. Where's Troy?"

Tate looked at Noah insolently. "You'll pay for that, Ramsey."

Noah looked at him like he would have gladly shot him where he stood. "Put it on my tab," Noah said.

He pushed Tate roughly to Lucas. Lucas put his gun in his back and urged him forward. "Start walking," he said.

Tate did, wiping blood off his mouth with the back of his hand. "You'll never leave here alive."

"You keep it up and neither will you. Now you shut up before I blast you," Noah said.

Tate went to the door in the corner of the room and opened it. It held another stairway leading up. Tate paused when he was almost at the top. Lucas was about to ask him why, when he threw open a trap door. Lucas felt the hair on the back of his neck stand up. Lucas froze where he stood while Tate hoisted himself out of the stairway, catering heavily to the shoulder Lucas shot him in. Tate escaped the confines of the stairway and Lucas heard what he was afraid of, feet padding across the floor and growling. A chain scraped the floor. Dogs. Lucas' lips were clamped together and he was holding his breath.

"What's the matter Lucas? Go!" Tony said, urgently.

Nicole leaned forward. "Oh, shit! Noah! They've got dogs up there," she whispered harshly.

"Fuck! Move, let me through." Tate turned and looked down at him smiling.

"Cain? Are you afraid of dogs?" Tate clapped his hands and stepped back, leaving Lucas face to muzzle with a snarling pit bull.

It shook its head at him ferociously, slinging its foamy spit across his face. Tate laughed. "Ha! Did you just piss your pants, Mr. Cain? Maybe I should let him go."

Noah spoke from just behind Lucas. "Let him go then, motherfucka!"

Tate grinned and let the pit bull go. The dog leapt into the stairway and Noah extended his arm and sprayed its ass with bullets. Lucas was hugely repulsed as the dog's blood and guts rained down on him.

Noah pushed past him. "Get your head right. I got you."

Noah leapt out of the hole like a fucking superhero, his gun blazing. Lucas summoned all the courage he had and came up after Noah. He was vaguely aware that Nicole, Leah and Tony had joined them. Lucas could not believe how shook he was. There had to be at least 12 dogs in here. His mouth was dry and his skin was crawling, but his hands weren't shaking, so he continued to fire. He was fine until two dogs ran at him at once. He dropped and aimed high, taking out the first dog, but the other dog came in low and lunged at him. Lucas didn't have enough time to bring the gun back down to shoot. The dog opened its jaws and went for his throat. Lucas lowered his arms in time to protect his neck, but the dog managed to lock its jaws on his forearm. The dog knocked him flat with the impact of the collision.

Lucas screamed and tried to pry the dog off with his other hand, but it was useless. The pit bull had locked on him. In an instant, he was nine years old again and this was no longer a pit bull, but a mastiff, and just like so long ago, this dog had latched onto him and he couldn't get it off. The dog growled deep in its throat. The pain and pressure of its bite was unbearable. He felt like he was reliving a memory. Lucas turned over and struggled to get to his knees. His muscles felt like rubber and he wondered, just as he'd done when he was a little boy, why no one was coming to help him.

Nicole danced into his line of vision, just as another dog launched itself at him from his left and knocked him down. Lucas hit the floor still trying to scream, even though the wind was knocked out of him. The dogs claws raked his face as it struggled for purchase on his moving body. Lucas put his head down as Nicole started shooting. The dog fell away without inflicting major damage, but Lucas felt a bullet pierce his forearm and go straight through. His arm burned like it had been dipped in acid.

Noah came up on her right and pushed her out of the way. "What the fuck are you doin'? Get outta the way! Turn your head, Luke. Turn your head!"

Lucas turned his head and Noah planted a foot on both sides of his body. He reached down and grabbed the dog's collar, sticking the business end of his weapon into the dogs ear. Noah squeezed the trigger, and Lucas was once again splashed with dog gore. Noah levered the pit bull's jaws open to release his friend. Lucas was breathing hard, holding his shot arm with the one that had been bitten, trying to figure out which one hurt more. He made it back to his knees and Noah and Nicole helped him stagger back to his feet. Tony put a hole in the last dog, then he and Leah joined them.

Karma II

Lucas decided the gunshot hurt more. Nicole had her hand on his bicep, trying to estimate the damage she'd done. Lucas pulled away from her roughly. "What did you shoot me for?" He hollered at her.

"She didn't mean to. It's clean, probably clot up in a minute," Noah said, and handed him his gun.

"Can you shoot?" Tony asked.

Lucas closed his finger over the trigger. He'd been in much worse pain than this. His shirt was slick and gummy with dog entrails, blood and brains. Lucas shuddered involuntarily and carefully removed it. He did a quick assessment of his forearms. Deep puncture wounds and some tearing through one, clean gunshot through the other.

They both hurt like hell, but nothing was broken. He flexed the arm with the gunshot. Blood ran slow. He glared at Nicole. She'd shot him in his goddamned shooting arm.

"I'm sorry. I didn't mean it."

"I know," he reclaimed some of his cool and pushed the vision of himself screaming like at bitch out of his mind. "Let's go."

Noah pointed his gun toward yet another door. "He hobbled his ass through there. I think Leah got him in the hip."

Lucas smiled. "You mean it wasn't you?"

Noah smiled back. He'd be severely pissed later when he looked in the mirror. The wood from the desk had scoured a nice amount of skin off the left side of his face high on his cheek. He had a good-sized laceration on the same side of his forehead and that eye was swelling up. He was also sporting a big purple bruise behind his left ear.

"I was a little busy savin' your ass, bro."

They started toward the door. Noah's left hand looked like he'd squeezed a tomato.

"You hit?"

Noah looked at his hand. "Not really. Flesh wound between the fingers."

It looked a lot more serious than that to Lucas, but he kept his mouth closed. He knew from experience, they were running on adrenaline now, they'd crash later. Leah was the only one who wasn't bleeding. She and Tony reached the door first and took up positions on either side of it. Nicole dropped into a police crouch, while Lucas and Noah raised their guns and took position behind her.

"Throw it open." Lucas said.

Leah threw the door open. It was a final hallway, with a final doorway that stood open. Sunlight poured down the stairs and puddled on the floor. This door led to the roof. Tony shook his head. "No good. It's the last way out."

Lucas looked at Noah. Noah was squinting from the

light, but he nodded. "Call it," he said quietly.

Lucas turned to Nicole. "Give location and radio for backup."

Nicole took out the radio and began her request. A shadow fell over the stairway. "Come on up, or we come down." Troy called to them. "Either way, you lose."

"Let's roll, Luke. I ain't dyin' down here in the dark," Noah said, "Let's go up before they ambush us."

Lucas went up the stairs with Noah right behind him. "When we get to the top, start shootin', No. I'll go left and low."

"Shit, you ain't gotta tell me twice."

Lucas jogged up the last few steps, then rolled out the door to his left, shooting low. Noah went right and swept his gun in the same half-circle as Lucas, aiming high. Noah rolled out of his sight and Tony popped up in his place. Lucas turned his head to look for Noah and saw him sprinting across the roof after Tate. Tate was hobbling, and he was moving pretty fast, but Noah was closing the distance. Lucas was right behind Noah.

Karma II

Noah was yelling at the top of his lungs. "Drop your weapon, Tate! Drop it or I will shoot you!"

Tate kept going, so Noah stopped running and leveled his gun. He blew out both of Tate's kneecaps and watched him go down like a ton of bricks. Tate's gun popped away from him and out of his reach. Lucas nodded approval. "Nice take down."

Noah smirked and nodded back. "Yeah. Sweet. Do me a favor and watch my back while I read this motherfucker his rights."

"You got it."

They gave each other a painful dap and Lucas took Noah's back. Lucas looked over at Noah and watched him walk, with his gun down, to Tate's prone and writhing form. It was a moment in time that found a second to burn itself into Lucas' mind before that dread feeling dropped down on him, hot and heavy.

There was a raucous volley of gunfire to Lucas' right as Griff's unit spilled out of the staircase like ants out of a hill. Noah turned his head in that direction, raising his gun on reflex. There were so many shots being fired, hearing anything else above the cacophony was damn near impossible. There was no way Noah could have heard Lucas as he ran toward him, screaming for him to look out. He only heard Troy sprinting at him, screeching a maniacal war cry, at the last second.

Troy wasn't holding a gun; he was gripping that goddamned machete he used to claim scalps. Lucas fired at him before he got too close to fire safely. Blood spurted from three places in his body. Lucas knew he hit him, but that lunatic kept running. Knowing Troy, he was probably too high for the pain to register. Nicole and Tony rolled in on Noah's other side, looking for a clean shot, but it wasn't happening because Noah was between them.

Everything happened at once. Troy pulled a pistol out of his waistband and shot Noah three times. Tate turned over, grinning like a demon, and fired his own alternate weapon at Tony and Nicole. They both went down immediately from the unexpected gunplay. Noah staggered back running his hands over his wounds. Lucas sprayed Tate across the face with a burst from his gun and his head was reduced to a red mess. Leah was suddenly beside him. She'd gotten a weapon from somewhere, because she was firing at Troy.

Troy lunged at him and Noah ducked his machete. Troy gripped the machete in both hands and brought them over his head. Noah grabbed his forearms and struggled with him to keep the knife from coming down. They spun around and fought for control like they were in a disordered dance. Lucas looked at Nicole. She wasn't moving. Leah read his mind. She pushed him roughly in Noah's direction.

"Go! Go save Noah! I've got Nick and Tony. Go!" Lucas raced to the macabre death dance, but he had no intention of cutting in. This was the end of Troy.

"Let go of the weapon, Troy!" He shouted.

Troy grinned at him and spit in his face. "Fuck you, cop bastard! Shoot me!"

"Your call, asshole," Lucas said.

He socked the muzzle of his gun between Troy's second and third ribs and pulled the trigger. Troy fell at once because Lucas had just shot his heart out. Noah collapsed onto his back, breathing hard. Blood was trickling out of the side of his mouth. The front of his shirt was soaked with blood. Lucas counted three bullet holes besides the one in his hand. One was high up on his shoulder, one right above his knee, and a very scary one in his chest.

Lucas dropped to his knees beside him. "Noah," was all he managed to say.

Grief and terror took over his heart.

"F-Fucker tried to kill me." Noah sputtered. "I think… I think he broke my… fuckin' leg."

Griff was standing over his shoulder barking orders into his radio. When he was done, he hunkered down next to Lucas and put his hand on his shoulder. "EMS is coming up the stairs as we speak. How is he?"

291

Karma II

"How the fuck does he look like he is?" Lucas said in a low voice.

The EMS crews started to emerge onto the roof. Lucas watched Leah run out and get two crews and direct them to Nicole and Tony. Tony was prone and Nicole was lying on her side next to him.

"Go on and see about her. I'll stay here with Noah," Griff said.

Lucas looked down at Noah and was alarmed that his eyes had slipped closed. He put two fingers on his neck and felt for a pulse.

"Noah?" He said, hesitantly.

Noah opened his eyes and gave him a very diluted version of his signature smirk. "I'm… I'm still here. Go on."

Lucas touched Noah's arm and got up. He went to Nicole, not wanting to leave Noah, but he couldn't be in two places at once. When he got there they were loading her onto a stretcher. They were already taking Tony downstairs. The EMTs were working on her and she wore a mask on her face. Leah moved aside and he stepped in.

"I'm here. Don't worry, sweetheart. I'm here."

Nicole pulled the mask away from her mouth with a blood-streaked hand. "How's Noah? He's… Troy shot him so close. He's still here, right?"

Lucas nodded. "Yeah. Noah's still here. He's hurt bad, Nicole."

"Jesus. We saw Troy and we tried to stop him, but Tate…"

"Tate's dead. So is Troy." Lucas said, and he knew it to be true because he'd killed them both himself.

"Good. Tony's hurt bad, too."

"I know. Where are you hurt?"

Karma II

She winced as an EMT shot something in her arm, another started an I.V. drip. "Right leg. Left hip. Left arm."

One of the EMT's moved in close. "We need to take her down now, buddy, and you need to get looked at now."

"I will," Lucas said, acknowledging the EMT.

He kissed Nicole full on the mouth and she kissed him back. "I love you. I'll see you at the hospital."

"You tell Noah I'm praying for him, and you have them check you out. Soon, Lucas. I love you. Promise me."

"I will and I promise."

He kissed her again and went back to where Noah was being moved onto his own stretcher. Lucas wasn't able to get close to him, because the EMT's were working feverishly. Noah was in distress and he wasn't cooperating. Griff was watching the scene grimly. Lucas was simultaneously shocked and terrified. He'd only left him for a moment. What the hell was going on?

"Take it easy, relax, relax!" The tech urged.

"Don't touch me! Get off!"

Lucas shouldered his way in and looked down at Noah. They'd cut his shirt away, revealing the holes in his chest. The one in his shoulder seemed very much like the one Lucas received from Simone. It most likely had broken his collarbone. The one in his chest was almost dead center and it was ugly. Lucas knew enough to be thankful that it was bleeding steadily, and not a gurgling wound. Blood was running out of his mouth and every time he spoke, it sprayed a fine mist. Lucas could see he was getting weak, but Noah had enough fight in him to keep the techs frustrated. He was fighting them with every ounce of strength he had left.

"If he's your friend, talk him down so we can help him," the tech next to Lucas said as he prepared a syringe.

Lucas took Noah's hand and leaned down to look him in the eye. "Cut it out, Noah. Stop fighting and let them help you."

Karma II

Noah looked up at him and the pain and worry in his eyes floored Lucas. Noah gripped his hand and his teeth chattered. "I'm scared, Luke."

Noah's voice was shaky and breathless, not his voice at all. Lucas felt despair sinking its teeth into him as he saw the panic in Noah's eyes.

"I know. I'm not leaving you, Noah."

Noah made an attempt at a smile and it tore at Lucas' heart. He tried to speak, but blood spluttered from his lips. Noah took a long shaky breath and tried again. "Looks… like I might be… leavin' you."

Lucas watched Noah's eyes dilate until his gray eyes seemed black in the space of 10 seconds. "No." Lucas whispered.

This shit could not be happening! Noah was fucking indestructible!

Noah turned his head. Tears slid out of his eyes. He was moaning. "I don't feel so good." Just like that, Noah's head fell back and his mouth dropped open.

"He's crashing! We're losing him! Move! Move!"

Lucas was pushed rudely out of the way as the crew set about saving Noah Ramsey. He couldn't even see Noah through the crowd of people working on him. Suddenly they were moving, racing toward the stairs, with one tech astride Noah, giving him chest compressions.

Lucas stood there in helpless shock as they took his dearest friend away, fighting to save his life. He instinctively folded his hurt arms across his chest and dropped his head, something he'd always done since he was a little boy, and willed himself not to cry. Someone grabbed him around the waist and he opened his eyes.

It was Leah. Her pretty face was awash with tears. She was sobbing so hard, she could barely stand up. "Oh, Lucas. Oh, God."

He put his arms around her and she collapsed against him, crying into his chest inconsolably. Lucas rubbed her back.

Karma II

"He's going to die!" She sobbed.

Lucas shook his head. "He's not. He won't."

His mind refused to let him believe that. Noah was tough as nails.

"I love him." She didn't have to convince Lucas.

"I know. So do I."

Griff watched them with sorrowful eyes. When he thought they were ready, he intruded, respectfully. "I think it's time to get to the hospital. Let's go."

Lucas placed his arm around Leah and started walking toward the car. With the cold grip of fear pressing down on him, Lucas nearly choked at the thought of losing Noah. He closed his eyes and willed the universe to keep his friend alive. Only time would tell if it was enough, and time certainly wasn't on Noah's side. The familiar tug of a loved one slipping away forced Lucas to close his eyes and do the only thing left in his power to do: pray.

♕ Triple Crown Publications

Order Form

P.O. Box 247378   Columbus, OH 43224

Name	
Address	
City	
State	Zipcode

QTY	TITLES	PRICE
	A Down Chick	$15.00
	A Hood Legend	$15.00
	A Hustler's Son	$15.00
	A Hustler's Wife	$15.00
	A Project Chick	$15.00
	Always a Queen	$15.00
	Amongst Thieves	$15.00
	Baby Girl Pt. 1	$15.00
	Baby Girl Pt. 2	$15.00
	Betrayed	$15.00
	Bitch	$15.00
	Bitch Reloaded	$15.00
	Black	$15.00
	Black and Ugly	$15.00
	Blinded	$15.00
	Cash Money	$15.00

Shipping & Handling
1 - 3 Books $5.00
4 - 9 Books $9.00
$1.95 for each add'l book

Total $_____

Forms of accepted payment: Postage Stamps, Personal or Institutional Checks & Money Orders. All mail in orders take 5-7 business days to be delivered.

♕ Triple Crown Publications

Order Form

P.O. Box 247378 Columbus, OH 43224

Name	
Address	
City	
State	Zipcode

QTY	TITLES	PRICE
	Chances	$15.00
	Chyna Black	$15.00
	China Doll	$15.00
	Contagious	$15.00
	Crack Head	$15.00
	Crack Head II	$15.00
	Cream	$15.00
	Cut Throat	$15.00
	Dangerous	$15.00
	Dime Piece	$15.00
	Dirty Red	$15.00
	Dirtier Than Ever	$20.00
	Dirty South	$15.00
	Diva	$15.00
	Dollar Bill	$15.00
	Ecstasy	$15.00

Shipping & Handling
1 - 3 Books $5.00
4 - 9 Books $9.00
$1.95 for each add'l book

Total $_____

Forms of accepted payment: Postage Stamps, Personal or Institutional Checks &
Money Orders. All mail in orders take 5-7 business days to be delivered.

♛ Triple Crown Publications

Order Form

P.O. Box 247378   Columbus, OH 43224

Name	
Address	
City	
State	Zipcode

QTY	TITLES	PRICE
	Flip Side of the Game	$15.00
	For the Strength of You	$15.00
	Forever A Queen	$15.00
	Game Over	$15.00
	Gangsta	$15.00
	Grimey	$15.00
	Hold U Down	$15.00
	Hood Rats	$15.00
	Hood Richest	$15.00
	Hoodwinked	$15.00
	How to Succeed in the Publishing Game	$15.00
	Ice	$15.00
	Imagine This	$15.00
	In Cahootz	$15.00
	Innocent	$15.00
	Karma Pt. 1	$15.00

Shipping & Handling
1 - 3 Books $5.00
4 - 9 Books $9.00
$1.95 for each add'l book

Total $_____

♕ Triple Crown Publications

Order Form

P.O. Box 247378 Columbus, OH 43224

Name	
Address	
City	
State	Zipcode

QTY	TITLES	PRICE
	Karma Pt. 2	$15.00
	Keisha	$15.00
	Larceny	$15.00
	Let That Be the Reason	$15.00
	Life	$15.00
	Love & Loyalty	$15.00
	Me & My Boyfriend	$15.00
	Menage's Way	$15.00
	Mina's Joint	$15.00
	Mistress of the Game	$15.00
	Queen	$15.00
	Rage Times Fury	$15.00
	Road Dawgz	$15.00
	Sheisty	$15.00
	Stacy	$15.00
	Stained Cotton	$15.00

Shipping & Handling
1 - 3 Books $5.00
4 - 9 Books $9.00
$1.95 for each add'l book

Total $_____

Forms of accepted payment: Postage Stamps, Personal or Institutional Checks &
Money Orders. All mail in orders take 5-7 business days to be delivered.

♛ Triple Crown Publications

Order Form

P.O. Box 247378   Columbus, OH 43224

Name	
Address	
City	
State	Zipcode

QTY	TITLES	PRICE
	Still Dirty	$15.00
	Still Sheisty	$15.00
	Street Love	$15.00
	Sunshine & Rain	$15.00
	The Bitch is Back	$15.00
	The Game	$15.00
	The Pink Palace The Set Up	$15.00
	The Set Up	$15.00
	Trickery	$15.00
	Trickery Pt 2	$15.00
	The Reason Why	$15.00
	Torn	$15.00
	Vixen Icon	$15.00
	Whore	

Shipping & Handling

1 - 3 Books $5.00
4 - 9 Books $9.00
$1.95 for each add'l book

Total $_____

Forms of accepted payment: Postage Stamps, Personal or Institutional Checks &
Money Orders. All mail in orders take 5-7 business days to be delivered.